W9-CFJ-253

Books by Victoria Malvey

Portrait of Dreams
Enchanted
Temptress
A Merry Chase
Fortune's Bride
A Proper Affair
Wedding of the Year

Published by POCKET BOOKS

WEDDING
of the YEAR

VICTORIA MALVEY

SONNET BOOKS
New York London Toronto Sydney Tokyo Singapore

For information regarding special discounts for bulk
purchases, please contact Simon & Schuster Special Sales
at 1-800-456-6798 or business@simonandschuster.com

This book is a work of fiction. Names, characters, places and
incidents are products of the author's imagination or are used
fictitiously. Any resemblance to actual events or locales or per-
sons, living or dead, is entirely coincidental.

An *Original* Publication of POCKET BOOKS

A Sonnet Book published by
POCKET BOOKS, a division of Simon & Schuster, Inc.
1230 Avenue of the Americas, New York, NY 10020

Copyright © 2001 by Victoria Malvey

ISBN: 0-7434-1884-0

First Sonnet Books printing December 2001

10   9   8   7   6   5   4   3   2   1

SONNET BOOKS and colophon are trademarks of
Simon & Schuster, Inc.

Cover art by Rachael McCampbell

Printed in the U.S.A.

To my nephew
Christopher Manuel Malvey
October 27, 2000

Another angel in Heaven.
Hold on to him tightly, Lindsey,
and know you are both loved very, very much.

Acknowledgments

A special thanks to my editor, Amy Pierpont, for her understanding and compassion during a difficult time in my life. Without her encouragement and empathy, this book would never have been finished. My thanks, Amy!

And another thank you to my agent, Pam Hopkins, for helping me face hard times and overcome them. As always, your support lent me strength and helped me get back on track.

Prologue

Godmersham, England
November 1828

You will perhaps say that the sinews and muscles of a bird are incomparably more powerful than those of man, because . . .

A loud noise broke Elizabeth's concentration. Glancing up from her book on Leonardo da Vinci's flying experiments, she saw the footmen lifting the heavy trunk again. As she watched, a second set of footmen passed with yet another traveling trunk.

Oh, no, Elizabeth thought, setting aside the book. Surely they weren't leaving for London already. Lifting her skirts, she rushed up the curved staircase, past the servants carrying boxes and trunks, and into her mother's bedchamber. Surrounded by utter chaos, her mother directed the servants with ease as she tossed gown after gown upon the bed, creating a colorful mound of garments.

"Be certain you pack that lovely feather hat I purchased just . . ."

"What's happening, Mama?" Elizabeth asked, praying she was wrong. Perhaps they were simply going on a trip to Scotland, or a jaunt across the moors.

Turning with a brilliant smile, Mama laid a shawl upon the gowns. "We're off to London."

"Already? Must we go to town so soon?" Elizabeth asked as the servants, laden with boxes, left the room. "Can't we wait until after Christmas?"

"I'm afraid not, poppet," her mother replied as she sorted through her enormous closet.

"London!" Catherine exclaimed as she entered the bedchamber. "We're heading back to town early?"

Their mother answered with a laugh. "I knew you wouldn't mind, Kit-cat."

"Mind? Heavens, no." Catherine bounded onto the bed. "Only an old muggins like Beth would mind."

A few blonde tendrils escaped their mother's elegant coiffure as she shook her head. "Elizabeth simply prefers the country, Catherine," she corrected, moving to join them on the bed.

"Indeed, I do," Elizabeth agreed, sending a teasing smile toward her sister. "*Some* of us have interests other than parties and nattering."

Catherine fell back onto the bed in a huff. " 'Nattering'? Only old ladies 'natter,' and I'm fourteen, not eighty."

"Very well then. What if I say you adore to talk about fripperies and other silly things all day long and well into the night until I fear my ears will burst?" Elizabeth countered, playfully tossing a pillow at Catherine.

"Come now, girls," their mother said, the sparkle

in her blue eyes belying the stern tone in her voice.

Catherine scrunched her nose at her sister.

"Young ladies do not make faces, Catherine."

Her mother's quiet reprimand made Catherine sit upright. "Sorry, Mama" she mumbled.

"And as for you," their mother said, reaching out to take hold of Elizabeth's hand. "While I know you love life in the country, you must remember that you'll have your first season next year, so it is best if you pay close attention to the actions of the debutantes in town."

"Don't remind me," Elizabeth groaned, closing her eyes. The mere thought of a Season made her cringe.

"Come now, darling. You will love it."

Mama's reassurances did little to ease the churning in the pit of her stomach. Though she might look exactly like her mother, Elizabeth couldn't have been more different. The ever-elegant Lady Margaret Everley, Countess of Shipham, was so vivacious, so charming, that Elizabeth didn't know of anyone who didn't like her. And while she might mirror her mother in looks, she was quite unlike her in personality; Elizabeth was shy, quiet, and preferred the company of her books to that of people.

Glancing at her sister, Elizabeth tried not to feel envious of Catherine and her ease with people. With her brown hair, gray eyes, and petite frame, she looked nothing like their tall, willowy mother. Yet, in personality, Catherine mirrored Mama. Both of them were so outgoing, so bright, so charming, when it was all she could do to converse with the neighbors.

"I can't wait for my Season!" Catherine pronounced happily.

"I know you can't, Kit-cat," their mother said with a laugh, reaching out to stroke her hair. "But you have three more years yet."

"Three?" she moaned. "Many girls debut at sixteen. Why can't I?"

"You know the answer to that as well as I," Mama replied softly. "Your father has decided his girls will have their first Season when they turn seventeen."

"I'd be perfectly content to wait a bit longer," Elizabeth offered hopefully.

Mama laughed brilliantly. "Knowing you, my darling Elizabeth, you would fancy skipping a Season all together." Leaning forward, she clasped Elizabeth's hands between hers. "I believe you'll surprise yourself with how much you will enjoy your debut. We'll go shopping for the perfect gowns on Regent Street, then ride along Ladies' Walk in Hyde Park to show off your new, smart riding habit, and the gentlemen will scramble to fill in your dance card." She smiled at Elizabeth. "Trust me, darling. Everything will be just fine."

"I believe you," she replied softly, knowing her mother would somehow find a way to help her overcome her shortcomings.

"Yes, don't worry, Elizabeth. All you have to do is stand there, looking utterly beautiful, and gentlemen will be swarming all over you," Catherine predicted gaily. "And as soon as I'm finally old enough, I shall join you and together we can attend every party, every soiree." Sliding off the bed, Catherine twirled around with her arms spread wide. "I'll dance until my feet hurt." She grabbed hold of the bedpost. "And I'll collect hundreds of offers from the finest bachelors until I decide upon my heart's true love."

Mama sighed heartily. "That's what I worry about with you, Cat. That you'll fancy yourself in love with some fleet-footed fortune hunter and, with your romantic nature, you'll be unable to see beyond your own fantasies to the truth." Leveling a somber look at Catherine, Mama pointed a finger at her. "But just as I'll help your sister to enjoy her first Season, I'll keep a close eye on you . . . to make certain you don't enjoy yours *too* much."

Catherine couldn't help but laugh at her mother's worries.

"What's this?" boomed Douglas Everley, Earl of Shipham, as he stepped into the bedchamber. "My girls are having a party without me?" He shook his head. "For shame on all of you."

With a soft laugh, Lady Margaret stood and, holding out her arms, moved toward her husband. "Not a party, darling. Just a little gathering."

Lifting her hand to his lips, Douglas smiled down at her. "Well, then, I suppose I shan't feel slighted at not being invited to join you."

"Good." Lady Margaret smoothed her hand down his waistcoat. "I should hate for you to feel slighted, Douglas, so I promise to invite you to any party we might have."

"Why don't we have one now?" Without awaiting a response, he swung his wife into his arms and began to waltz her around the room as he hummed aloud.

Lady Margaret laughed up at her husband as he spun her across the gleaming floor.

"Join us, girls," Douglas shouted gaily before resuming his tune.

Giggling, Catherine held out her arms to Elizabeth and they began to twirl around the room as well.

"You're a terrible dancer," Elizabeth said, her smile taking the sting out of the words.

"So are you," Catherine returned brightly. "But I'm not the one who has to learn how to dance by next year."

1

London, England
November 1830

Comfortably ensconced within the soft cushions of the library chair, Elizabeth studied da Vinci's theories on astrology, the same theories that had caused the Church to declare him a heretic. Feeling slightly nervous that her father might discover her reading such controversial information, Elizabeth glanced around the brocade-covered wing of her chair . . . and caught sight of Catherine, tiptoeing across the floor toward the door that connected the library to their father's study. "Cat?"

Catherine skidded to a halt. "Shhhh," she whispered testily as she moved the last few paces to the door.

Elizabeth might have managed to ignore her sister's odd behavior if Catherine hadn't then leaned forward and pressed her ear against the door. "What are you *doing*, Catherine?" Elizabeth exclaimed, unable to believe her sister would eavesdrop upon their father.

Twisting around, Catherine pressed a finger to her lips. Even from across the room, Elizabeth could see annoyance brightening her sister's eyes. "Do you want me to get caught?" Catherine hissed.

"Of course not, but still, Catherine, it's not right to listen to Papa's private conversation," Elizabeth protested softly.

"It most certainly is when Papa's discussion concerns me." She waved her hand. "Now quiet down, Elizabeth, so I can hear what they're saying."

Her curiosity now overriding her disapproval, Elizabeth set aside the astrology charts. "To whom is he speaking?"

"Lord Dunham."

It took a moment of thought, but Elizabeth finally placed the name. "Is he that foppish dandy with reddish hair?"

Catherine shot her an exasperated glance. "Only *you* would describe one of the most eligible gentlemen of the season in such a despicable fashion."

Elizabeth rose from her chair with a decidedly unladylike snort. "If he's considered one of the most eligible gentlemen, it is little wonder I have yet to find someone who interests me."

"That's not the reason at all, Elizabeth, and you know it." Catherine shook her head. "You're far too busy burying your head in all of your books and silly experiments to even consider entertaining a suitor."

"The gentlemen of the ton aren't exactly beating down the door to court me," Elizabeth pointed out.

"Only because you don't give them a chance to get to know you."

"I do so," Elizabeth protested. "Why, just last evening I spoke with Lord Connor about the complications I was encountering in designing a catapult."

Glancing over her shoulder, Catherine rolled her eyes.

"Good heavens, Elizabeth, gentlemen don't wish to discuss gadgets and gears at a ball!"

"Then what do they want to discuss?" Elizabeth asked, genuinely at a loss.

Catherine shrugged. "Most gentlemen don't really require *actual* conversation. If you simply look fascinated with whatever they're saying and add an occasional nod, they find you fascinating."

"How could that be?" Elizabeth countered, even more confused than before. "Are gentlemen really interested in an empty-headed miss who does nothing more than hang on their every word?"

"For the most part," Catherine agreed with a firm nod.

"If that's what gentlemen really want, then I fear I am doomed to spinsterhood," Elizabeth predicted.

"Pshaw," Catherine said, waving her hand dismissively. "All you need is to find the perfect gentleman who appreciates all of your fine qualities."

No, what she needed was a miracle. Elizabeth dropped her book onto the chair she'd recently abandoned. "What I need is someone who can help me to fit into society, someone who loves me, someone who can teach me how to successfully converse at parties, someone who can help me belong."

"You belong now," Catherine countered. "After all, you're the daughter of an earl."

Shaking her head, Elizabeth continued, "That's the *only* reason I'm accepted. It doesn't help me to feel a part of society. It's as if everyone simply sees me and dismisses me as a brainless, vapid lady. Worse still, I don't know how to dispell their mistaken beliefs. Even you have to admit, Cat, that I'm woefully bad at conversing with people or thinking up those witty replies you toss out with such ease."

"Carrying on polite conversation is a skill like any other," Catherine pointed out. "Which means it can be learned."

"I've been out two seasons, Catherine, yet I am no closer to mastering that particular skill than I was on the eve of my debut," Elizabeth said, trying not to allow the panic she felt to come into her voice. After seeing her parents' marriage, Elizabeth wanted to marry, to have children, to achieve the happiness her parents had found. "I doubt I shall ever find a suitable gentleman in town. They are all far too sophisticated, too glib, to ever take an interest in a country girl like me. Perhaps I'd be better off returning to our country estate and searching for a husband there. I know I'm far more comfortable in the country than I've ever been in town."

"But then I'd never see you," Catherine cried. "I couldn't bear that, so we shall simply have to find a suitable gentleman here in town."

"How?" Elizabeth asked. "It's not as if I haven't tried to find a husband here, but apparently it is not meant to be."

Catherine sighed deeply. "If only Mama were still alive, she would have helped you find the perfect husband."

Mama. Her name alone brought the familiar ache to Elizabeth's chest. Memories of Mama growing weaker and weaker, until she became bedridden, assailed Elizabeth. In her mind's eye, she could still see her mother wasting away, fading slowly, then finally, after a few months, simply giving in to the consumption.

Mama's death had devastated their family, destroying them all. Even now Papa was a shadow of his former self, while she and Catherine tried to negotiate the difficult waters of polite society unscathed.

"Perhaps that is true," Elizabeth conceded, "but even if Mama *were* still alive, it wouldn't change the fact that I'm pitiful at traversing the social world."

"Not pitiful, merely inexperienced."

Smiling at Catherine's protest, Elizabeth shook her head. "If I haven't gained any experience in two years, then I hold little hope for the future. I think it best that I resign myself to the fact that I shall be the loving, old maiden aunt to your children."

"My goodness, Elizabeth, you can't give up hope that . . ." A loud burst of laughter came from behind the closed door to their father's study. "What's going on in there?" Catherine mused softly before lifting a finger toward Elizabeth. "Hold on a moment, Elizabeth, while I try to figure out what Papa's saying." And with that, Catherine turned and pressed her ear against the door once again.

Elizabeth didn't see the point of returning to their conversation, as she knew that Catherine—with her rosy outlook on life—would never acknowledge the hopelessness of her situation. But before Elizabeth could bid her sister a swift farewell and leave the room while Catherine was distracted, the door to Papa's study opened, sending Catherine stumbling forward . . . and right into Papa's chest.

"I thought I might find you here," he remarked dryly as he grasped Catherine's shoulders and steadied her.

"Why, Papa . . ." Catherine began, her voice altering as she smoothed down her skirts. "I was just coming in to see you."

Papa lifted a brow in reply, causing Catherine to shift beneath the pointed look.

"Well, I *was,*" she protested. "While I know it might appear that I was trying to eavesdrop upon your private conversation, that's not the case at all. I was simply, er, trying to ascertain if you were alone or not before I entered your study."

"A knock would have sufficed."

Catherine bit her lower lip. "Perhaps, but it still would have been interrupting you if you were engaged with a visitor."

"You, my darling Cat," began Papa, leaning forward to tweak Catherine's nose, "have always been an abominable liar."

"I'm not lying," Catherine replied weakly. "Elizabeth was here; she can tell you that . . ."

Laughing, Elizabeth lifted her hands. "Oh, no, Cat. Leave me out of this mess, thank you very much."

With her back to Papa, Catherine scowled at Elizabeth's refusal to cover for her.

"Then again," Elizabeth began softly, unable to keep from teasing her sister, "perhaps I should tell Papa that you were . . ."

". . . about to inquire after his guest," Catherine interjected, cutting off Elizabeth's confession as she spun about to face Papa once more. "Who called upon you this early, Papa?"

"As if you didn't hear each and every word I said," Papa replied with a laugh.

"In truth, Papa," Elizabeth began, finally coming to her sister's aid. "I doubt if Catherine overheard more than a few moments of your conversation before you opened the door."

Catherine nodded quickly, immediately latching onto Elizabeth's explanation. "It's true, Papa."

Their father's lips twitched, but he didn't argue the point further. Instead, he clapped his hands together. "So, Catherine, would you like to hear what Lord Dunham had to say?"

All assertions of innocence were immediately dropped as Catherine stepped forward eagerly. "Yes, Papa."

"He offered for your hand."

"And?"

"I graciously declined his offer."

Disappointment warred with annoyance upon Catherine's face. "Without even discussing the matter with me?"

"I believe that is my right," Papa said smoothly, clasping his hands behind his back.

Catherine shook her head fiercely. "Since I'm the one he offered for, I believe I should be the one to decide if he is refused or not."

Papa tilted his head to the side. "You seem more upset that I didn't consult with you first than over the loss of a match with Lord Dunham."

"Well, of course I am," Catherine retorted. "I would have refused him as well . . . but it should have been *my* choice."

"Heaven save me," Papa muttered under his breath. "You've received at least two dozen proposals since your debut, Catherine. Did you actually expect me to consult you on each and every one?"

"Absolutely."

Papa rolled his eyes. "Then you'd best become used to disappointment, for I have no intention of doing that."

"You're being so unreasonable, Papa!" exclaimed Catherine, looking toward Elizabeth. *"Please* help me reason with him."

It was all Elizabeth could do to hold back her smile over Catherine's dramatic plea. "I don't hold much hope to sway Papa in this matter, Cat. After all, you know how he is when he sets his mind to something."

Glumly, Catherine nodded. "An unmovable force."

"Precisely." Lifting one shoulder, Elizabeth added, "Besides, I don't see why you are so upset about this, Catherine. Not *one* of the gentlemen Papa refused was someone you would have actually considered marrying. If I remember correctly, you said that you found Lord Dunham to be a bit of a bore."

With typical flair, Catherine threw her hands up in the air. "Well, *you* know that, Elizabeth, but I never told Papa how I felt about Lord Dunham." Dropping down into a chair, she looked up at Elizabeth. "For all he knew, I could have considered Lord Dunham my perfect mate."

"With his preference for outlandishly bright jackets, his affected lisp, and his habit of using snuff until you weary of the snorting noise he makes, I highly doubt anyone would think him a perfect mate, much less a man of intelligence like Papa," Elizabeth assured her sister.

"Thank you for coming to my defense, Elizabeth," he said before turning his attention onto Catherine. "As for you, my youngest, I shall continue to do what I consider best for you."

Elizabeth could tell by Catherine's expression that she was biting back a remark.

"And you need to socialize more, Elizabeth," Papa continued as he turned his sharp gaze onto her. "If you became more interested in town life, you might find you actually enjoy social outings."

"I hold little hope for that, Papa," murmured Elizabeth.

His expression let her know he didn't believe a word of her denial. "Then I think you underestimate yourself. At the ball tonight, I don't want to see you off by yourself in a corner or chatting with the elderly ladies." He leveled a finger at her. "You are to dance, laugh, and generally enjoy yourself with other young ladies and gentlemen."

"But . . ."

"No 'but,' Elizabeth." Leaning forward, he pressed a kiss upon her forehead. "Why don't you show the ton how special you truly are?"

Elizabeth bit back her groan. "Yes, Papa."

"Thank you." Stepping back, he gestured toward the door. "Now why don't the two of you go prepare for our evening at Almack's?"

"With pleasure," Catherine said, wrapping her arm through Elizabeth's. "I'll even help Elizabeth choose her gown."

Alarm flared within Elizabeth as she remembered the deep bodices of the gowns Catherine had insisted upon ordering for her. Having learned her lesson, it had been the first and last time Elizabeth had sought her sister's fashion advice. "I'm perfectly capable of choosing my own attire, Cat."

"Of course you are, silly," Catherine replied with a knowing grin. "But it will be much more fun if I help." Turning wide eyes onto Papa, she asked, "Don't you agree, Papa?"

"I most certainly do." He patted Elizabeth's arm. "You won't regret allowing Catherine to help you."

Oh, but she already did, Elizabeth thought, as Catherine tugged her out of the room. "I'm not going to wear one of those indecent gowns you ordered without my approval," Elizabeth warned her sister. "And you won't be able to change my mind."

Catherine laughed brightly. "We'll see, Beth."

Elizabeth scowled at her sister. "You don't fight fair."

"Not when your happiness is at stake, Beth."

"Happiness?" Looking down at her gown, Elizabeth adjusted the fichu she'd put around her shoulders to help hide her low décolletage. "What on earth would make you believe I'd be happy standing here in Almack's with my . . ." Unable to voice the word out loud, she merely waved toward her bosom. ". . . exposed."

"You're hardly exposed," Catherine returned. "Especially not since you insisted upon wrapping that horrid shawl around your shoulders."

"A fichu is a perfectly acceptable accessory to any gown."

"Perhaps when you're an elderly matron, but not when you're trying to attract a husband."

"I believe I've made my feelings on *that* subject very well known."

"Come now, Beth," Catherine began, concern darkening her eyes. "Surely you don't wish to be alone when you're . . ." She broke off her sentiments as Lord Hutton joined them.

"Pardon the interruption, Lady Catherine, Lady Elizabeth," he murmured politely, bowing to each of them in turn, "but I've come to claim my dance, my lady."

Holding out her hand, Catherine graciously accepted his proffered arm. As she watched her sister walk away, Elizabeth bit back a sigh and glanced down at her woefully empty dance card. Only a few dances were claimed . . . and most of them by elderly gentlemen who were friends of Papa's.

Another sigh escaped her as she lowered the card and lifted her chin. "It doesn't matter," she murmured softly to herself.

"Of course it does."

Startled, Elizabeth spun around to face the gentleman who had spoken from behind her. Though she felt herself grow warm with embarrassment, she refused to allow this stranger to see her chagrin. "Excuse me?" she said so coldly that ice practically dripped off the two words.

Grinning wickedly, the gentleman pretended to shiver as he rubbed his arms. *"Brrrrr,"* he retorted.

Determined to ignore him, she turned back around and resumed watching the dancers.

"Ah, the direct cut." His voice floated over her shoulder, but she refused to give in to the urge to glance back at him. "If this is how you treat a gentleman, it is little wonder that you're standing here all alone."

"A gentleman?" she scoffed, unable to remain silent for one moment longer. "Sneaking up behind a lady, eavesdropping upon her, then daring to address her without an introduction are hardly the actions of a gentleman."

His laugh was low and outrageously appealing. "Lord, you do possess a tart tongue, don't you, my lady? Lucky for you, I am a stalwart soul and not easily put off."

Flustered, Elizabeth forgot her resolve to ignore him and looked over her shoulder. Immediately she wished she hadn't, for his grin made her insides jittery. With his dark hair, handsome blue eyes, and dashing features, he was precisely the sort of attractive gentleman who left her feeling awkward and gauche. "You presume far too much if you consider me lucky for having to suffer your overly familiar person, sir." Struggling to maintain her cool poise, she faced front again. "I am not in the habit of speaking with rakes."

"A rake, am I?" he murmured softly, stepping forward until he stood beside her. "Now it is you who presume too much. Perhaps I am merely another person who understands what it is like to be utterly alone in a crowd."

A gasp broke from Elizabeth as she stared at him in amazement. "P-p-pardon me?"

"I believe you heard me quite well." His smile softened. "I saw you standing here, all alone, wistfully watching the dancers, and I couldn't help but be moved by the sadness in your expression."

Hope, fragile and pale, bloomed within her, but she squashed it ruthlessly. "What could a gentleman such as yourself possibly know about being lonely?"

"A gentlemen such as myself?" he repeated, an eyebrow curving upward. "Do you mean a rake like me?"

No, she meant someone so handsome, so self-assured, so . . . appealing.

Mistaking her silence, the gentleman nodded sharply. "Perhaps I misunderstood you, my lady, for anyone who can't look beyond the appearance of a person is undeniably shallow."

His remark touched her deeply. Here she'd stood, judging him, put off by his handsome appearance, and unwilling to credit him with true emotions. Good Heavens! She'd treated him just like the ton treated her. As the gentleman took a step forward, she reached out, clasping his arm, and brought him to a halt. "Forgive me, my lord. I didn't mean to offend you."

For a moment he merely gazed down at her, then a corner of his mouth tipped upward. "A prettier apology I've never received," he murmured as he brought her hand to his lips. "Still, I would rather you afford me the honor of this dance."

Not waiting for her reply, he tucked her hand into his elbow.

Elizabeth tried to dig in her feet, but her kid slippers found no toehold upon Almack's gleaming wooden floor. "No, please," she pleaded softly. "I fear I lack the skill to dance."

The corners of his eyes crinkled as his smile broadened into a grin. "Don't worry, my lady, for I shall guide you through every step."

Aware of the weight of the stares they were garnering, Elizabeth reluctantly began to walk beside him. She dreaded making a fool of herself upon the dance floor, but this gentleman left her with no choice. If she struggled and caused a scene, the dragons of Almack's might revoke her voucher.

And being dragged onto the dance floor would certainly constitute a 'scene.'

"If you insist I dance with you, I should at least know your name, my lord," Elizabeth said as she took up position in the quadrille.

Even his appealing grin did little to ease the hard knot of apprehension in the pit of her stomach. "Forgive my oversight. I was so taken with you that I quite forgot a minor triviality such as introductions."

The charming response caused another flutter inside her. "Luckily it isn't too late to rectify that mistake."

"Lord Richard Vernon at your service, my lady." He tilted his head at the introduction. "And you are . . ."

"Horrible at dancing," she returned as she stumbled against him.

Instead of the annoyance she was expecting, Lord Vernon tossed back his head and laughed aloud, drawing more than a few gazes. "Very well then, you may keep your name a secret." As they dipped closer in the dance, he whispered into her ear. "Besides, I do so love a woman of mystery."

Elizabeth stumbled slightly at the teasing remark, but caught herself before she could make another misstep. While she wished she hadn't let him know how desperately unsettling she found him, she had to forgive herself that one tiny display. After all, his outrageousness was something she'd never before encountered. Perhaps all the men of the ton weren't so dreadfully dull.

Still, this banter was a skill she'd never learned, and she found herself searching for something to say that wouldn't make her look like a naive country miss.

Thankfully, the dance came to an end a few moments later, saving her the need to devise a sparkling comment.

"Would you care to join me in a refreshment, my mystery lady?"

In her tongue-tied state, she'd thoroughly embarrass herself if she spent any more time in his presence. Needing to collect herself, Elizabeth shook her head, pushing aside her regret. "While I appreciate the offer, my lord, I believe it might be best if I return to my sister."

"The loss of your charming company will forever wound me," he said, dramatically pressing a hand to his heart.

Oh, Lord, how was she supposed to respond to that remark? Offering him a wavering smile in farewell, she gathered her skirts and stepped around him. She hadn't even made it a foot away when he called out to her.

"Perhaps you should adjust your fichu," he suggested. "I'd rather you not share that delightful view with any gentleman other than myself."

A gasp broke from Elizabeth as she glanced down to see that her fichu had completely slipped from one shoulder, fully exposing her plunging neckline. His soft chuckle only added to her unsettled emotions.

Feeling her cheeks burn, she clutched the dangling material to her chest as she hurried away to the ladies' chamber to repair her person . . . wondering all the while at the odd desire she had to tear off the fichu and face him, bold and wild, letting him look his fill.

Dear Heavens, what was happening to her?

Watching the fair lady scurry away, Richard continued to chuckle as he made his way off the dance floor. When he'd come to Almack's this evening, he'd had no intentions of dancing with anyone, much less forcing some lady he'd never before met to dance with him. He'd only come at his mother's request.

He shook his head as he imagined what his brother, the noble Lord John Vernon, Marquess of Wykham, would have said about this latest escapade. Lord, he'd have to hear about his brash behavior for hours on end. No, John would never be able to understand the reason he'd pulled that blonde goddess onto the dance floor with him. Instead, his brother would look at him in bafflement.

Hearing her sigh as she'd watched her companion step away with a dance partner, Richard had seen, felt, and heard her utter loneliness. And, hell, he knew just how lonely a person could feel, even in the most crowded of rooms. Though he'd admitted this dark secret to her, she hadn't believed him. Instead, she'd judged him and decided he was a rake. While it was true that he was considered a rake by reputation, for some odd reason he'd thought that this woman who understood what loneliness was might be able to see beneath the facade to the man inside.

And just when he thought she'd dismissed him, she surprised him by offering him a pretty apology and accepting his offer to dance. Her shy response intrigued him, and he promised himself he'd discover her name before the night was through.

Still smiling, he glanced around for his mother, hoping she might be able to identify the blonde beauty. Scanning the edges of the room, he was lost in the search for his mother until someone tapped him upon the shoulder.

"You certainly seem to take pleasure in setting the dragons atwitter. Whatever have you done now?"

The amused observation came from his elder brother, John. Grinning broadly, Richard looked around to see that several members of the ton were staring in his direction. "One must make the most of their strengths," he observed.

John's expression grew sober as he looked at Richard. "The ease with which you astound the ton isn't a strength."

"Shall we say it's a gift then?" Richard countered swiftly.

"More a curse than a gift, I'd warrant." John clasped his hands behind his back. "Until last year, I'd worried whether you'd ever tire of the wastrel lifestyle you'd embraced. But you have quite admirably reclaimed your dignity." His brows furrowed. "What I can't understand is why you continue to act the rake? Why don't you behave—"

"This isn't the time or place for this conversation," Richard interrupted. "Now if you'll excuse me, John, I see Mother across the room, and I need her help in identifying someone for me."

"Perhaps I can help," John offered. "With your . . . more adventurous pursuits this past year, you've spent little time at these affairs, but I've attended most of them."

"Naturally," Richard remarked with a laugh. "After all, you must fulfill all the social obligations befitting your station."

"Why is it that whenever you speak of my preference for polite behavior you always end up making me sound like a priggish bluenose?"

"Because you're fast becoming one," Richard returned, trying to soften his words with a smile. "Really, John, I'm starting to worry about you."

John rocked back on his heels. "Isn't that ironic?"

"Yes, but it doesn't change the fact that I worry you are becoming too set in your ways, too rigid . . . too much like Father."

"I shall take that as a compliment," John said smoothly.

"It wasn't meant as one," Richard muttered, shaking his head. "Father could barely crack a smile on his best days. Is that really what you want to become?"

A side of John's mouth quirked upward. "As long as I have you around, I doubt it would be possible to give up smiling. You're just too bloody entertaining, Richard."

Richard rolled his eyes. "You're deliberately missing my point, John. You should heed my warning and start to live a little before you turn around and find you're a crotchety old man with no wife, no children, no friends."

Amusement brightened John's expression. "Well, at least I'll still have you, brother."

"Fine, then. Make light of this, John," Richard replied. "I'm too busy trying to discover the identity of my mystery lady to spend more time arguing with you now."

"I offered to help," John reminded him.

"Very well." Searching the ballroom again, Richard spotted his dance partner sitting along the far wall, next to one of Almack's patronesses. "The one seated next to Lady Sefton."

At a glance, John nodded. "That is Lady Elizabeth Everley, the daughter of the Earl of Shipham."

Elizabeth. Richard turned the name over in his mind. From what he could tell of her nature from their brief acquaintance, he acknowledged that the name fit her well: formal, cool, and yet still soft and feminine.

"Would you like an introduction?"

Imagining the lady's response, Richard began to grin as he nodded. "Lead the way."

2

Douglas Everley, Earl of Shipham, stepped into the grand ballroom and looked around for his daughters. With one quick glance he found Catherine, wearing a wide smile as she danced with Lord Allen. Unfortunately, his Elizabeth wasn't dancing, but rather sitting against the rear wall next to one of the patronesses of Almacks.

Sighing, he made his way over to his eldest daughter, wondering with each step what it would take to make her more interested in attracting a gentleman's attention. "Pardon the interruption, my lady, but I wonder if I might have a word with my daughter," he said, bowing low.

The grand dame tipped her head graciously. "Certainly, my lord."

Before he could escort her to a more private area, Elizabeth blurted, "I danced earlier, Papa. I kept my promise; I swear I did!"

"Lady Elizabeth did indeed dance earlier, my lord," began Lady Sefton. "In fact, I was just now warning her about that particular gentleman . . . if one can apply that term to Lord Vernon."

Douglas frowned slightly, trying to place the familiar-sounding name. "Lord Vernon, you said?"

Her elaborate headpiece bobbed as Lady Sefton nodded. "Exactly. Lord Richard Vernon, younger brother of the delightful Marquess of Wykham."

"Ah, yes," Douglas murmured. "I am acquainted with the Marquess, but have never had the pleasure of meeting his sibling."

"I'm quite certain you would find it a pleasant experience if you ever were to meet Lord Vernon, for he is a charming devil." Lady Sefton waggled her fan at Elizabeth. "Which is precisely why you should stay far away from him, young lady," she pronounced in firm tones. "That rapscallion seems to know precisely what to say to a lady to make her believe he knows her very soul."

"Come now, Lady Sefton," began Douglas with a smile. "I've yet to meet a gentleman who possessed that particular ability."

"As you said, my lord, you've never met Lord Vernon." Snapping her fan open, Lady Sefton fluttered it against her chest as if she were about to become beset with vapors. "Why, two seasons ago, he ruined the reputation of a young debutante with his silvered tongue and sweet compliments, enticing her into improper behavior. The poor dear thought Lord Vernon in love with her, foolish chit that she was, only to discover that he'd done it all on a wager." Lady Sefton made a *tsk*ing sound as she slowly shook her head. "Of course, it was far too late for her by then, and her shamed parents were forced to wed her off to some country baron. And that is only *one* tale from Lord Vernon's wicked past," she finished.

"There are more?"

Douglas watched the color drain from his daughter's face as she listened to Lady Sefton's gossip.

"*Much* worse," announced Lady Sefton.

Undoubtedly providing the mavens of Almack's with all the fodder they desired, thought Douglas, tired of listening to gossip. "Elizabeth, I'm in dire need of refreshment." Offering Lady Sefton a polite nod, he assisted his daughter out of the seat. "Excuse us, my lady."

Bowing her head in acquiescence, Lady Sefton immediately turned toward her companion on her left. "It would be a dreadful shame to allow Lord Vernon to ruin another girl, especially one as . . ."

Having heard enough, Douglas tugged Elizabeth away from the gossip. When she stumbled, he looked down at his daughter, alarmed by her pallor. "Elizabeth? Are you feeling ill?"

Confusion darkened her gaze as she slowly shook her head. "H-h-h-he seemed so nice."

"I don't doubt he did," Douglas agreed, squeezing Elizabeth's hand in comfort. "And he might be precisely what he seemed to be. You can't listen to idle gossip, Elizabeth. I prefer to judge a man upon his present actions, not his past ones." Still, he knew from experience that, more often than not, gossip stemmed from a grain of truth, and if one bit of that horrid tale he'd just heard from Lady Sefton was true, then he would have to ensure he steered his daughter far away from this Lord Vernon.

Glancing up, Douglas noticed the Marquess of Wykham approaching, and at the marquess' side was a gentleman who, from the look of him, was the infamous brother. "It looks as if I'm about to get the opportunity to finally meet this notorious gentleman."

Beside him, Elizabeth moaned softly.

"Good evening, my lord," John said as he held out his hand to Lord Shepham. "It's been quite a while."

"Indeed." Lord Shipham accepted the outstretched hand with a shake. "You are looking well, Wykham."

"I can say the same to you, sir." Placing a hand upon his brother's shoulder, John drew Richard forward. "Might I have the honor of presenting my brother, Lord Richard Vernon?"

"A pleasure," murmured Lord Shipham, with a smile that didn't quite reach his eyes.

The reaction didn't surprise Richard. Obviously the man had heard of his reputation. Biting back a curse, Richard glanced at Elizabeth to see if her father had spoken to her about his past.

Gone were the shy smiles and warm glances. Instead, the ice maiden had returned . . . and this time, Richard feared he wouldn't be able to melt through the frozen wall that surrounded Elizabeth once again.

A resigned sigh escaped Richard as she lifted her chin and pointedly looked away from him. So much for finding someone who understood him, he thought, as Lord Shipham introduced Elizabeth to John.

"A pleasure to make your acquaintance, Lord Wykham," Elizabeth murmured to John, dipping into a curtsey. Pointedly ignoring him, she didn't even bother with a polite greeting. If he'd had any doubts about how much she'd heard about his past misdeeds, they were gone now.

An awkward silence descended upon the group until

Lord Shipham cleared his throat. "So, Lord Vernon, how did you meet my daughter?"

Richard instinctively adopted the pose of rakish ennui he'd perfected years before. "I walked up to her and introduced myself," he said blithely.

"Introduced yourself?" John muttered under his breath. "Good Lord, Richard, what were you thinking?"

"I believe I was thinking that the lady was in need of a dance partner."

John let loose a long-suffering sigh. "Please forgive my brother his boldness, my lady. Despite his frequent lapses in propriety, I assure you he is well-bred."

"Well-bred?" Richard laughed. "Lord, John, you make me sound like a hunting hound. Next thing I know you'll be offering to show her my teeth."

Lord Shipham stiffened. "Your comment makes me question the statement altogether, sir."

John sent Richard a quelling look, then offered a reassuring smile to Lord Shipham. "Pardon my brother, sir. His humor is an acquired taste."

"So I see."

Humiliation burned inside Richard as he tried to keep the flush of embarrassment from staining his cheeks. Lord, why did he let his anger get the best of him? And why the devil had he been so disappointed in Elizabeth's rejection of him in the first place? Acknowledging the utter rudeness of his behavior, Richard offered his own apologies to Lord Shipham. "Please pardon my . . ."

"Excuse us," Lord Shipham interrupted, directing his comment toward John, "but I promised my daughter refreshment." And with that, Lord Shipham tugged Elizabeth away, leaving Richard staring after them in frustration.

"Why do you persist in behaving so poorly, Richard?" John asked wearily. "Would it kill you to let others know that you truly *are* a gentleman?"

Swallowing the lump of humiliation stuck in his throat, Richard shrugged one shoulder. "I don't know; I've never tried."

"It's past time you did," John said quietly.

Staring after Elizabeth, Richard released a sigh. "Perhaps you're right."

John nudged him. "Perhaps?"

The long-time jest made him smile. "Sorry, I forgot. You're *always* right, aren't you?"

"And you're always the clever one, Richard." John put a companionable hand upon Richard's shoulder. "Now, why don't we see if we can find a cigar and a drink?"

"Lead the way."

As her father led her out of the ballroom, Elizabeth struggled to contain her need to scream. How could she have been such a fool? Like a naive country girl, she'd been taken in by Lord Vernon's glib statements, allowed his words to touch a chord deep inside her and make her believe he felt the same way she did in society.

Instead, however, he'd been playing a game. Like a master magician, he'd gazed into her, seeking out her weakness, and used it to disarm her. When she thought of how he'd spouted all that nonsense about not judging him by his appearance, she felt even more foolish. She'd just been duped by a master.

Well, she'd certainly shown him that she wasn't so easily deceived. As soon as she'd snubbed him, Lord Vernon had dropped his mask, allowing her to see the caustic, jaded libertine he'd hidden from her during their first meeting. He played the part of offended gentleman like a premier actor from a Drury Lane theatre.

The thought of forcing another polite smile tonight made Elizabeth want to groan. Pressing a hand to her temple, Elizabeth offered her father an apologetic smile. "I'm feeling a bit fatigued, Papa, and would like to return home now."

"Certainly, my dear," he murmured immediately. "It's near dawn anyway, so why don't I collect your sister and we'll all be heading off."

Though she didn't want to spoil Catherine's fun, Elizabeth knew she wouldn't be able to bear another chance encounter with Lord Vernon. Promising herself that she would explain it to Catherine when they arrived home, Elizabeth nodded to her father. "I shall wait here for you."

A few moments later, her father returned with Catherine in tow.

"I still don't understand why we can't stay for the last hour, Papa," protested Catherine.

"Sorry, Cat, it's my fault," Elizabeth said, saving her father from explaining. "My head is beginning to pound."

Catherine nodded understandingly. "Almack's can be so overwhelming." Without another word, they collected their wraps and allowed their father to escort them outside.

"I saw you conversing with the Marquess of Wykham and his brother, Lord Richard Vernon," Catherine began the moment the carriage door closed.

Before Elizabeth could answer, their father chimed in. "Indeed we were. I'm acquainted with the marquess through a business venture we both invested in."

"From all accounts, the two gentlemen might very well look like brothers, but their disposition couldn't be more different," Catherine said, undoubtedly relaying the latest gossip. "So tell me, Elizabeth, what did you think of the proper marquess and his devilish brother?"

"Apt description."

Catherine's eyes widened. "My, my. Do tell."

Regretting her impulsive remark, Elizabeth shrugged lightly. "There's nothing to tell, except to agree with what you've already said. Lord Wykham was indeed very proper and charming, while his brother made no attempt to curb his rakish manner."

"I quite agree," their father stated firmly. "The younger pup struck me as being rude and far too puffed-up."

Remembering Lord Vernon's deceit, Elizabeth agreed with her father's assessment wholeheartedly. "Since Lord Wykham behaved in a most decorous manner, I found it a bit startling to think them brothers."

"Why?" Catherine questioned, tilting her head to the side. "Do you think that just because they are family they should act the same? After all, you and I disprove that theory, Elizabeth, for we are as different as night and day."

"True," Elizabeth conceded with a small frown.

Their father smoothed a hand down his vest. "So, you were taken with the marquess, were you, Elizabeth?"

There was an odd note to Papa's question. "To say I was taken is an exaggeration. Lord Wykham simply impressed me with his manner."

"Ah, but perhaps with a little nudging we can change your being impressed to being taken," Catherine said brightly.

"I've long since given up hope of that, Cat," admitted Elizabeth, holding in a sigh of regret. "I've yet to find someone who I wish to marry."

"You'll find someone soon," predicted their father, patting Elizabeth's arm comfortingly.

"Even if I don't, it won't be disastrous." Shaking her head, Elizabeth tried to make her sister and father understand. "I will be perfectly content back in the countryside, where I can read, pursue my experiments, and live my life exactly as I desire."

Papa looked stunned as he sagged back against the carriage seat. "You don't mean that, Elizabeth."

"Oh, but I do, Papa." Leaning forward, she placed her hand upon his knee. "Why must I marry in order to be happy?"

"Because if you don't, you'll be alone." A haunted shadow darkened his expression. "And there is nothing worse than being lonely."

Knowing he was thinking of Mama, Elizabeth hurried to reassure him it was different for her. "I know you miss Mama terribly, but it won't be like that for me. I've never been in love, never felt a part of someone, so I won't feel as if I've lost something."

"I . . . I don't know what to say to you, how to convince you that you're wrong," Papa said finally.

"I'm not wrong." As the carriage rolled to a stop, Elizabeth straightened in her seat. "Will you consider what I've said tonight, Papa?"

At Papa's nod, Elizabeth leaned across the seat to press a kiss upon his cheek before following Catherine from the carriage. Undoubtedly he would consider her words, see the wisdom in her argument, and release her from attending these foolish events . . . and suffering the presence of foolish men.

He'd never felt more . . . defeated.

Douglas slumped onto his bed, feeling ancient and completely, unbearably alone. And to think that this was what Elizabeth desired. To come up to her lonely bedchamber every night, to never know the passion of marriage, the companionship of a spouse. He shook his head.

"Difficult evening?"

Sighing, Douglas turned his head to see his wife . . . or rather her ghost . . . sitting in a chair near the fire. "Lord, Margaret, I miss you so damn much," he said, his voice breaking on the last word.

Sadness shifted over her face. "I know," she murmured softly. "That's why I'm still here with you."

He wanted to go to her, to sweep her up into his arms and take comfort in her softness, but he knew from experience that she would simply fade away. On the eve of her death, she'd come to him, looking strong and healthy, and he'd rushed to hold her—only to find his arms unable to close around her ethereal form. Still, he was glad for her company every night, and if the price was this ache to touch her once more, he could easily live with it rather than live without her at all.

"I don't know what to do with our girls," he admitted as he moved to sit across from Margaret. "While Catherine enjoys collecting proposals, Elizabeth wants nothing to do with the gentlemen of the ton." He rubbed his hands over his face. "She told me this evening that she didn't care if she ever married."

"Oh, dear," murmured Margaret. "That would not be good for our Elizabeth."

Resting his elbows upon his knees, Douglas leaned forward. "No, it wouldn't. She would continue to lose herself in her books, growing ever more distant." He shook his head. "Even now, I find it difficult to reach her."

Margaret's eyes darkened. "But you were always close."

"I know," Douglas admitted softly. "After your death, I spent hours in my room, talking to you, and though I am loathe to admit it, I failed to help our girls with their grief. And when I finally roused myself to regain an interest in their lives, I'd discovered I was no longer needed." Our girls turned to each other, becoming much closer than before. And while that is wonderful, I now feel as if I'm outside of them, an observer looking into their lives." He sighed heavily. "While Catherine seems open and affectionate, I sometimes wonder if her flitting from one gentleman to the next is a way to avoid becoming too attached to any one gentleman. And as for Elizabeth, well, she simply stopped wishing to interact with anyone."

Nodding, Margaret remained silent for a moment before replying. "Then you must help Elizabeth to find a way to overcome her shyness, and help Catherine settle her affections upon a special gentleman."

"How?" he asked, feeling helpless.

A soft smile brightened her features. "With the right incentive, you can inspire the girls to try to find their perfect match."

"Like I found with you."

Tears glittered in Margaret's eyes. "Yes, like we found with each other."

At that moment, Douglas swore he would have sold

his soul for one more kiss with his wife. Struggling his way past the intense emotions flooding him, he refocused his thoughts onto his daughters. "Now all we need to do is figure out how to inspire them."

Margaret's angelic smile tipped upward with devilish intent. "I do believe I have just the thing."

With a laugh, Douglas settled back in his chair. "Do tell."

3

"Excuse the interruption, Master Richard, but the shipment of flour just arrived."

Setting down his pen upon the open ledger, Richard rose from his chair to glance out the window at the dozens of people bustling about the wharf despite the early hour. "Excellent. Fifty boxes, right?"

"All nice and tight," agreed Mr. Perth, the head foreman for Richard's business.

"Tell the captain I shall be right down to settle the account." After Mr. Perth nodded and hurried from the room, Richard returned his attention to the busy wharf. Satisfaction settled deep into his gut as he realized he'd made his mark upon this place. Little had he known, when he'd won this pretzel business in a card game, that it would come to mean so much to him.

Pretzels. Lord, who would have ever guessed that there was so much money to be made in little bits of baked dough? Richard laughed out loud. When he'd first won the business, he'd scoffed at it, thinking that the only value the business might have would be in the building and machines. After all, who in their right mind would want to be a bloody pretzel maker? Indeed, he'd had every intention of simply selling it off to replenish all the monies he'd lost at the gaming tables, but when he'd come to tour the place, to get an idea of its value, something about the busy workroom had appealed to him. Richard smiled at the memory. Even Mr. Perth had looked at him with resignation, viewing him as a dandy with far too much time on his idle hands. Worst thing was, Mr. Perth had been right.

In an impulsive act, Richard had decided to try and make a go of the business. Much to his surprise, the merchant next door, Aaron Burnbaum, had taken him under his wing and taught him the fundamentals of running a business. On the advice of his new friend, Richard had approached the local pubs, given them a few samples to try, and had, in the end, signed most of them on as customers. Then he'd expanded his business to the continent. Who would have guessed that the Germans, who created the pretzel after all, would consider an imported English pretzel a delicacy?

He didn't know why the Germans craved his pretzels, nor did he care. All he knew was that he'd expanded this business until it had begun to thrive and had been making money, hand over fist, ever since. His success in this venture had long since replenished his accounts, and while he now had the financial security he'd desired, he had no wish to walk away from the business. Indeed not.

This was *his*.

It was a pity he couldn't tell anyone from the ton of his foray into a common business venture. Hell, even *he* had considered the factory a grand farce . . . only the jest turned out to be on him. He could only imagine the reaction if he looked at a pompous bluestocking and told her he was running a pretzel factory. Not only would he become the laughingstock of town, but he'd also be ostracized from society.

And even though John was thrilled that he was no longer consumed with rakish pursuits, Richard knew his brother would prefer if he sold the business and reinvested the profits into a more gentlemanly venture. Something where he kept his hands clean. Glancing down at his ink-stained hands, Richard smiled, remembering how dirty he'd felt from his past debaucheries when he would think nothing of drinking himself into a stupor and falling into a strumpet's bed. He'd never imagined that by dirtying his hands with good honest toil from a hard day's work he'd finally feel clean.

Richard shook his head. Lord, he didn't have time to be caught up in such self-indulgent thoughts. After all, he had a business to run.

Pounding the nail into place to secure the arm of the catapult, Elizabeth lost herself in her new experiment. When a hand touched her shoulder, she yelped in surprise, dropped the hammer, and spun around, pressing a hand to her chest. "Catherine," she rasped, trying to get her pounding heart to slow. "I didn't hear you come in."

"Obviously." She smiled sheepishly. "Sorry about scaring you, Elizabeth. I tried knocking, but you didn't hear me over your hammering." Peering over Elizabeth's shoulder, Catherine gazed down at the table. "What are you working on now?"

Elizabeth gestured toward her half-completed catapult. "I'm trying to recreate a miniature version of da Vinci's catapult, but shifting the measurements and keeping the weight in alignment is proving difficult. So, I'm trying to secure . . ."

"Please, Elizabeth," interrupted Catherine, holding up her hands. "Simply stating that you're building a small catapult would have sufficed."

"Sorry." Lifting one shoulder, Elizabeth tucked her hands into the pockets of her leather work apron. "I tend to get carried away whenever I talk about my experiments."

"I know you love it." Catherine wrinkled her nose as she looked around the small shed. "I don't understand *why* though. Look at this place, Elizabeth. Every corner is crammed with old bits of rubbish. It is beyond me how you can spend so much time in here."

"Then we're even, for I can't begin to fathom why you enjoy spending so much time at parties," Elizabeth countered.

Catherine smiled at that point. "Yes, I suppose we are even."

Retrieving her hammer, Elizabeth hung it from a nail on the wall. "Did you come to visit me or did I forget another soiree?" she asked, knowing how often she lost track of time here in her workshop . . . and how often Catherine needed to pull her out of this haven and direct her to dress for a social outing. "I hope I don't have another dull obligation, because I'm really making strides on this machine and I'd like to spend more time on it."

"Perhaps later." Catherine reached down and untied Elizabeth's apron. "Papa wishes to speak with us in his study."

"He does?" Surprise filled Elizabeth as she lifted her apron over her head and hung it on a nearby peg. "Is something the matter?"

Catherine shrugged her shoulders. "I don't know; he wouldn't say a word other than to ask me to fetch you."

"Do you think we might be going back to the country?" Elizabeth asked hopefully.

"Not unless you plan on leaving me behind in town."

Tipping her head to the side, Elizabeth pretended to be considering the idea.

With a laugh, Catherine clasped Elizabeth's hand and they walked out of the workshop.

As soon as they entered their father's study, he rose to his feet, greeted them, and asked them to sit in the two chairs across from his wide desk before resuming his seat behind his desk. The formal seating arrangements struck Elizabeth as odd. In the past, whenever their father wished to speak to them, they would sit in the cushioned chairs near the fireplace.

"Thank you for fetching Elizabeth," he said to Catherine.

"You're welcome, Papa." Folding her hands in her lap, Catherine asked quietly, "What did you wish to speak with us about?"

"Your futures." Their father took a deep breath, as if bracing himself. "I think it's time I helped . . . guide you."

Elizabeth blinked in surprise. "Guide us?"

Nodding, their father placed his elbows on his desk and leaned forward. "Let's discuss your future first, Catherine. You wish to marry, don't you?"

"Of course," she replied automatically.

"Then why have you failed to settle upon one gentleman?"

Having wondered the same thing herself, Elizabeth waited for her sister's reply.

"Because this is my first season and I wished to enjoy it unfettered," Catherine explained. "I will, however, decide upon a husband before the end of the season."

"Very good." Their father's gaze shifted onto Elizabeth. "And what of you, Elizabeth?"

She shifted in her chair. "What of me, Papa? I don't seem to attract many gentlemen," she pointed out.

"Because you aren't trying."

Stiffening, Elizabeth shook her head. "That's not true. I *do* try. It's just that I can't converse with Catherine's ease."

Papa's expression softened. "Then you need to try harder, Elizabeth. Despite your assertions that you would be perfectly fine living as an old maid in the country, I don't wish that for you . . . which is why I've devised my plan."

"Plan?" Elizabeth asked apprehensively. "What plan?"

"Your greatest strength, Elizabeth, is your love for your family, so I'm going to help you tap into that strength to help you overcome your shyness." Clearing his throat, their father continued. "I will not allow Catherine to marry before you, so if you wish to grant your sister's dearest wish, you will indeed begin to exert yourself at social affairs and settle upon someone to wed."

A gasp broke from both Elizabeth and Catherine.

"You can't be . . ."

"Surely you don't mean . . ."

Papa raised both of his hands, cutting off their simultaneous protests. "My mind is made up on this matter. Catherine, you will only marry after your sister does."

"But what if she *never* marries?" Catherine wailed. "It's not fair."

"Don't worry, poppet," reassured Papa. "Elizabeth loves you and she will do anything . . . even marry . . . to ensure your happiness." He gave Elizabeth a challenging stare. "Isn't that right?"

A fierce denial was on the tip of her tongue, ready to fly, when Elizabeth glanced over at her sister's anxious expression. Her father had neatly set the trap in place, and now she was caught. "How can you do this to us, Papa?"

"As someone who loves you and is concerned for your future, I feel I have no other choice." He laced his fingers together. "I'm doing this for your own good, Elizabeth."

"My own good?" Thrusting back her chair, Elizabeth stood, forcing herself not to sway beneath the weight of her crushing disappointment. Her beloved father had unexpectedly become her adversary. "Please, Papa," she whispered brokenly. "Please don't do this to me."

Father closed his eyes as if in pain. Slowly, his lashes lifted, and in the depths of his gaze, Elizabeth saw his rigid determination. "All I'm trying to do to you, Elizabeth, is help you find happiness. I know you so well, darling, and if you are properly motivated, you can apply yourself diligently. You need to consider this my way of motivating you to work on your socializing skills and seek out a partner."

Pressing her hands against her rolling stomach, Elizabeth whispered, "And what if I fail?"

"You won't."

Elizabeth wished she had an ounce of her father's conviction. "You would risk Catherine's happiness?"

Their father shook his head. "I don't believe I'm risking anything. I have faith in you, Elizabeth."

"This isn't right, Papa," protested Catherine, coming to stand beside Elizabeth. "You shouldn't put this pressure upon Elizabeth."

"I feel as if I've been left no choice."

The firm tone of their father's voice shattered Elizabeth's last whisper of hope, leaving behind a horrid sense of betrayal. "It's no use, Cat," Elizabeth said slowly. "We have no choice but to accept his dictates, regardless of how unreasonable they might be, and pray that he hasn't destroyed our future happiness in the process."

Catherine's brows drew together. "But . . ."

"There's no use in arguing," Elizabeth repeated as she straightened her shoulders. "Let's leave Father to his machinations."

As soon as the girls left the study, Douglas dropped his face into his trembling hands. Dear God, he prayed he hadn't done anything to harm their chances at happiness. Did he have the right to play God with their lives? Of course, he did. He was their father.

The queasiness in his stomach settled. It would be all right; it *had* to be all right.

The noon hour was only minutes away when Richard stepped down from his carriage. Brushing at his coat, he soon gave up the futile effort to wipe away the flour that had spilled on the fine silk. Still, the money he'd made today alone would purchase more than a few new jackets. Warmed by the thought, he slowly made his way up the front steps.

Lord, he was exhausted, but then he'd earned the right to be tired. He'd gone from Almack's to his office, where he'd worked through the night in order to make the ship sailing for Germany on the morning tide. And while he'd found the morning's work incredibly satisfying, that feeling did little to alleviate the weariness sinking into his bones.

A groan broke from him when he spotted John's carriage waiting in front of his townhouse. *Wonderful,* Richard thought. All he wanted was his bed; he didn't have enough energy for even a brief conversation with John. But since his brother had already arrived, he'd have to find the strength somewhere. Sighing wearily, he continued to trudge up the steps and into his home.

"Good day, John," Richard said, purposely injecting a light note into his greeting as he dragged himself into the parlor. "What brings you by so early?"

John shot an incredulous look out the window at the bright noon sun. "Hardly early, Richard, but then again, most of us seek our beds sometime during the night."

Dropping into a chair, Richard propped his aching feet onto a stool. "Couldn't," he said. "Had a shipment that needed to go out this morning."

A frown darkened John's expression. "Don't you have employees who take care of that for you?"

"Of course I do, but one of my men was ill."

"So you took his place?"

The incredulous question made Richard smile. "Precisely."

"Good God, man, look at yourself." Striding over to Richard, John fingered an edge of his flour-coated jacket. "You're filthy, covered in flour, and exhausted."

"You forgot to mention satisfied," Richard added quietly.

Stepping back, John took a seat across from Richard. "I'm certain you are, Richard. I will be the first one to admit that I'm proud of the way you turned your life around . . . without any help, despite my many offers."

A side of his mouth quirked upward. "Just because I didn't accept any of your offers for financial aid doesn't mean I didn't appreciate them."

"I know," John assured him. "And now I can see that it was best that you *didn't* accept any money from me to replenish your accounts."

"True enough, because I wouldn't have appreciated a bloody farthing of it." No, if he hadn't been so financially desperate to consider running a pretzel company, he might still be mired in debauchery.

"You're right." John leaned forward. "But perhaps it is time to consider selling the company and sinking those funds into a more . . . acceptable venture."

"Why? You don't like having your brother being known as the Pretzel Man?" Richard asked, stung by John's remark.

"Don't take offense, Richard. I merely want to help you."

Swinging his feet off the stool, Richard sat upright. "I didn't need your help before and I don't need it now. I like getting my hands dirty and creating something wonderful. I'm proud of what I do."

"If you're so proud, then why do you persist in acting the rake?"

John's quiet question took the wind from his sails. How could he respond? Because whether or not he admitted it to John, part of him *was* humiliated that he was now a pretzel maker.

"That's what I thought." John settled back in his chair. "If you sold the factory and invested the money, then you wouldn't need to fear someone finding out. Many gentlemen now actively participate in their investment ventures.

You could show the ton who you really are, Richard, and not have to hide behind a facade."

It was true, Richard knew. It was the perfect solution to everything. But there was only one hitch.

He *liked* owning the pretzel company.

"What you fail to understand, John, is that I don't wish to give it up. I'd rather play the lecherous dandy in order to hide my business. Besides, I so rarely go out to social events anymore."

"Because you're spending all your time at that factory."

"Ah, but it's time well spent." Standing, Richard retrieved a rolled parchment from the sideboard. "Look at what I've designed to improve the production of the factory." Spreading the paper out on top of the table, he gestured toward the sketch. "This is a strip of leather that lays on top of a set of rolling pins. My men can place the pretzels on this belt, then, by pulling on this rope here, can send them onto the next station without breaking the flow of production."

Placing a hand upon the drawing, John captured Richard's gaze. "You're becoming consumed by this, Richard. Last night was the first time you've gone to Almack's in over a year," he pointed out.

A laugh broke from Richard. "First you're concerned about me because I'm wasting my life, and when I finally pick myself up, you're starting to worry that I'm not spending enough time at frivolous parties?"

"Attending social outings isn't frivolous," insisted John as he sat back again.

"I know, I know; it's a social obligation." Richard rolled up the parchment. "Besides, however would you find a suitable bride if you didn't scour the marriage mart."

It was John's turn to laugh. "Trust me when I say that finding a bride isn't one of the reasons I attend soirees."

"You can't be serious." Yet when Richard looked at his brother, he saw John was indeed serious. "Why on earth not?"

"Because the last thing I want right now is to be saddled with another responsibility."

Responsibilities like him, Richard realized. Ever since their father died, John had been shouldering the tremendous burden of maintaining the estate. "Fine pair we are," Richard murmured, smiling at his brother. "I have no desire to wed because I'm far too busy, and you don't want a wife because you wish for a taste of freedom." He tipped his head to the side. "Wonder who will get the lauded title of Marquess of Wykham if you don't produce an heir?"

"No need to think on that further, because I do have every intention of fulfilling that obligation." A grin split John's face. "Just not right now."

Richard returned his brother's smile. "Fair enough." But somehow the idea of John as man-about-town didn't seem, well, like John. "What if you happen to meet a woman who seems perfect for you? What if tomorrow you met a lady who made you feel free instead of burdened?"

John's smile dimmed and he remained quiet for a long moment. "I honestly don't know. If there were such a lady, perhaps she would still this odd sense of restlessness I've been feeling lately."

"She just might," Richard agreed. "Besides, if you marry, you'll be far too busy to worry about me." And that would be one less burden for John to worry about.

"While that might be the case, I don't expect to find the perfect woman tomorrow," John said confidently.

No, Richard thought, hiding a smile, but perhaps here was one thing Richard could do for John.

Without conscious thought, Elizabeth headed toward the one place that had always provided her solace. Her workshop. Slamming open the door, she struggled to control the tightening in her chest, to retain a semblance of calm in front of Catherine, who had followed her.

"What are we going to do?" Catherine whispered, clutching her skirt.

The fact that Catherine didn't even seem aware that she was wrinkling her dress spoke volumes about her distress. Elizabeth shook her head, at a loss as to how to get them out of this mess. "I don't know," she replied honestly. "Maybe after Papa's had a while to consider . . ."

Before she could even finish her thought, Catherine interrupted. "No, he won't," she stated emphatically. "You know Papa. When he makes up his mind, he doesn't change it. Ever."

"You're right," Elizabeth admitted, though it galled her to do so. Looking around her workshop, she wished that devising the solution to this problem was as easy as figuring out the next step in her experiments. She stilled at that thought, before slowly murmuring, "Then we'll just have to find a way *around* his dictate."

Hope brightened Catherine's gaze as she released her gown. "Around? How do you mean?"

Biting her lower lip, Elizabeth gestured to the part-laden shelves of her workshop. "Whenever I reach an impasse in an experiment, I don't try to find a way to change the problem; I try to find a way around it." She could tell by Catherine's expression she didn't understand, so Elizabeth struggled to find the right words. "For example, if I'm building a machine and the bolt the diagram says to use doesn't fit, I don't try to force it. Instead, I find a new one, or sometimes I even redesign the entire joint to make it work better."

Catherine furrowed her brows. "I still don't understand what that has to do with the fact that Papa insists you marry before I do."

"All I'm saying, Cat, is that there has to be a way around this problem, and all we need to do is consider it from all angles and figure out a different approach." Elizabeth smiled for the first time since hearing Papa's horrid pronouncement. "Don't worry, Cat. I'm very good at finding ways around problems."

Catherine's expression didn't lighten. "Figuring out a problem with a few bolts is a much different thing than devising a way to outsmart Papa."

Her sister had a point, Elizabeth conceded, but she thrust her doubt aside. Positive thinking was what was needed here. *That's right,* she assured herself. With enough positive thinking, she could find her way around any problem.

Especially when her sister's future happiness depended upon it.

Walking into White's was one of the hardest things Richard had forced himself to do in a very long time. Still, he'd found himself tossing restlessly upon the bed this afternoon when he should have fallen into an exhausted sleep. Thoughts of his poor behavior toward Lord Shipham and Elizabeth had raced through his head, keeping him from his much-needed rest.

There were times, Richard admitted as he tugged

upon his waistcoat, that this new moral consciousness of his was a bloody pain in the arse. After having called upon Lord Shipham at his house, Richard learned that Elizabeth's father had come to White's . . . and so he'd followed.

Spotting Lord Shipham near the fireplace, Richard took a fortifying breath and headed toward him. Three steps away, Richard stopped and cleared his throat, causing Lord Shipham to glance up from his paper. The cold expression on his face did little to encourage Richard.

"Pardon the interruption, my lord, but I wondered if I might have a word with you," Richard began in his most polite voice.

"I'd rather not," Lord Shipham returned bluntly. "I'm quite enjoying my moment of solitude."

Despite the response, Richard forged onward. "I assure you, my lord, it will only take a moment of your time." Before Lord Shipham could say another word, Richard sat down beside him. "Currently, I find myself in the awkward position of having to apologize to you."

Lord Shipham raised an eyebrow.

Taking this as a positive response, Richard continued, "Last night I was blatantly rude to you and your daughter. My actions were not those of a gentleman and I offer my most sincere apologies."

Still, Lord Shipham remained silent.

The man's unblinking stare was bloody unnerving, Richard decided. Lord, he'd been a fool to come here, offering up an apology like a miscreant. Feeling his cheeks warm, Richard rose without another word and turned on his heel.

"Sit down, Lord Vernon, and allow a man a moment to respond before you race off."

Surprised, Richard resumed his seat.

Folding his paper, Lord Shipham gave Richard his full attention. "When you get to be my age, Lord Vernon, there's not much that surprises you." He pointed at Richard. "But your apology did. And since you were so forthcoming, I feel I must admit that, after having heard the gossip about your past behavior, I might have been quick to jump to conclusions about your behavior."

"That is most generous of you to admit, sir."

"Not generous, just honest," Lord Shipham corrected. "And for a man who prides himself on taking stock of a person's character rather than heeding the tainted tales of a few very bored old women, it isn't an easy thing to admit."

Richard couldn't help but laugh. "Though I'd like to assure you that all the stories you've heard were falsehoods, I find myself unable to do so . . . and remain honest."

The corners of Lord Shipham's mouth tilted upward. "Of course you can't. Don't know of many young gents who haven't reveled a bit before settling down." Leaning forward, Lord Shipham admitted, "Before I wed, I'll wager the gossips had a tale or two about my . . . adventures."

Relief eased the tightness in Richard's chest as he sat back in his chair, enjoying the company of Lord Shipham. Perhaps it wasn't such a bad thing after all to allow people to see the man he'd become.

"Now why don't we order up a few brandies, and I'll tell you about the time I rode a horse into Lord Hammond's country home on a lark."

"That sounds like a tale I simply must hear," Richard replied with a laugh.

Lord Shipham's gaze sharpened. "And then when I'm done, you can tell me why you behaved like such a bastard last night."

Nodding, Richard lifted his hand to beckon a server. "Fair enough."

"Excellent." Setting aside his paper, Lord Shipham leaned back in his chair as well. "In fact, why don't we begin with your explanation before we start swapping tales of misdeeds?"

Richard decided that the only way to handle this situation was with complete honesty. "Very well, sir," he began, "earlier that evening, I'd come upon your daughter, Lady Elizabeth, standing alone in the ballroom, and invited her to dance. Though she declined my invitation, I'm afraid I insisted she join me." He glanced at Lord Shipham to measure his response to that bit of information. When he realized Lord Shipham wasn't scowling, it gave Richard the courage to continue. "While she was shy, your daughter seemed to enjoy my company and, naturally, I found her charming."

"Naturally," Lord Shipham agreed, a corner of his mouth quirking upward.

Encouraged, Richard finished his tale. "But when we were formally introduced, she acted so cool . . . undoubtedly because of the tales she'd heard. While I understood the reasons behind her reception, I had little liking for her coolness, which is why I behaved so abominably."

Lord Shipham considered the admission for a moment. "So you set out to prove that all the stories she'd heard about you were true, since she seemed so determined to believe them."

"Precisely," Richard said, relieved that Lord Shipham

at least understood the reasons behind his behavior. "Still, that doesn't excuse my rudeness to you and your daughter."

"No," Lord Shipham agreed, "but it certainly makes it understandable."

Lord Shipham's reaction was so different from the one he'd imagined that Richard found himself struggling to take it all in. He'd thought Lord Shipham might accept the apology at best. Yet here he sat, as the man ordered two brandies for them, seemingly at ease with Richard's apology. More surprising still was the odd sensation of satisfaction sinking into him.

Perhaps there was something to fulfilling gentlemanly obligations.

"Now, I believe I was going to tell you one of the misdeeds from my past."

Richard settled back to enjoy the tale. . . .

4

"Have you devised a way around Papa's scheme?" whispered Catherine from behind her fan.

"No, but don't worry, Cat. I will," Elizabeth reassured her sister. Indeed, she'd been turning the problem over in her head all afternoon and was no closer to a solution. Closing her eyes, she rubbed at her temple.

"Well, if you don't think of something soon, we'll have to begin to concentrate on finding a gentleman for you to wed." Catherine touched Elizabeth's arm. "I know you said you didn't find anyone appealing, but surely there's *someone* here that you might find suitable."

Elizabeth shook her head. "If he's in town, I've yet to meet him."

"What of the gentlemen I saw you with yesterday? The Marquess of Wykham and his brother." Her eyes brightened. "The Marquess is a fine-looking fellow."

Elizabeth nodded slowly. "True, and he was a perfect gentleman . . . unlike that odious brother of his."

"Odious, am I?"

Elizabeth started at the voice behind her. Gritting her teeth, she glanced over her shoulder. "Still making it a habit of eavesdropping upon ladies' conversations, I see," she said coolly. After all, he could hardly expect a warm welcome after he'd played her for a fool.

Stepping around to face them, Lord Vernon grinned wickedly at her. "If I stopped, I'd miss out on all the interesting gossip fluttering about town these days." His gaze shifted onto Catherine. "I don't believe we've had the honor," he murmured, bowing low. "Richard Vernon, at your service, my lady."

Catherine dipped into a curtsey. "Lady Catherine Everley."

Lord Vernon's brows arched upward. "Everley?" He glanced between the two ladies. "Are you sisters or cousins?"

"Sisters . . . though you couldn't tell by looking at us," Catherine returned with a laugh.

"True enough, but then beauty comes in all different forms, does it not?" The charming smile he bestowed upon Catherine grated on Elizabeth's nerves.

Well, she wasn't about to allow the cad to deceive her sister the way he'd deceived her! But before Elizabeth could issue a word of warning to her sister, the marquess joined their group.

"Good evening, Lady Elizabeth," he said smoothly, bowing to her.

"And to you as well, sir." Gesturing toward her sister, Elizabeth murmured, "Might I introduce my sister, Lady Catherine?"

Once again, Lord Wykham dipped into a bow. "A pleasure, my lady."

"I didn't know you were coming to the Swanson's musicale this evening," Lord Vernon remarked.

Lord Wykham shrugged lightly. "Neither did I, until Mother asked me to escort her."

Elizabeth watched the interplay between the two brothers with interest. Lord Wykham's affection for his brother was evident.

"You could have sent a note around to me and I would have taken her," Lord Vernon offered.

"I did," Lord Wykham remarked dryly, "but you'd already left for the evening." He lowered his voice before admitting, "While I hold my mother in the greatest esteem, it is somewhat of a family secret that I absolutely abhor musicales."

Laughing, Lord Vernon placed an affectionate hand upon his brother's shoulder. "I've told John that I've been working on a design for a machine that alters any singer's voice into that of a songbird."

Elizabeth knew Lord Vernon was teasing his brother, but his comment about designing a machine intrigued her. "What sort of machine were you considering, my lord? I've not heard of components that you can assemble to actually change sound."

Catherine nudged her ribs—hard—before she trilled a charming laugh. "Come now, Elizabeth. What on earth do you know about machines and the like?"

In an instant, Elizabeth remembered her unfortunate penchant to get lost in discussions that were utterly inappropriate for polite society. Still, she thought mutinously, it wasn't as if she started the conversation this time!

Lord Vernon's brows drew together as he gave Elizabeth a pointed look. "You certainly sounded as if you knew what you were speaking about."

Dear Heavens! She'd done it now. Shaking her head, she laughed nervously. "I was merely teasing."

"But . . ."

The marquess cut off his brother. "Why don't we let this discussion rest, Richard?" he suggested in a tone that left it clear that the question was *not* a suggestion. "Will you accord me the honor of escorting you to your seat, Lady Elizabeth? I'm sure my brother would be delighted to lead Lady Catherine as well."

"It would be my pleasure," Elizabeth murmured politely, accepting his proffered arm. Smiling at her sister in farewell and giving Lord Vernon one last glance, she allowed Lord Wykham to lead her into the music room.

Blast it all! Richard fumed, watching Elizabeth walk off with his brother. Why the devil wouldn't John allow him to speak with her further on this matter of machines? The woman had certainly spoken like she was interested in the discussion. Though perhaps she was merely making fun, as she'd claimed, Richard conceded, holding back a sigh.

"I couldn't help but notice, Lord Vernon, that your brother seemed most taken with my sister."

Too stunned by the notion, Richard couldn't hold back his exclamation. "John, taken with Lady Elizabeth?"

A delicate frown curved upon Lady Catherine's features. "I don't know why you sound so astounded, my lord. It would be an advantageous match." Leaning forward, she confided, "My sister is most concerned with conducting herself in a manner befitting a lady."

"Naturally. Why wouldn't she be?" he asked, puzzled by Lady Catherine's remark.

Flustered, Lady Catherine hurried to explain. "I only

meant that, despite her fascination with . . . with machines and the like, she truly is a proper lady."

"Fascinated with machines?" The notion intrigued Richard more than he cared to admit, but he could tell from Lady Catherine's blush that she'd not meant to reveal that particular truth.

Lady Catherine dismissed the question with a wave of her hands. "While my sister does tinker with machines occasionally, I assure you it is *merely* a hobby."

Even still, he knew of no other lady in society with such a wonderful hobby. "Does she design her own machines then, or does she . . ."

"Please, sir," Lady Catherine said, glancing around quickly. "I prefer that my confidence not be bandied about the ton, utterly ruining my sister's chances of a suitable match. It is, after all, her greatest wish to be accepted unconditionally by society."

Which made him completely wrong for Elizabeth.

That stray thought startled Richard. It wasn't as if he'd had any true interest in Elizabeth. No, he assured himself, he was merely intrigued by the notion that she might share his passion for machines.

"Bearing that in mind, you can understand that my sister would never disgrace your brother's good name in any manner."

The hopeful note in Lady Catherine's odd comment baffled Richard. "Since your sister and my brother aren't connected at all, I fail to see where this might be relevant."

"I'm merely commenting upon any future developments." Lady Catherine leaned even closer to whisper, "I feel most certain that our siblings would make a fine match."

The workings of this woman's brain confounded Richard. "How can you make a statement like that when they've only met twice?"

Lady Catherine's eyes sparkled. "Because I can *sense* these things, my lord."

Richard laughed at the idea. "If that's true, then you'd make a bloody fortune as a matchmaker."

"That's highly unlikely, as I'd never ruin my reputation by going into trade," Lady Catherine replied with a smile.

It was all Richard could do to keep his smile in place. "Certainly not," he agreed, feeling rather ill. "You'd never lower yourself in that manner."

"Indeed. However that doesn't prevent me from aiding my sister with my ability to sense the perfect match."

The perfect match? Elizabeth and John? Somehow the very idea set off a jarring note inside Richard. Perhaps Lady Catherine overestimated her ability, for the two seemed ill-suited. While he might find Elizabeth's hobby intriguing, he knew his brother would not. Besides, he thought with a nod, the two seemed far too similar to ever suit.

Though he didn't know Elizabeth well enough to judge, Richard did know his brother, and someone interested in following the dictates of society was *not* what John needed. No, John needed to marry someone who would help him bend a little, make him a bit crazy, entice him to toss aside society's rules and do something for the sheer pleasure of it.

Hell, even Lady Catherine would better suit John.

Startled by the thought, Richard gazed down at Lady Catherine. Why not? After all, this woman had approached him, a virtual stranger, and proposed a matchmaking scheme between their siblings, so she obviously didn't concern herself overly much with abiding by the way these things were usually done.

"So, will you help me to arrange for our siblings to spend time together?" she asked, her expression hopeful.

Turning the question over in his head, Richard examined it from every angle. If he agreed, it would naturally bring Lady Catherine into close proximity with John, as she would undoubtedly escort her sister. Then, John could discover for himself that Lady Catherine was the perfect lady for him.

Of course, if John failed to take notice, Richard could always nudge him in the right direction. The four of them could begin to attend the same functions, and he could engineer it so John ended up with Lady Catherine and he ended up with Elizabeth. Not a bad trade at all.

A twinge of guilt plucked at Richard as he realized he'd be duping Lady Catherine. Still, when she was happily in love with his brother, she'd forgive his duplicity . . . especially if he helped find a suitable match for Elizabeth.

It was, Richard thought, the perfect solution.

"Well, my lord?" Catherine prodded. "Will you help me?"

Richard smiled politely. "It shall be my pleasure."

A happy smile brightened her features. "Splendid. When shall we begin?"

Holding out his arm, he said, "No time like the present."

She placed her hand upon his forearm. "Indeed not. What shall we do first?"

"Since we know that they are seated together, I believe we should find seats nearby, and make sure that they become properly acquainted."

"Perfect."

* * *

Thanking God that the first movement was finished, John shifted in his seat, praying that the next piece Miss Swanson chose would be blessedly shorter.

"That was lovely," Lady Elizabeth whispered to him as she leaned closer.

Lovely? If one enjoyed the caterwauling of a dying animal perhaps. Still, John nodded politely in agreement. "A most interesting interpretation of Mozart's work."

Lady Elizabeth gave him a smile before returning her attention to Miss Swanson again. *The perfect, refined lady,* John thought as he watched her.

Just the lady to help his brother battle his demons.

Warming to the idea, John examined the pairing in his mind. Lord knew, she seemed to interest his brother. Just this evening, he'd had to stop Richard from pursuing the idea that Lady Elizabeth might share his interest in machinery. If she was truly interested in Richard's odd tinkerings, that was an added bonus in John's mind.

She also might convince Richard to sell that ridiculous pretzel factory and invest in a more acceptable venture, one that didn't coat his jackets in flour. Still, he first needed to discover her attitude toward trade, to see if she could accept Richard.

The more John considered the idea of finding a bride for Richard, the more he liked it. While getting married might not be right for him, it seemed the perfect solution for Richard. Settling back in his chair, John reaffirmed his vow to see his family settled, then he could travel, see the world, take a tour of the continent . . . experience freedom for the first time in his life. The very thought intoxicated him.

As Miss Swanson pounded at the ivory keys, John

began to devise a way to nudge his brother toward the elegant Lady Elizabeth.

It was all Elizabeth could do to keep from clapping her hands over her ears to drown out the sound of Miss Swanson's playing. The bothersome noise made it hard for her to sort through her thoughts. Straightening in her chair, Elizabeth tried to ignore the singing and focus on the brilliant idea that had struck her when Lord Wykham had escorted her into the music room.

He was the solution to her problem.

If she simply spent time in Lord Wykham's company, then perhaps her father would be convinced that she was interested in marrying the marquess. While she was busy maintaining her deception, Elizabeth could use that time to help Catherine find a husband.

Elizabeth snuck a glance at Lord Wykham . . . and tried to push away that niggling feeling of guilt building inside of her. It wasn't very nice of her to be thinking of using Lord Wykham for her own means, but she didn't feel as if she had any choice in the matter.

After Catherine found her true love, Elizabeth would convince her papa to allow Catherine to marry first. Surely he couldn't refuse if he saw Catherine was in love with her future husband and that Elizabeth had developed what appeared to be serious intentions toward Lord Wykham.

Of course, once Catherine was safely wed, Elizabeth could bid Lord Wykham a fond farewell and retire to the country in peace and happiness. All in all, it was the perfect plan.

But she still didn't like the idea of deceiving Lord Wykham. Biting her lower lip, she turned other possibilities over in her head, only to come around to the same place. The problem was she couldn't justify using Lord Wykham for her own means. Sighing, she glanced at him again. He'd been a true gentleman and she couldn't repay his kindness with deception.

That left her with only one choice. She could speak with him privately, tell him of her plight, and pray he would agree to assist her in solving the vexing problem she and Catherine were having with their father. But why would he agree to help her? She couldn't help wonder.

Perhaps he would help her because he was, to his very core, a gentleman who was raised to believe in aiding a lady in need.

The trick would be to convince him of her need.

Deciding there was no time like the present, Elizabeth took a bracing breath. "Pardon my forwardness, my lord, but I wonder if I might have a private conversation with you."

Surprise registered in his eyes. "Of course," he replied after a moment. Pausing to clap as Miss Swanson came to the end of the second movement, Lord Wykham stood and escorted her from the music room.

On her way out the door, Elizabeth saw her sister sitting beside Lord Vernon and Lord Conover. Catherine glowed as she exchanged conversation with the two gentlemen. Elizabeth found it troubling to see Lord Vernon with her sister. After all, the man was a known lothario who preyed upon young fanciful girls like Catherine . . . like herself. As soon as they arrived home, Elizabeth promised herself she would tell Catherine about Lord Vernon's sordid past. . . .

Dismissing Lord Vernon forcibly from her thoughts, Elizabeth focused upon Catherine. Just the sight of her sister's smile strengthened Elizabeth's purpose as she followed Lord Wykham out the door.

Their father had been right about one thing. She would do anything for her sister.

Glancing down the hallway to be certain no one was around, John shut the door to the Swanson's study and turned to face Lady Elizabeth. He was all too aware that their departure must have raised more than a few eyebrows. He had no desire to have anyone interrupting this private meeting. With this in mind, he turned the lock and, striding over to the windows, closed the curtains, shielding them from prying eyes.

When he faced Lady Elizabeth once more, he noticed the alarm in her gaze. Flushing slightly, he gestured toward the curtains. "I didn't wish for us to be observed; lord knows what kind of gossip that would generate."

"Very clever," she acknowledged softly.

He could tell she was nervous from the way she was fiddling with the ribbons on her gown. "You wished to speak with me," he said, giving her an opening.

Nodding, she cleared her throat. "I know I've only met you twice and this will seem extremely forward, but I have a problem, of a rather delicate nature, so . . ."

"Why don't you just tell me what the problem is? I promise not to think ill of you," he said, cutting off her fumbling attempt at explanation.

"Very well." She took a deep breath. "You met my sister, Catherine, earlier this evening. Well, I adore her naturally, so when my father said that she couldn't marry before I did, I felt it called for drastic measures."

Lord, was the woman proposing? Now it was his turn to be nervous. "I don't know if . . ."

"Please let me finish. If I don't get this out, I don't know if I'll still have the nerve to say it," she said. "You see, I have no desire to marry for anything less than love."

Her simple statement settled the unease churning in his gut, for after two meetings, it was safe to assume the lady wasn't in love with him.

"The problem is that, despite my best efforts, I seem unable to find a gentleman who suits me. My sister, on the other hand, has no shortage of suitors, and I believe she will easily find someone she wishes to marry, so I thought, I wondered, if perhaps you might aid me in a slight . . . deception."

He raised his eyebrows. "Pardon?"

A brilliant flush spread across her features. "I know it's a great deal to ask this of you, but as I said before, I'm desperate. If my father believes I have . . . feelings for you, he might allow my sister to wed before me as long as he assumes that I will marry soon afterward."

"Then when your sister is safely married, you and I will appear to have a parting of the ways," John finished for her.

"Exactly." She gave him a tremulous smile. "You *do* understand."

"Understanding and agreeing are two different things, my lady," he said stiffly. "I have little liking for devious schemes."

"So do I, but what choice has my father left me?" She held out her hands. "Don't you think it unfair that he punish my sister because of my wish to avoid a hasty marriage? I certainly do."

While John agreed with her on some level, he also understood that a man would take drastic measures if it would benefit those he loved. "Perhaps you could speak with your father, explain how you feel, and he would change his mind."

She dropped her arms to her sides. "I've pleaded with him, reminded him that he promised he would never arrange an unwanted marriage for us and that I've never found someone who interests me, but he refuses to listen. He is set in his course." She gazed up at him. "Will you help me?"

John looked at Lady Elizabeth, weighing her plea. While he disliked the thought of deceiving her father, he had to admit that Lord Shipham seemed to be asking quite a lot of his daughters. Besides, John thought, if he spent time with Lady Elizabeth, then he would be able to arrange for Richard to spend time with them as well.

Turning away from her to keep his whirling thoughts from reflecting in his expression, John continued to tie together his thoughts. Perhaps if she spent time with Richard, she would discover a kinship with him that would lead to love. Lord knew their peculiar interest in experiments alone made them seem well-matched, for he didn't know of anyone else who shared that particular hobby.

If he agreed to her plan, there might be additional benefits for all parties involved. Lady Elizabeth might find love, Richard might finally find the acceptance he'd been lacking, and he might gain freedom from his worry over his younger brother.

Lifting his chin, he turned back to face Lady Elizabeth. "Very well, my lady. I will help your cause."

"Thank you," she said in a rush. "This means so much to me. You are truly a gentleman, my lord."

"It is my pleasure to come to your aid," he murmured in return. Especially if everything worked out as he hoped.

5

"I noticed you spent quite a bit of time with Lord Wykham," Papa commented as he spread cream upon his scone.

Pausing to sip at her tea, Elizabeth tried to project a nervous excitement. "Indeed," she murmured, interjecting just the right amount of gushing into the word.

Father's eyes lit up. "Splendid. It does my heart good to see you finally show interest in a gentleman."

"She didn't say she was interested, Papa," said Catherine, setting down her teacup with a clink. "Allowing a gentleman to escort her into a musicale and being interested in him are two completely separate things."

"Actually, I did find him most charming." Elizabeth dabbed at her mouth with her linen napkin. "He was quite entertaining."

"Entertaining?" exclaimed Catherine, obviously stunned. "I found him to be somewhat . . . staid."

Elizabeth laughed at her sister's remark. "If you compare him to the dandies and rakes you prefer, then perhaps you might find him staid. However, I assure you his conversation was quite stimulating."

"I knew I was right to urge you to seek out a suitable husband, Elizabeth."

"*Urge*, Papa?" she countered dryly. "I believe the word is blackmail."

He waved his hand. "Such an ugly word, Elizabeth."

"But most appropriate."

Rising to his feet, Papa leaned down to press a kiss onto her forehead, then one onto Catherine's as well. "Perhaps," he conceded as he straightened, "but what's a little blackmail among family, if it's done for the finest of reasons?" Chuckling, he tugged down his cuffs. "Thank you for sharing tea with me, girls. Please excuse me, as I promised Lord Esterville I would meet him this afternoon."

Elizabeth gave her father a pointed look. "You are simply trying to slip out because you find the conversation uncomfortable." She lifted a shoulder. "Guilt is never a comfortable emotion, Papa."

Reaching out, he tapped Elizabeth on the nose. "Mind that sharp tongue of yours, girl, or you might scare off the marquess."

Since he wasn't really interested in her, there was little chance of that. Still, to her father, she smiled and nodded. "I shall try."

At the pliable answer, Catherine stared at her suspiciously, but Papa failed to notice anything amiss. Bidding Papa farewell, Elizabeth took another sip of her tea as she returned Catherine's gaze.

"What are you up to, Elizabeth?"

Elizabeth grinned at her sister's perception. "Do you remember when I said that we needed to find a way around Papa's edict?" At Cat's nod, she continued, "Well,

I've figured out a way to do it. The Marquess of Wykham."

"Lord Wykham?" Catherine exclaimed. "How on earth can he be the solution to our problem?"

"Because he has agreed to pose as my suitor." Taking a sip of her tea, Elizabeth waited for her sister's incredulous response. It wasn't long in coming.

"He's *what?*" Catherine shook her head as if unable to comprehend the new development. "Are you saying that the stuffy marquess agreed to this plan?"

"Yes."

Confusion darkened Catherine's gaze. "But that's so unlike him."

"How would you know? You only met the man last night," Elizabeth pointed out.

"Because it doesn't take a long acquaintance to figure out if a gentleman is of a staid or adventurous nature," Catherine returned quickly.

"Well, apparently you're going to have to rethink your logic, for Lord Wykham wasn't at all what you imagined him to be." Elizabeth smiled over her sister's astonishment.

Bewildered, Catherine tapped her fingers against the table. "Perhaps there's more to Lord Wykham than I thought."

Elizabeth gave her sister a pointed look. "Perhaps?"

Rolling her eyes, Catherine said, "Very well then. I'll admit I was too hasty in judging Lord Wykham."

Elizabeth moved onto the next part of her plan. "Now that we agree upon that point, we need to shift our focus back onto our problem. While Lord Wykham has generously agreed to help us, that only gains us some time. We still need to concentrate on helping you find the perfect husband."

"The perfect gentleman for me is someone witty, entertaining, and unfailingly charming."

Catherine's immediate response made Elizabeth smile. "You don't worry about trivialities like loyalty, steadfastness, or common sense, then."

"And you've just described a deadly dull fellow," Catherine stated as she nibbled at a scone.

Elizabeth's amusement died. "You really need to be more practical, Cat. Many spendthrifts are enjoyable to spend time with, but hardly marriage material."

Dusting off her fingers, Catherine rolled her eyes. "True, but then the reverse is true as well; not all gentlemen are dull and boring." She smiled brilliantly at Elizabeth. "What we need to do is find someone who is both steadfast *and* entertaining."

"That's quite a tall order, Cat," Elizabeth pointed out.

Her smile shifted into a full-fledged grin. "Who ever said finding the perfect husband would be easy?"

"This affair is deadly dull, isn't it?" Catherine whispered behind her fan.

Elizabeth glanced around the room. "I've certainly been to more lively gatherings. I've still no idea why Papa insisted we attend."

Catherine perked up when she saw Lord Vernon before her. Unfortunately, his brother was standing alongside him. "Good evening, Lord Vernon," she said, offering her hand.

"It is a good evening indeed, now that I have been accorded the pleasure of seeing you, Lady Catherine."

Bowing over her hand, he straightened and repeated the gesture with Elizabeth. "And you as well, my lady."

Catherine noted with interest that her sister tugged her hand away quickly. Looking at Elizabeth's flushed features, Catherine grew more intrigued by her sister's response to Lord Vernon. She continued to watch Elizabeth as she greeted Lord Wykham. This time, Elizabeth's features remained cool and polite, as if the marquess didn't affect her one way or the other.

Now that she knew about Elizabeth's lack of interest in the marquess, her plans of matchmaking shifted in an instant. Tilting her head to the side, Catherine wondered if Lord Vernon would be perfect for Elizabeth. Perhaps he irritated her sister now, but at least he managed to evoke a true, passionate response from her.

It might be interesting to push the two of them together and see what happened . . . which meant getting the boring Lord Wykham out of the way.

"My lord," she began, pasting a smile upon her face, "it is wonderful to see you again."

Lord Wykham bent stiffly over her hand, not even bothering to press a kiss upon the back of her gloved fingers. "The pleasure is all mine."

The polite return made Catherine want to roll her eyes. Instead of the charming repartee his brother managed, the marquess seemed only able to give her practiced responses. Forcing herself to remember her main objective in addressing Lord Wykham, Catherine kept her smile firmly in place. "I could very well argue that point, my lord, but I shall refrain."

His brows shifted together slightly, as if she'd confused him with her reply.

Sighing softly, Catherine decided to simply work toward leaving Elizabeth alone with Lord Vernon. "I find myself a bit parched," she murmured, pressing a hand to her throat.

Lord Wykham nodded once. "Most understandable, as it is rather warm in here."

Apparently the marquess wasn't one to pick up on subtleties. "Quite so. I would dearly love a glass of punch."

"Punch? I thought Lady Andersen preferred to serve lemonade."

Astounded by his answer, she could only gape at him for a moment. Lord, was the man a buffoon as well as a dullard? Practically gritting her teeth, Catherine again forced another laugh. "I can see that you prefer to jest with me," she said smoothly. "But seriously, my lord, I simply must have a refreshment of some sort if I wish to avoid fainting." Deciding it was time to be blunt, she asked, "Would you escort me into the parlor to fetch some refreshments?"

"Certainly, my lady." Offering his arm, he bid his farewells to Lord Vernon and Elizabeth. Victory soared through Catherine as she allowed the marquess to lead her away. She only hoped Elizabeth appreciated her sacrifice, Catherine thought, as she engaged Lord Wykham in conversation.

"I never understood the appeal of the strong, silent type, my lord," she began flirtatiously, "but you're beginning to help me understand."

Watching her sister walk away, Elizabeth was too stunned by Catherine's behavior to notice Lord Vernon move to stand at her side. My goodness, for having proclaimed Lord Wykham a dullard, Catherine certainly seemed interested in spending time in his company. But why? Elizabeth couldn't understand the reason behind her sister's unexpected actions. After all, she'd told Catherine that Lord Wykham was going to show interest in her in order to give Catherine time to find her perfect mate. Why then did her sister go off with him?

"This is a surprising turn of events."

Lord Vernon's remark brought Elizabeth from her thoughts. "Indeed," she agreed as she shifted away from him.

"A pleasant surprise, though." His gaze sharpened. "I think your sister suits my brother quite well."

"Do you?" Elizabeth considered the match for a moment. Had Catherine decided to give Lord Wykham a second chance because she realized she'd judged him too quickly? Perhaps that was the reason behind her behavior.

"I do, indeed. Your sister has the sort of engaging personality that will help my brother to put aside his rigid beliefs." He grinned at Elizabeth. "John can often be most trying in his arrogance."

Perhaps Lord Vernon was right and their siblings would be perfect for one another. What then of her grand plan to accept Lord Wykham's assistance in posing as her suitor? How could he be both her suitor and court Catherine at the same time? The whole mess was becoming so jumbled.

Besides, it also meant that her sister was away from Lord Vernon, which was a good thing, for she'd forgotten to inform Catherine of his disreputable past.

"Are you woolgathering or did I offend you with my remark about John's arrogance?"

Returning her thoughts to the present, Elizabeth

flicked open her fan and gave Lord Vernon a pointed stare. "I was merely thinking that the trait must run in the family."

Lord Vernon laughed aloud. "I say, Lady Elizabeth, I do find your tartness refreshing. Shrewish as well, but refreshing, nonetheless."

"Shrewish, is it? From you, Lord Vernon, I shall consider that a compliment." She narrowed her eyes. "Undoubtedly you prefer the simpering misses with their inane conversation and dull twitterings."

"Then why do I seem to find myself in your company so often these past few days?"

"I'm uncertain," she replied. "Perhaps you are finally demonstrating a bit of good taste."

"Along with a healthy dose of tolerance, I suppose."

"Why don't you leave then, if you find me so odious?"

"I wonder that myself." His grin was devilishly appealing. "I find myself oddly entertained by your waspish comments. Luckily for me, when it comes to being tolerant, I happen to be close to sainted."

Laughter escaped her before she could hold it back. "You? Sainted? From our brief acquaintance, Lord Vernon, I must admit that I find that difficult to believe."

"You wound me."

She tapped her fan against her cheek. "Come now, my lord. I highly doubt a few words could cause harm to . . . someone of your reputation."

"Someone of my reputation?" Lord Vernon asked, a grin splitting his features. "Do you mean someone arrogant? Or do you consider me the worst of rakes once again? I fear the subtlety of your insult escapes me."

Lifting her chin, Elizabeth boldly met his gaze. "I

shall leave it to you to decide upon the proper description, for I've been assured by the matrons that either one will suit."

Lord Vernon crossed his arms and stared at her for a long moment.

"What are you staring at?" Elizabeth finally asked, fighting the urge to squirm under his gaze.

"A fool." His features hardened as he leaned closer. "Of all people, I would think that you'd understand how gossips exaggerate everything. They say that you disdain conversation, that you are cold and unpleasant, and that you hold yourself above everyone."

She shook beneath his heated accusation.

"You can't deny that there are elements of the truth in that harsh bit of gossip any more than I can deny there's truth in the gossip you heard about me," he rasped, his gaze cold and forbidding. "Still, I was willing to ignore the gossip, to take you on your actions rather than your reputation, and I thought you would do the same." He shook his head. "I was wrong. Perhaps I'm the fool instead of you."

His words shamed her. "No, I'm the foolish one," she admitted quietly. "When you danced with me, I felt as if you understood me, as if you understood about being lonely in a crowd. But when Lady Sefton told me of your reputation, and how you always seemed to know exactly what to say to a lady to disarm her, I thought that you'd figured out what to say to make me soften toward you and you were simply toying with me."

Slowly, he shook his head. "I wasn't toying with you at all. I do understand all about being lonely."

Staring at him, Elizabeth realized she was afraid to believe him, afraid that he was just telling her what she wanted to hear, afraid that she would trust him only to be disappointed later. But what if he was telling the truth? What if he *did* understand, and she'd pushed away the only other person who could empathize with how she felt? Her fear of that mistake was greater than her fear of believing him.

Taking her courage in hand, she offered him a smile. "Let's begin again," she said simply. "I'm Elizabeth Everley."

Warmth flooded his features as he clasped her hand within his. "Richard Vernon."

The horde of people milling about seemed to fade into the background as she gazed into Richard's eyes, lost within the blue depths.

"Good evening, Vernon. Haven't seen you about lately."

The interruption jarred them from the magic of the moment. Swiftly, Elizabeth drew her hand back. She blinked in surprise as Richard's expression hardened into a polite mask. "Morrow."

Curious over Richard's reaction, she gave the gentleman a second look. With styled blond hair, dapper manner of dress, and a bored glaze in his pale, blue eyes, the gentleman appeared to be a rake of the first water.

"Will you introduce me to your lovely companion, Vernon?" the man asked smoothly.

For a moment, Elizabeth thought Richard would refuse the request, but finally he said, "Lady Elizabeth Everley, might I present Anthony Cole, Viscount Morrow?"

After only the briefest hesitation, Elizabeth offered Lord Morrow her hand. As his fingers curled about hers, she was oddly relieved that she wore gloves.

"An honor, my lady," Lord Morrow murmured as he straightened.

"It is a pleasure to make your acquaintance, my lord," she returned coolly, pulling her hand free.

Lord Morrow tugged down on his vest. "So, tell me, Vernon, where have you been hiding these days?"

"I've been busy." The stiffness in Richard's words reminded Elizabeth of Lord Wykham's manner of speaking.

"Too busy to visit your old haunts, eh?" He glanced over at Elizabeth. "Still, if the lovely Lady Elizabeth is the reason you've been hiding yourself away, then I'd completely understand your absence. She is a pretty bit indeed."

Richard drew back his shoulders. "That is hardly the remark a gentleman makes in the presence of a lady, sir."

If Richard hadn't been so serious, Elizabeth would have burst out laughing at his rigid manner. Imagine, the rule-bending young lord commenting on Lord Morrow's lack of gentlemanly graces.

"Lord, aren't you the uppity one now?" sneered Lord Morrow.

A look of utter disgust twisted Richard's features, before he recovered his poise. "Excuse us, Morrow, but I claimed this dance with Lady Elizabeth."

Before Elizabeth could even comment, Richard curled his hand beneath her elbow and steered her toward the dance floor. As they took their positions, he murmured, "I apologize for subjecting you to that unpleasant scene."

Elizabeth lifted her eyebrows. "I don't believe *you* did. After all, Lord Morrow approached you, leaving you little choice but to speak with him."

"That's true enough," Richard conceded with a terse nod. "Though I suppose I could have walked away."

"And left me alone with him?" Elizabeth smiled softly. "You would never abandon a lady to suffer Lord Morrow's company alone."

"So you've gained a measure of trust in me?" he asked quietly.

Elizabeth leveled a measured look at Richard. "Not as of yet, but I've decided to give you the chance to earn my trust."

His laughter burst from him, a vibrant sound that drew the attention of the other dancers. "Then I see I shall have to do my best to never disappoint you, my lady."

"I believe you're up to the challenge."

His grin widened. "I most certainly am. Would you like to shock everyone present and waltz with me?" he whispered to her.

"You are utterly incorrigible, Richard," she retorted with a smile.

"Ah, but you're addressing me as Richard now, so that leads me to believe you are attracted to incorrigible men." He twirled her about in a wide circle. "Luckily for me, that sort of behavior comes easily."

Clutching his shoulder, Elizabeth spun around the dance floor with him. Lord, she didn't want to be so completely charmed by Richard, but she was.

How she was.

6

Left with no choice, John followed Lady Catherine out into the garden. "This really isn't proper, Lady Catherine."

"Oh, for Heaven's sake, Lord Wykham. I promise to refrain from offending your person."

He couldn't help but wince at the sarcasm in her response. "I don't mean to sound priggish, but . . ."

Lady Catherine's loud sniff told him all too clearly that she did indeed find him priggish. Well, even if she didn't possess the good sense to realize he was merely being sensible, he knew it was his gentlemanly duty to point out how this innocent turn on the veranda could jeopardize her reputation.

"Lady Catherine," he began in the stern tone he usually saved for Richard, "I must insist that we return to the ballroom, as it is most unseemly to be alone with you. While the reasons behind this demand seem to have escaped you, I assure you, my lady, that they are quite valid."

Lady Catherine's sigh spoke volumes. "I appreciate that you are concerned with my welfare, my lord, but I am not worried about anyone's reaction if we are discovered. After all, it is not as if we are in a torrid embrace."

John grew flushed at the mere thought of holding this unique creature in his arms. "Indeed not."

At his reply, Lady Catherine shrugged lightly. "Exactly. So, if anyone wanders by, we can simply tell them that I was feeling a bit faint and you escorted me outside for a breath of fresh air."

"Very well, but only for a little while. If we're supposed to be taking a breath of fresh air, that excuse only justifies a short absence."

"Ahhh, yes, most practical of you, my lord. But how can you be practical on a night such as this?" Spreading her arms wide, Lady Catherine spun around twice. Coming to a stop, she rested her hands against the balustrade and gazed up into the night sky. "This is a magical night. I can feel it. It's a night meant for love, stolen kisses, and passionate vows of unending devotion." She gave him a wry smile. "Yet all you can think of is what people might say."

John stiffened as her words hit their mark. "You needn't mock me."

Turning around, she leaned back against the stone balustrade. "I'm not mocking you, Lord Wykham. If anything, I feel rather sorry for you."

"What?" He was the Marquess of Wykham, a reliable, wealthy fellow who garnered respect from the highest nobles in the land . . . and this chit of a girl felt sorry for him! How preposterous.

"If you can't see the magic in this night, you must not see it at all." She shook her head. "Your life must be pitifully dull and boring."

"My life is neither dull nor boring."

He could tell by her expression that she didn't believe

him. "Very well, then. Tell me one thing you've done this past week that has been spontaneous."

"I . . . well, I . . ." For the life of him, John couldn't come up with a single thing he'd done that hadn't been planned. Finally, he remembered calling upon Richard. "I paid an unscheduled visit to my brother," he said triumphantly.

"Oh, my," she murmured with a sarcastic lilt in her voice. "One whole visit with your brother. How adventurous of you."

John drew back his shoulders even further. "My life suits me perfectly."

"I know . . . which is what makes it all the worse." She released another deep sigh. "Have you ever done something bold, something unexpected, something totally spontaneous?"

"Of course," he retorted firmly, despite the fact that he couldn't think of even one time to support that assertion.

"Very well, then, my lord," she murmured. Hearing the challenge in her voice, he braced himself for what she'd say next. Even in the dark, he could see the glint in her eyes. "Then perhaps you would like to dance with me."

"Here?"

"Of course." Holding out her arm, she began to dance with an invisible partner. "You should learn to enjoy life, Lord Wykham."

It alarmed him to realize just how alluring her offer was, to know that he would like to gather her in his arms, forsaking all sense of propriety and reason for a sweet moment of pleasure. "You're being awfully presumptuous, Lady Catherine. I happen to enjoy my life."

She stopped dancing, allowing her arms to fall to her

sides. "Do you truly enjoy it? Or do you merely find it comfortable?"

"What is the difference?" he countered swiftly. "I happen to *enjoy* being *comfortable.*"

Her brilliant laughter teased at his senses. "Quite the clever answer, my lord."

John shook his head, completely at a loss as to how to deal with Lady Catherine. "I believe we should return to the ballroom," he finally said.

"Before anyone notices we are gone?"

"Precisely," he replied, pleasantly surprised at her grasp of the situation.

Lady Catherine sighed dramatically. "I don't suppose I could get you to take a walk around the garden with me then?"

"No, I don't suppose." Obviously her insight into the ramifications was fleeting. John held out his hand. "Please allow me to escort you back into the house."

Tilting her head to the side, she studied him for a long, silent moment. "I know you can't possibly enjoy life with such a staid attitude . . . and the fact that you can't even comprehend the difference between a comfortable existence and really living saddens me." She shook her head. "For how can you ever correct the problem if you can't even understand it."

Good Lord! He found transcribing Latin far easier than trying to understand this vexing creature. "Will you please allow me to escort you inside?" he demanded in frustration.

"What if I said no? What if I preferred to . . ."

Unable to make her see reason, John ignored her questions and simply reached out, clasped her elbow, and began to guide her toward the glass doors.

"What on earth do you think you're doing?" she demanded, trying to tug away from his grasp.

"Escorting you back into the ballroom," John ground out, not even trying to hide his annoyance. "Since you won't listen to reason, you leave me no choice but to perform my gentlemanly duties without your consent."

"Dragging me into the Anderson's townhouse is hardly the action of a gentleman."

"On the contrary, Lady Catherine, it is precisely how a gentleman should proceed when a lady is in danger of destroying her precious reputation." He glanced down at her. "It amazes me that you're related to Lady Elizabeth. Did she get all the sense in your family?"

"I've had all I can take of your irksome person," she muttered softly.

As he opened the door, John allowed Lady Catherine to sweep in before him. "I can assure you, my lady, I share your sentiment."

Lifting her chin, she marched away without bidding him farewell. Just as well, John thought, watching the brunette beauty weave her way through the crowd, for she tested the limits of his restraint.

Lord, she'd test the restraint of Saint Peter himself.

Comforting himself with that fact, John forgave himself his boldness in escorting her inside without her permission. After all, it was obvious that the chit had no concept of what was best for her reputation. Indeed, he'd helped guide her into the proper actions. He'd behaved like the perfect gentleman.

Then why did he feel this odd sensation inside him, as if he'd just lost something? Pushing aside the bothersome thought, John headed toward the study to enjoy a brandy and cigar. Hopefully, he'd given Richard enough time alone with Lady Elizabeth to aid their romance.

If not, that was Richard's problem.

"How was your evening?" Catherine asked as she sat down on Elizabeth's bed. "Lady Andersen mentioned that you danced with Lord Vernon twice . . . and in a row, no less."

Elizabeth wrapped her arms around her drawn-up knees. "The reason I danced with him in the first place was to escape the presence of a most horrid gentleman."

"Horrid?" Catherine lifted her eyebrows. "But I thought Lord Wykham was with me."

Laughing, Elizabeth shook her head. "I thought you agreed that you'd judged Lord Wykham too hastily."

"Indeed I had," Catherine conceded as she smoothed her nightgown over her curled legs. "But now that I have spent more time with him, I'll stick with my original opinion of him. Come now, Elizabeth, even you must admit that Lord Wykham would tempt anyone to see if they could get him to unbend."

"Why would you wish to provoke him?"

Catherine shrugged lightly. "I don't know. It's just that, tonight, I wanted to see if he'd act less staid and dull."

"Less like a gentleman?"

"No . . . more like a person." Catherine waved her hands. "Enough about him. You've yet to tell me why you danced *twice* with Lord Vernon."

"As I said, I accepted his invitation to dance simply to escape that horrid Lord Morrow," Elizabeth explained. "Then Lord Vernon and I got into a . . . discussion, so I wasn't even aware of beginning a second dance."

Catherine clasped her hands against her chest. "How lovely that you were swept away by Lord Vernon."

" 'Swept away' is hardly the phrase I'd use," Elizabeth corrected. "Though I must admit that I enjoyed Richard's company far more than I'd ever expected possible." She hugged her knees closer. "It's odd that I didn't particularly like the man, yet tonight he made me want to trust him." Elizabeth thought of how he'd overcome her determination to avoid him. "It's also amazing how easy it is for me to converse with him. I'm so often at a loss for words, but with Richard, I always know what to say."

"Richard, is it?"

Elizabeth felt her cheeks warm.

Catherine sighed softly. "That's wonderful."

The scariest part for Elizabeth was that she'd indeed felt wonderful this evening. "I hope I'm not making a terrible mistake," she admitted to her sister.

"I doubt you are," Catherine assured her. "In fact, the more I think of the two of you together, the more convinced I become that it's a perfect match."

Elizabeth gave her sister a weak smile. "Then why am I so scared?"

"Because I imagine falling in love can be frightening." Catherine tipped her head to the side. "Why else would they refer to it as *falling?* Somewhere along the line, someone must have figured out that it can hurt."

Elizabeth had to laugh at her sister's observation. "All I pray is that if I do indeed fall, I don't fall too far."

"Good evening, Margaret," Douglas said cheerfully as he pulled off his cravat. "I'm glad you're here."

"I come every evening, Douglas," she pointed out.

"That you do, my love." Unbuttoning his vest, he tossed it over the back of his changing screen. "And I look forward to seeing you every night." He paused in removing his shirt as he looked fully at his wife's ghostly form for the first time since entering the room. "Why do you seem so pale this evening? Indeed, you actually look like a ghost."

"That's because I am one."

His wife's beautiful smile tugged at his heart, making him think of all he'd lost. "I know, my darling, but usually you appear before me looking quite . . . solid."

Margaret lifted her eyebrows. "Solid? I assure you, Douglas, I am lighter than ever."

He laughed at her quip. "True enough, love, but that's not what I meant. You usually look as if you were alive and with me once more, as if I could walk up to you and hold you in my arms." He shook his head. "But this evening, I can almost see through you. You actually *look* like a ghost for the first time."

She gave him a knowing smile. "How lovely," she said softly, offering no further explanation. However, before he could question her, Margaret asked, "How did our plan work with the girls?"

"Splendidly," replied Douglas, his jovial mood brightening again. "Have you ever met the Marquess of Wykham and his brother, Lord Vernon?"

Margaret's brow drew together. "I believe so. Wasn't the marquess that spendthrift who used to make the silliest wagers over foolishness like who could toss a rock the furthest?"

"That was the current marquess' father," Douglas corrected. "If you recall, the old boy passed away when his eldest son, John, was only a lad, but that didn't stop John from taking over the family fortunes and refilling the coffers despite his tender age." Douglas sat down to remove his boots. "Quite an admirable fellow."

"And which one of our girls has caught his eye?"

"That's just the thing, Margaret," Douglas said as he set his second boot down by the bed. "I'm not sure."

Margaret frowned slightly. "How can you not be sure? To which girl does he pay attention? Elizabeth or Catherine?"

"Both," Douglas admitted with a laugh. "Last night, he spent time with Elizabeth, but tonight he spent quite a bit of time with Catherine."

"He sounds like a philanderer of the worst sort!" exclaimed Margaret.

Douglas shook his head. "He's quite the steadfast fellow."

"A steadfast person doesn't play with two girls' hearts at once."

"Who said he was playing with their hearts?" Douglas asked incredulously. "I merely said he seemed interested in our daughters. After one meeting, it is highly unlikely that the hearts of our daughters are in peril."

Margaret appeared somewhat mollified by his reply. "I suppose that's true enough, but I still don't like the thought of him leading our daughters into believing he might be interested in them."

"Well, then, you won't like it any better when I tell you his brother, Richard, is doing the same thing."

"*What?*"

Douglas grinned at his wife. "Indeed, last night he spent time with Catherine and this evening with Elizabeth."

"Are you telling me that those two brothers *switched* our daughters between them?"

"Yes," he replied simply, settling back to await his wife's explosion.

It wasn't long in coming.

Thrusting to her feet, Margaret glared down at him. "And you merely stood by and watched them trade our daughters as if they were common trollops?"

"I did nothing of the sort," he assured her. "You are making far too much of this, Margaret. Now, please take a seat, as looking up at you is causing a crick in my neck."

With a disgruntled huff, Margaret settled back into her chair. "I don't like thinking that these two gentleman are toying with our daughters . . . and I'm not around to do anything about it."

Understanding softened Douglas. "I know you regret not being able to guide our daughters through this, but I assure you, they seem to be doing fine these past few days. Elizabeth is more animated that I've seen her in years, while Catherine seems more contemplative that ever before. Whatever these brothers are doing, it is a good thing for our girls."

"But which daughter will end up with which brother?"

"Who cares?" Douglas retorted with a laugh. "As far as I'm concerned, there are two girls and two gentlemen, both respectable and upstanding, so it really doesn't matter who winds up with whom." He lifted a shoulder. "The way I see it, what we have here is a no-lose situation."

Smiling softly, Margaret shook her head. "In matters of love, Douglas, things are *never* that easy."

* * *

The next morning, with her maid in tow, Elizabeth entered a crammed, dark shop filled with broken parts and pieces from various machines and other sorts of devices. The tiny room smelled of oil, dirt, and mildew.

She was in Heaven.

"Good day, Lady Elizabeth," greeted the proprietor as he came bustling out from the back room. "It's always a treat when you honor my shop with a visit."

"Thank you, Mr. Dunfee," she said, smiling at the old man. With a scraggly beard, flyaway gray hair, and his bent, thin body, he looked more like a gnome than a man, but his warmth, charm, and generosity made up for his lack of stature. "Though I know I was just here a few days ago, I'm in the midst of a project and needed a specific piece to make my experiment work."

He nodded sagely. "I know just what you're saying, my lady. You get set on finishing something and there's no stopping you until you do."

"Precisely," she replied warmly, feeling more comfortable in the dark confines of the shop than in the spacious glory of a ballroom.

"Then you just enjoy yourself and poke around to your heart's content, Lady Elizabeth." He gestured toward the back room. "I'll be in there, unloading a new shipment if you need me."

"Thank you, Mr. Dunfee." Giving him a smile in farewell, she turned toward the jumbled parts lying on the table in front of her.

"Can I be of assistance, my lady?" asked her maid, Alice.

Glancing toward the young girl, Elizabeth almost laughed out loud at the disgusted, yet determined expression on her face. "No, thank you, Alice. I'm just going to putter around the shop, so if you prefer to wait for me in the carriage, that is fine with me." She waved toward the open doorway. "Mr. Dunfee is here with me."

Elizabeth could tell from Alice's expression that she was torn between staying with her mistress and escaping the odorous, cluttered room. Apparently, Alice's sense of smell won the battle. "Very well, my lady. I shall be right outside with the footman."

As soon as Alice scurried out the door, Elizabeth tugged off her gloves, stuffing them haphazardly into her reticule, and began to sift through the treasures. Grease soon stained her fingers and smudged her dress, but Elizabeth felt happier than she had all week.

Well, she thought, *that wasn't entirely true.* Last night, matching wits with Lord Vernon had been most enjoyable as well.

"I'd hoped to find a treasure here today, but not one as delightful as you."

At the sound of Richard's voice, Elizabeth spun around, startled to find him standing in the open doorway to the back room.

"My lord," she gasped. "What on earth are you doing here?"

A corner of his mouth quirked upward. "I was just about to ask the same thing of you, Lady Elizabeth."

She searched for an answer that would make her presence in this shop acceptable, but she couldn't think of one. "I . . . I was just looking for a piece I need to complete an experiment I'm working on," she admitted, finally settling upon honesty.

"Experiment?" Richard lifted his brows. "I thought

you told me you didn't know anything about machines, that you were only teasing."

Embarrassed at having been caught in a fib, Elizabeth felt her cheeks heat. "I didn't wish to admit my penchant for tinkering with machines."

"Perfectly understandable," he replied amicably. "Besides, your sister mentioned it for you."

"She *what?*" she exclaimed.

"Last night she told me all about your hobby; I'm quite certain she didn't mean to, but I'm afraid I flustered her and she let this piece of information slip. I assured her she could trust me not to reveal your hobby to the ton."

Elizabeth hoped Cat's trust wasn't misplaced.

"Now, tell me—what sort of experiment would bring a lady such as yourself to a humble shop like this?"

"I'm trying to build a catapult," she replied.

"A catapult?" he asked, surprise coloring his tone. "Did you design the machine all by yourself?"

Eagerly, she answered his question. "I took the original design from Mr. da Vinci's treatise, but I'm in the process of sizing it down."

"Really?" Richard's enthusiasm touched a responding chord within her. "Isn't it hard to get the measurements exact?"

"Yes, but I'm managing," she agreed, thrilled at having found someone who shared her passion for experiments. "I'm having a problem finding a bolt to secure the arm of the sling."

"It's amazing how one small part can make such a huge difference in the outcome of your experiment, isn't it?"

"Yes, it is." The freedom of discussing her hobby exhilarated her. "And what of you? Why are you here?"

Shrugging, Richard retrieved a J-shaped pipe from a nearby table. "Since I enjoy tinkering as much as you, I often tour Mr. Dunfee's shop just to see if he's gotten in any unusual parts." Seeing her look of confusion, he hastily added, "It's not as if I'm in trade or anything."

"Heavens, no!" Elizabeth exclaimed. "Even the mere suggestion of going into trade would be enough to get you ostracized *forever.*"

Glancing away, Richard set down the pipe. "Indeed, it would," he agreed finally. "Perhaps it would be best if you kept my interest in machines to yourself."

"If you will return the favor," she replied quickly. "It wouldn't do to have the patronesses of Almack's finding out about my . . . habit. Especially when it took me so long to obtain a voucher in the first place."

"I'm glad we could reach this understanding, for it would do my reputation as a rake irreparable harm if anyone were to discover I had other pursuits aside from gaming, drinking, and womanizing."

"Heaven forbid," she responded with a laugh. Brushing back a loose strand of hair, Elizabeth inadvertently touched her cheek with her finger, leaving a blackened streak behind. She glanced down at her oil-stained hands before looking back at Richard. "I've just made a mess, haven't I?"

"A particularly lovely one at that," Richard said cheerfully. Stepping forward, he produced a handkerchief from his pocket. "If I may?"

At her nod, Richard held her chin between his forefinger and thumb and gently wiped her cheek with the cloth. "There you are, Elizabeth, as good as new."

His use of her first name made her overwhelmingly aware of his nearness. Suddenly, she felt out of breath, as if she'd been running for a long way. Startled, she looked up into his face, allowing her gaze to slide over his aquiline nose, his well-molded lips, his perfectly cut cheekbones. She'd thought him handsome from the first moment she saw him, but never as breathtaking as he looked now. Something about the seriousness of his expression tugged at her insides.

When his gaze shifted to capture hers, she gasped lightly at the intensity filling his blue eyes. The soft stroking of the cloth slowed, becoming more of a caress, as he held her gaze.

"Elizabeth," he whispered, leaning forward until mere inches separated them.

The urge to close the distance between them swept over her. For the first time in her life, she wanted to feel a man's kiss, to explore the burgeoning desire inside her. "My lord," she began softly as she shifted another inch closer.

His eyes sparkled with amusement. "Richard," he corrected her.

Dropping her gaze onto his curved lips, she allowed herself to fall into her emotions. "Richard," she said breathlessly, her lips remaining parted as she watched him move even closer, trembling in her eagerness to experience her first kiss.

"Lady Elizabeth," called Mr. Dunfee from the back room. "Would you mind stepping back here for a moment? I think you might be interested in a piece I just received."

Mr. Dunfee's call broke the spell binding her to Richard. With a sharp intake of breath, she jerked herself out of his arms, stepping back and pressing her hands to her burning cheeks. "I . . . I . . ."

"Lady Elizabeth?" called Mr. Dunfee, popping his head through the doorway. "Would you care to see my find?"

Tearing her gaze away from Richard's taut features, she nodded to Mr. Dunfee. "Y-y-yes, I would, sir."

As the proprietor disappeared back into the second room, Elizabeth tried to compose herself. "I should go now," she whispered softly.

His eyes darkened. "I know."

Tremulously, she smiled at him. "It's wonderful to know you share my passion for tinkering, Richard, and even more comforting to know you will hide my secret," she confided. "After all, the worst thing that could possibly happen to either one of us is someone finding out about our hobby."

The hand he'd raised froze an inch from her cheek, before he let it drop to his side. "The opinion of the ton means that much to you?"

"Of course," she replied automatically. "I've been trying to gain acceptance for three years now. I wouldn't do anything to jeopardize what success I've achieved so far."

"No," he murmured softly. "That would be utter folly."

Pressing her fingertips to her lips, Elizabeth couldn't hide the burst of happiness inside her. "When will I see you again?" she asked, unable to hold in the question.

The way Richard drew back confused Elizabeth. "I don't know," he said in an oddly stiff voice.

"Oh." Feeling self-conscious, she rubbed her hands on her skirts, ignoring the stains she left behind. "Of course you don't," she stuttered, before continuing awkwardly.

"Very well, then. I shall simply bid you a good day, Richard." Turning on her heel, she hurried into the backroom, leaving Richard behind.

He couldn't get out of the blasted shop fast enough to escape his thoughts. The image of Elizabeth gazing at his mouth, her lips softened and parted, her eyes darkening with the beginnings of desire pounded through him, making Richard slam the door of Mr. Dunfee's shop behind him.

Blast the woman, he thought, as he stormed past her waiting carriage and down the street. He'd been looking forward to dallying in the shop, wandering amongst the various parts to see if he could find something of use for his factory, but the moment he'd seen Elizabeth, all thoughts of work were erased from his mind.

He'd been intrigued by her interest in dirty machine parts and downright charmed by the streak of grease she'd left upon her skin. Ah, yes, her skin. That soft flesh had beckoned him for a longer, more intimate touch. Under his hands, Elizabeth had turned into a gentle, giving female, eager to sample the delights of desire.

But the desire she felt was for the man he appeared to be, not the man he actually was. His ears still burned with her shock at the very notion of being associated with trade. She sought acceptance from the ton and, if he aligned himself with her, he would destroy her hopes. For the moment society discovered his secret, his pride in being a pretzel maker, for God's sake, he would, as Elizabeth predicted, be ostracized forever.

And, as much as he wanted her, he knew he'd be the worst thing that could happen to Elizabeth. No, it would be best for Elizabeth's welfare if he stayed as far away from her as possible.

Lost in his thoughts, Richard didn't notice the approach of another gentleman until he literally bumped into him. "Pardon me, sir . . . Morrow!"

Viscount Morrow smoothed the shoulder of Richard's jacket. "The apology should be mine, old chap. I'd hoped to run into you."

Richard's mood soured even more. First, realizing he had no future with the intriguing Elizabeth, now a chance meeting with the debased Viscount. Whenever he ran into Morrow, it brought back memories of his past debaucheries. Shaking off the unwanted thoughts, Richard reminded himself he was no longer the rakehell he'd once been. "If you'll excuse me, I . . ."

"Surely you can spare an old friend a moment of your time?" Morrow said, reaching out to clasp Richard's arm.

He looked pointedly down at Morrow's hand until the man released him. "We were never friends," he said coldly.

"I seem to remember us haunting the same gaming hells, then sharing a hackney to a brothel."

"Another time, another place, . . . another man," Richard finished softly. He still found it difficult to think on all the things he'd once done in his misguided youth.

Morrow scowled darkly. "You look the same to me."

"Look again then, for I assure you I have left those foolish pursuits behind." Thrusting his hand through his hair, Richard sighed deeply. "While I often accompanied you on the quest for lecherous pleasures, Morrow, I never considered us friends."

Though Morrow's features grew mottled with anger,

his tone remained civil. "You often lent me blunt back then. Isn't that the conduct of friends?"

"I purchased a doxy for you, Morrow, or spotted you a bit of money for a game." Richard lifted a shoulder, thrusting away the memory of just how much money he used to toss carelessly about . . . and how quickly he ran through his generous inheritance. Looking down at Morrow's face, Richard could see the puffiness that accompanied a drinking binge and the dark circles under his eyes from lack of sleep. This man represented all that he wished to forget in his past . . . and Richard was willing to do anything to make him go away. "What do you want with me, Morrow?" he finally asked.

Morrow shifted on his feet. "I'd hoped you would float me a loan for a few days. I've gone to some of my other friends, but they seem to be in the same predicament. You see, I've run into a bit of bad luck and . . ."

"No explanation necessary," Richard said, cutting off Morrow's explanation. He knew all too well how easy it was to fall into a "bit of back luck" . . . and how hard it was to find a way out of the hole. Well, he had finally found his way out, managed to shake the dirt off himself, and had rebuilt his life. Still, he knew the panic that Morrow must be feeling at the moment, the desperation when you feared society would find out just how far you'd sunk. Wearily, Richard nodded slowly. "Very well, Morrow. Send your card around to my address and I'll be certain my man-of-business arranges for a transfer of funds into your accounts."

A broad grin split Morrow's face as he slapped Richard on the shoulder. "You are a king among men, Vernon."

Richard reached out and tugged Morrow's fingers off his shoulder. "In the future, you should approach someone else for assistance."

Apparently Morrow was too relieved by Richard's offer to take offense at his remark. "Naturally, Vernon. I'll not bother you again."

Bidding Morrow farewell, Richard hastened away, satisfied that he'd freed himself from another piece of unwanted history.

7

When his mother stepped into his study, John put down his pen upon the open accounting ledger and rose to his feet. "This is an unexpected pleasure," he murmured, escorting her to one of the chairs facing his office desk.

"Thank you, dear," she said before gesturing toward his open ledgers. "Though I do hope I'm not disturbing you."

Despite the fact that he'd been deeply engrossed in balancing his estate books, John hurried to reassure his mother. "Of course not," he said before settling into the seat opposite her. "To what do I owe the honor of this visit?"

"I wish to discuss the latest gossip with you."

John groaned softly. "You know I don't . . ."

"About you and the Everley girls."

His protest died unspoken. "What are the gossips saying?"

"The *ton* is abuzz with your courtship of the Everley girls."

"My *what?*"

Her blue eyes, so like his own, danced with mirth as she settled back into her chair. "I have your attention now, don't I?"

"Most assuredly. Now please explain, Mother."

"I visited my good friend, Eugenia Weatherby, this afternoon for tea and heard an earful about my sons and their recent behavior."

Though he wanted to urge his mother along, John knew from experience that she took her own sweet time telling a story.

"Apparently, all of polite society has taken note of the interest both you and Richard have shown in the Everley ladies." Smoothing down the ribbons on her dress, her mother paused for a moment. "Yet no one seems to know which son prefers which daughter, for, according to gossip, you and Richard have spent time with each of the girls over the past two nights."

John chose his words carefully, not wishing to give his hopelessly romantic mother hope that there was anything of depth between him and either one of the Everley ladies. "While it might be true that I have conversed with both Lady Elizabeth and Lady Catherine over the past few days, I have not directed undue attention toward them."

His mother twirled a ribbon around her finger. "According to Eugenia, you escorted Lady Elizabeth into the musicale, then the two of you were missing for a while . . . leading everyone to believe that you snuck off for a moment of private conversation. Last night, you were seen obtaining refreshments with Lady Catherine, then no one caught sight of either you or the lady for quite some time." She lifted her eyebrows and gave him a pointed look. "I do believe that qualifies as undue attention, John."

Cursing the growing warmth in his cheeks, John tried to keep his voice level. "Escorting a lady into a musicale or for refreshments are hardly acts that declare an interest in courtship," he pointed out calmly.

From his mother's skeptical expression, John knew she didn't accept his protest. "Come now, John," she began softly. "I'm your mother. I know when you're deliberately dissembling and, I assure you, there's no need. I've longed for the day when you'd forget your responsibilities for a few moments and enjoy the company of a young lady. There's no need to hide your interest in one of the Everley girls from me."

"I'm hiding nothing," he stated firmly, rising abruptly. Thrusting his hands into his pockets, John began to pace across his study floor. "Good God, mother, the *last* thing I'm looking for at this moment is a wife. If you must know, I'd spoken with Lady Elizabeth because I felt she would be a fine match for Richard, a sensible lady who would help him settle down a bit. As for Lady Catherine . . ." He broke off with a harsh laugh. "I pity the man who marries that lady. She's far too romantic, too unconcerned with appearances, too . . . too . . ."

"Exciting?"

"Yes. No!" he corrected himself as soon as he realized what he'd said. But from the avid gleam in his mother's gaze, John knew his correction had come a moment too late. "Please try to understand, Mother. I have no wish to burden myself with more responsibility. I'm hoping Richard weds and I can be reassured he's settled and happy; then I can tour the world. I'll walk through the Coliseum in Rome, tour the isles of Greece, climb the Alps." John walked behind his desk, running his hands along the back of his office chair. "For as long as I can remember, I've been sitting here, in this very room, focusing on caring for the family and . . ."

"Dreaming of escape," his mother finished softly. Her eyes shimmered with unshed tears. "Oh, my darling John, I'm so sorry to have placed such a burden upon you at such a tender age."

He shook his head. "You didn't place anything upon me," he assured her. "I took hold of it on my own and haven't a single regret over these past years. All I'm saying is that, before I settle down and take on the additional responsibility of a family, I wish to travel, to explore the world outside of England for a while." He shrugged lightly. "When I've had my fill, I shall return and marry someone sensible, someone practical, someone with whom I can settle into a comfortable life."

Indeed he'd never even consider marrying a woman who thought nothing of asking a gentleman to dance in moonlight. A shimmering memory of just how tempted he'd been to take Catherine up on her offer, to sweep her into his arms, to toss caution aside and claim what she so tauntingly offered, swept through him.

Forcibly, he stilled his now racing heart. He needed to remember what he wanted out of life and not allow himself to be tempted from his path . . . regardless of how alluring the lady might be.

"You've been particularly quiet this afternoon."

At Catherine's remark, Elizabeth redirected her gaze from the carriage window toward her sister. "Sorry. I was just thinking about my visit to Mr. Dunfee's shop today." And of her encounter with Richard.

Catherine's gaze sharpened upon her face. "Did something happen?"

"Nothing of mention," she said vaguely. Despite their close relationship, Elizabeth didn't wish to discuss her confusion over Richard's odd behavior. At least not until she'd sorted through the mess herself.

"Must you go there?" their father asked with a shake of his head. "It is a dangerous section of town."

Elizabeth patted her father's hand comfortingly. "Trust me, Papa. I'm perfectly safe when I go in our private coach with a few servants. Besides, while the shops on Bond Street might offer me anything from hats to boots, not one can provide me with a machine gear."

"Thank Heaven," Catherine replied with a smile. "I don't think I'd enjoy a society that was focused on the experiments of da Vinci."

Elizabeth raised a brow. "If the ton were ever to become fascinated with da Vinci's works, we'd have to rename London and call it Utopia."

Their father joined them in laughter as their carriage rocked to a stop in front of the theater. As they alighted from their conveyance, Elizabeth paused for a moment, taking in the grandeur of society's elite dressed in their finest. Glancing down at her own plain white dress, she felt as she always did when amongst the ton—dowdy and awkward, a peahen amongst swans. In her own environment, surrounded by machinery parts, Elizabeth always felt confident and comfortable; yet here, out in the social world, she felt utterly inadequate.

Drawing back her shoulders, Elizabeth hid her shaky nerves, retreating behind a wall of cool reserve when she saw Lady Atherton sailing toward them.

"Lord Shipham! How wonderful that you and your lovely daughters could attend this evening's performance." She offered their father her hand, smiling in a manner that struck Elizabeth as being completely false.

"Your presence only enhances my enjoyment of the evening," Father murmured as he bent over Lady Atherton's hand.

A laugh fluttered from the matron. "My gracious, you are ever the charmer, my lord."

"You inspire that in a gentleman, my lady."

Father's return almost had Elizabeth rolling her eyes. With all the flowery falsehoods tossed about, it was little wonder she had a hard time functioning in polite society.

Catherine, however, suffered no such inadequacies. "Lady Atherton," Cat exclaimed as she stepped forward. "It is wonderful to see you here." She offered the matron a sweet smile. "I am so looking forward to seeing Miss Newton's performance in Mr. Shakespeare's *Taming of the Shrew.* Everyone says she is simply marvelous."

"Indeed, she is," gushed Lady Atherton. "Stunningly brilliant."

Elizabeth tried to enter the conversation. "I believe the credit should be given to Mr. Shakespeare, for it is his words that move people."

Lady Atherton sniffed in derision. "Without the talents of a gifted actress, the play would be a very dull affair." She gestured toward the door. "If you'll excuse me, I believe I'll take my seat," she said before walking off.

The fact that she'd offended Lady Atherton was clear, but what remained uncertain in Elizabeth's mind was *how* she'd upset the lady.

"Oh, Elizabeth, how *could* you?" sighed Catherine.

"How could I what?" Elizabeth shook her head. "I don't know what I said to upset Lady Atherton."

Leaning closer, Catherine explained, "Lady Atherton considers herself the premier patroness of theater."

Still at a loss, Elizabeth shrugged lightly. "So why did I offend her by pointing out Mr. Shakespeare's talent?"

"Because you belittled Miss Newton's talent in the process." Catherine nudged Elizabeth's arm. "And, if you'll remember the conversation we had at the Mortimer's tea last week, Lady Weatherby mentioned that Lady Atherton sponsored Miss Newton."

Elizabeth closed her eyes as the depth of her faux pas sank in. "So it is only natural that Lady Atherton would be offended by my suggestion that it is Mr. Shakespeare's play that has everyone atwitter, rather than Miss Newton's performance."

"Precisely."

Shaking her head, Elizabeth looked at her sister. "Even when I try to be polite, I end up making a horrid gaffe." She sighed in exasperation. "Is it little wonder that I prefer my experiments? I'm a dismal failure at this."

"Come now, Elizabeth," interrupted their father. "You simply need a bit more practice, then I'm certain you'll be able to hold your own with even the most intimidating matron."

"If I continue to offend people like Lady Atherton, soon there won't be anyone left to practice upon, Papa," Elizabeth pointed out wryly. "So, now that I've managed to upset one of the most powerful hostessess in all of London, my evening has truly begun. Shall we take our seats and I'll see who I can offend next?"

"Why don't we do the first part of your suggestion and avoid the second?" Father asked with a laugh.

Offering his arm to both her and Catherine, their father led them into the beautiful theater and to their private box without further incident. Breathing a sigh of relief, Elizabeth sank down into her chair and waited for the play to begin. From the moment the curtains lifted, Elizabeth found herself so caught up in the wildly entertaining story of Petruchio and Kate that, by the intermission, she'd completely forgotten her mishap with Lady Atherton.

"That was wonderful, wasn't it?" Elizabeth turned toward her sister and father with a smile. "I vow I am quite breathless to see how it will end."

"I think . . ." Catherine began, only to break off her reply when a lady stepped into their box.

"Oh, my goodness," she exclaimed, pressing her hand to her stomach. "Forgive the intrusion; I seem to have stumbled into the wrong box."

Though Elizabeth couldn't ever remember meeting the lady, she looked oddly familiar to her. Trying to place her, Elizabeth noted the woman's blue eyes, dark hair that was touched with only a few gray streaks, the familiar curve to her cheeks.

"It's quite all right," their father said, rising to face the attractive woman. "I consider it our good fortune that you happened upon our box, Lady Wykham."

Lady Wykham! Richard's mother. Immediately Elizabeth saw the strong resemblance between mother and son.

"I thank you for your welcome, my lord." She offered their father a pretty smile. "Do I have the pleasure of addressing the Earl of Shipham?"

"Indeed, you do." Their father bowed to her. "Douglas Everley, Earl of Shipham, at your service." Straightening, he gestured toward Elizabeth and Catherine. "And might I present my daughters, Lady Elizabeth and Lady Catherine?"

Gliding forward with a grace Elizabeth could never hope to match, Lady Wykham reached out to warmly clasp their hands. "I'm pleased to have the chance to meet both of you, as I've heard we have quite a bit in common."

Elizabeth frowned at the woman in confusion. "Pardon?"

"My sons," she prodded softly.

Immediately, the memory of Richard bending close to her and her desire to experience his kiss raced through her, completely flustering Elizabeth. "Ummm, yes, indeed," she stammered, before pulling free of Lady Wykham's hold. "Please excuse me, my lady, I need to . . . to . . . refresh myself." Not waiting for a reply, Elizabeth hurried from the box.

In the corridor, Elizabeth leaned against the wall, pressing her hands against her eyes, fighting the urge to race down to their carriage and run home to the safety of her workshop. What had she been thinking to rush away from Lady Wykham like some stuttering, foolish chit? Now Richard's mother probably thought her to be a complete imbecile.

Not only would it hinder her hopes of using John as a cover, but it also bothered her to think Lady Wykham would speak poorly of her to Richard. Indeed, she wanted Lady Wykham to think well of the entire family, just in case the interest Elizabeth sensed between Catherine and the marquess bloomed into a true affection. Lord, it was all so confusing!

Dropping her hands to her sides, Elizabeth moved down the corridor toward the lady's parlor. She'd gone no more than a few steps when she caught sight of Richard leaning against a pillar, chatting with Lord Hampton. Good Heavens! With a gasp, Elizabeth stepped into a nearby box, pulling the curtains closed behind her, hoping Richard hadn't seen her. After all, what would she say to him? *Good evening, my lord, so glad I didn't kiss you this afternoon, despite the fact that I can't stop thinking about what it would have felt like to kiss you.* Oh, yes, that would play well.

"Good evening, Lady Elizabeth."

Startled, she spun toward Lord Wykham. "Good evening, my lord."

He'd risen from his chair, but still stood near the balustrade. "Are you enjoying the performance?"

"Yes, very much so," she replied, relieved he was far too much of a gentleman to ask why she'd stepped unbidden into his box.

"You seemed to enjoy it."

His comment caused her to lift her brows in question.

A dull flush stained his cheekbones. "I happened to notice you and your sister were only three boxes down when I took my seat."

Moving forward, she leaned over the rail to gaze over at her family's box. Her father stood conversing with Lady Wykham and Catherine. "Perhaps that's why your mother got mixed up and entered our box by mistake."

"My mother's in your box?" Immediately, he leaned out and glared across the expanse. "So she is."

The grim tone to his voice surprised Elizabeth. "It's

quite all right," she assured him. "Your mother's most charming."

"For a guileful snoop," he muttered as he turned toward Elizabeth. "What did she say to your sister?"

"My sister?" Elizabeth shook her head. "Nothing, but then I left almost immediately after your mother arrived, so . . ."

"Please excuse me, Lady Elizabeth."

Before the last syllable had left his mouth, Lord Wykham strode from the box, leaving her alone. She'd only had time to blink twice before she saw him reappear next to his mother. The tight cast to his expression told of his inexplicable annoyance.

An excited whisper in the next box made Elizabeth glance over her shoulder . . . to meet the gaze of none other than Lady Atherton. Elizabeth looked away quickly, only to notice that almost everyone had their eyes trained upon her or the scene unfolding in her family's box.

As the lights flickered, signaling the start of the second half of the performance, Elizabeth turned to return to her family's box when she heard Richard's laugh from right outside the curtain. She wasn't ready to face him yet. Stepping backward, she pressed against the wall, praying that Richard wouldn't enter the box.

With the way today had been going, she should have known better than to waste time on hope.

Richard entered the tiny room and came to an abrupt halt when he caught sight of her. Elizabeth heard the rush of whispers from the people watching them. She closed her eyes briefly, wishing the ground would open up and swallow her whole. It was bad enough that she had to face Richard after melting in his arms, but to be forced to confront him under the watchful scrutiny of vicious gossips was more than she could bear.

Thankfully, the lights to the theater dimmed completely, bringing blessed darkness to the box and a cacophony of disappointed groans from the people watching them.

"Elizabeth."

The softness of his voice surprised her. Slowly, she opened her eyes to peer at him through the shadows. "I . . . I . . ." Realizing she didn't have any idea what to say to him, she finally ceased her awkward stammering and fell silent.

His movements appeared slightly awkward to her, but she shook her head, dismissing the notion as a trick of the light. "Where did everyone go?"

The easy question loosened her tongue. "Both your mother and Lord Wykham are visiting with my father and sister," she replied, her nerves settling.

"In your box? Well, that's certainly unexpected," he remarked easily, before settling into a chair. "As for me, I'm going to enjoy the second half of this fantastic play." A side of his mouth tilted upward as he glanced back at her. "Are you going to join me, or do you plan on cowering there for the remainder of the performance?"

His challenge sparked an immediate response. "Cower?" she returned briskly. "I was merely trying to accommodate your girth when you entered the room."

"My girth." Richard laughed brightly as he patted his flat stomach. "Indeed."

She couldn't help but smile at his reaction.

"Now stop being so ridiculous and take a seat, Elizabeth."

Surprisingly enough, she didn't take offense at his direction. It was as if his laughter had restored the easiness between them, making it seem as if the near-kiss in Mr. Dunfee's shop had never occurred. Tilting her head, she gazed at Richard, thinking how he could infuriate her one minute, make her want to kiss him the next, then do an about-face and simply make her feel like a friend.

Without another moment of hesitation, she settled into the chair next to Richard and watched the play.

8

From the stiffness in Lord Wykham's posture, Catherine feared the man would do permanent harm to his back if he didn't loosen up. Instead of simply sitting back and enjoying the play, he sat there, poker straight, as if the witty play were pure torture for him.

Sighing, she redirected her attention onto the stage, but her interest in the play was gone as well. Needing a few moments alone, Catherine leaned forward to whisper to her father when she lost her balance. Tipping to her side, she caught herself on the nearest object.

John's thigh.

He flinched beneath her hand, as if she'd harmed him in some way. Perhaps he simply didn't wish anyone to touch his sainted person. Rolling her eyes, she released him and balanced herself upon the back of her father's chair. "I'll be right back, Papa," she whispered, before rising and heading toward the exit of their box.

"Do you need an escort, Lady Catherine?" Lord Wykham asked as she reached the curtains.

"No, thank you, my lord. I wouldn't wish to make you suffer my presence for a moment longer than absolutely necessary," she replied softly, then slipped out into the corridor.

Twisting around in his seat to face front, John tried to control the seething emotions roiling around inside of him. What was it about Catherine that bothered him so? He felt torn between lecturing her on her inappropriate behavior . . . and kissing her senseless. At this moment, the latter held greater appeal.

He glanced back at the stilled curtain, waiting for her to reappear. Another minute went by before John leaned forward to Lord Shipham and said, "Excuse me, my lord, but your daughter hasn't returned yet."

"Hmmmm," Lord Shipham murmured, his attention still fixed upon the stage.

Hmmmm? What kind of bloody answer was that? Wasn't the man worried that his daughter hadn't come back to the box? The rational side of John reminded him that she'd only been gone a few minutes and that it took far longer than that for her to reach the lady's parlor. Still, his emotional side wanted nothing to do with reason.

Rising, John tugged down on his vest. "Don't concern yourself, my lord. I shall provide her with safe escort," he said, before hurrying after Catherine.

Lord Shipham grinned as he watched John leave the box. "Safe escort?" he murmured to Lady Wykham.

"Ah, yes, thieves and miscreants abound in the theater," she countered, her eyes sparkling with amusement. "I do believe we have a romance on our hands, my lord."

"Oh, I do hope so," he replied. "In fact, I'm praying we have more than one."

Lady Wykham's brows lifted. "Then you think my Richard and your Elizabeth are . . . interested in one another."

"I predict all of the ton will be wondering the very same thing tomorrow," he said, pointing toward the Wykham box. "Look over there."

Following the line of his hand, Lady Wykham caught sight of Richard and Elizabeth, sitting next to one another, alone in the box. As she watched, Richard leaned over to say something to Elizabeth, who tossed back her head in laughter. Smiling, Lady Wykham returned her attention to Lord Shipham. "Splendid," she pronounced. "Don't you agree?"

"Absolutely," he returned emphatically. "I do believe the connection between our houses would be a fine thing, my lady."

"Indeed, it would." Folding her hands upon her lap, Lady Wykham continued, "And when they wed, it will be the wedding of the year."

"When who weds? Richard and Elizabeth, or John and Catherine?"

She lifted one shoulder. "Does it truly matter? Either match will be met with abounding enthusiasm from the ton." Her hand swept toward the other boxes. "See how everyone is looking toward the Wykham box, watching your daughter and my son? The romance between our children is the premier gossip these days, and everyone who is anyone is speaking of it."

"That's true enough," Lord Shipham agreed readily. "If even I've heard snippets of it, then it must be on everyone's lips."

"I assure you, it is. So, you see, my lord, if these romances culminate with a wedding, it will be *the* event of the year."

"That matters not one whit to me as long as my girls are happy," Lord Shipham said.

Lady Wykham nodded succinctly. "I couldn't agree with you more."

In perfect agreement, Lord Shipham smiled at Lady Wykham, who gave him a contented smile right back, then they both settled back to enjoy the remainder of the play.

Striding down the corridor, John headed for the lady's parlor to collect that troublesome woman. *It was his duty as a gentleman,* he told himself, ignoring the taunting laugh he heard within his head. Only by chance did he glance down the staircase . . . and caught a glimpse of rose silk.

Catherine.

Breaking stride, he leaned over the banister just in time to see her glide off the last stair and toward the outer door. Surely even she wouldn't be foolish enough to go outside without escort. Then he remembered that just last night she'd been perfectly prepared to do that very thing if he hadn't agreed to escort her.

A creature of impulse like Catherine would do whatever took her fancy, regardless of the inadvisability of the act.

Cursing beneath his breath, John raced after her, taking the stairs two at a time. As he headed outside, the brisk night air did little to cool his frustrations. One swift look around, and he located Catherine as she strolled aimlessly through the gardens alongside the theater.

Uncertain of what he would do once he got his hands on her, John stormed toward the unsuspecting Catherine.

* * *

"Poor Petruchio," Richard commented as the last scene unfolded before them. "To be stuck with that shrew for the rest of his life."

"Poor Petruchio nothing," countered Elizabeth. "He should praise Kate every day for being such a strong woman, to make him realize that she's his partner, his mate, rather than his handmaiden."

As the curtain drew closed, Richard rose, unaware he had stepped upon Elizabeth's gown, and began clapping. But when Elizabeth tried to follow suit, she was stopped short by her skirt, the abrupt motion sent her off balance, and caused her to stumble.

"Elizabeth?" Immediately, Richard reached for her. "Are you hurt?" he asked, running his hands down her arms.

"I don't think so," she murmured as she tried to regain her composure. "I'm afraid I twisted my ankle."

Concern darkened his blue eyes. "Why don't you stay still for a few minutes?"

"I feel so foolish," she admitted softly.

Richard kneeled down in front of her and began to gently press his fingers against her ankle. "Tell me if this hurts."

Elizabeth opened her eyes and met his gaze. "No . . . no, really, I'm fine," she assured him.

Looking into Richard's face as the shadows enfolded them closer, Elizabeth again felt the stroke of desire for Richard. Unconsciously, she parted her lips, offering him silent invitation to gift her with his kiss. As his gaze dropped to her mouth, Elizabeth felt her heart race in anticipation.

"Elizabeth," he rasped, his head dipping lower. "We shouldn't."

"I know," she murmured in reply as she lay her hands on his shoulders.

Arching upward, she met his descending mouth eagerly. His lips molded against hers, shaping, sculpting, teaching her the tenderness of a first kiss. Unbidden, a moan rose to her lips as she instinctively tilted her head to give him better access to her mouth.

Richard's groan vibrated through her as he accepted her invitation, slanting his head to deepen the kiss. As his tongue swept inward with passionate intent, Elizabeth curled her arms around his neck, pulling him closer. At the feel of his chest pressing against her sensitized breasts, Elizabeth exploded with desire, entwining her tongue with his, eliciting another groan of passion from Richard.

Shifting to the side, Richard slid his hand down her cheek, trailing his fingers along her collarbone, to tease the edge of her bodice. Hunger arose within Elizabeth. She'd never known she could feel like this, never believed a kiss could make her want so much more. Every inch of her body tingled and her senses were heightened. Beneath her fingers, his hair felt so silky. The scent of heated flesh tantalized her, making her yearn for more. She'd never before felt so connected with anyone, as if they were one desire, one thought, one need. They even breathed as one.

A soft moan escaped her when Richard broke off their kiss to scrape his teeth along her arched neck. Shivers chased through her, running downward toward her core. Her fingers clutched at him, urging him onward, as he slowly made her way down toward her aching breast.

His hot breath washed over her as he laved at her skin before drawing it deeply into his mouth with an erotic kiss. Elizabeth pushed herself upward toward him, giving herself over to him with utter abandon, wanting more, wanting . . .

The roar of applause rose upward, jarring her from the haze of yearning. As if awakening from a dream, Elizabeth opened her eyes to stare up at the ceiling of the theatre box. Her blood chilled at the realization that she was compromising herself in a very public place where her father, Richard's mother, or any number of people could find them at any moment.

She now used the fingers she'd threaded through his hair in passion to pull his head up. The blaze of desire she saw in his eyes made her catch her breath, but another shout of praise from the audience reminded her of their position. "Oh, God," she rasped softly. "What are we doing?"

His brows drew together. "Elizabeth?"

But she was too mortified to respond to the confusion she heard in his voice. "Please, release me," she said urgently, glancing at the door, not noticing how he blanched at her order. "What was I thinking?" she continued under her breath.

Immediately, Richard stood, keeping his back to the open balcony as he smoothed his waistcoat. "I believe you were thinking that you enjoyed my kiss."

Scrambling to her feet, Elizabeth pressed against the wall, praying she would blend into the curtains and no one looking at their box would notice her slightly disheveled state. "Yes," she replied slowly. "I was enjoying your kisses." But instead of the statement bringing warmth, it made her feel cold and bereft. Of course she'd enjoyed his kisses. He was a rake, after all, the consummate seducer of women. Under his experienced touch, she'd fallen victim to her own foolishness. And while she might believe he was more than a rake, Richard admitted he'd earned his reputation. She also couldn't forget how he'd almost kissed her in Mr. Dunfee's shop, then pulled back abruptly, almost as if he'd been toying with her. "But then," she pointed out in what she prayed was a reasonable tone, "I'm merely one of many who has enjoyed them, aren't I, Richard?"

He flinched as if she'd hit him. But in the next instant, his expression shifted into a confident mask, making her believe she'd imagined the initial reaction. "One of a great many." Straightening his cravat, he paused to run his fingers through his hair . . . hair that she'd mussed . . . before sauntering toward her. "Anytime you wish to indulge again, my lady Elizabeth, please let me know," he murmured as he ran a lazy finger along her bodice.

Struggling for composure, she slapped his hand away. "Thank you, my lord, but I believe in the future I shall restrain my base urges. Some of us are capable of resisting debauchery."

A disappointed light flickered in his eyes, before he lowered his lids, shielding the expression in their blue depths. "So speaks the woman who lay moaning in my arms just a few moments ago," he said. "For someone who reveled in my . . . debauchery, you are hardly in the position to judge me, madam."

His mouth, the same mouth that had invoked such a heated response within her, thinned into a cold line as Richard stared down at her for one long minute before turning on his heel and striding from the box.

Her fragile facade crumpled the moment he disappeared. Hiding her face in her hands, Elizabeth allowed her tears to spill onto her palms. She welcomed the pain, anything to hold back the cold that threatened to overtake her. For a few precious moments, she'd felt . . . glorious.

She was a fool.

In the corridor, Richard fought the urge to return to the box when he heard Elizabeth begin to cry. God, she must think him a bastard.

Which meant he'd accomplished his goal.

When she'd given herself over to him with such sweet passion, he'd become lost in her, in the moment, forgetting everything but the splendor of her in his arms. It was only after the desire had waned and she'd looked at him with shock that he'd remembered he was everything she didn't want.

And that had angered . . . and saddened him.

Her accusation that she was only one of many had struck a nerve, hurting him more than he'd ever thought possible. It had also provided him with the perfect opportunity to thrust a wedge between them, to ensure that Elizabeth would stay far away from him.

It was for the best, he told himself over and over again. She wanted to belong, to be part of society, while he knew he would be unwelcome at every house once the truth of his new profession became common knowledge. Gritting his teeth against regret, he forced himself to move away from the box, leaving Elizabeth to her tears.

While she might feel a twinge of pain now, Richard knew he was saving her from a great deal more.

That knowledge, however, didn't make him feel any less the bastard.

* * *

"What the devil do you think you're doing out here all alone, Catherine?"

A startled yelp escaped her, but Catherine's alarm faded when she saw Lord Wykham. "What do you mean by scaring me like that?"

"I scared you?" His expression was grim. "Do you have any idea what fate could have befallen you out here, all alone?"

The words in his initial question echoed through her head. "You called me Catherine," she said with a pleased smile. "So the high and mighty Lord Wykham unbends long enough to drop the proper address."

He looked at her incredulously. "My God, surely you can't be so utterly . . ." Grabbing her by the shoulders, he pulled her toward him. "I reprimand you for risking not only your reputation this time, but your safety as well, and all you can do is mock me for calling you by your Christian name?" He lifted her up until she stood on her tiptoes, pressed against his chest. "Have you no sense, woman?"

Catherine stared in fascination at the changes in him. Gone was Lord Wykham, the staid gentleman who wouldn't raise his voice to a lady, and in his place was John, this breathtaking tempest of a man whose emotions seethed within him.

A lock of thick black hair fell across his forehead as he brought her another inch closer. "Well, have you?"

But a reply, any response at all, was beyond her as she stared at him, utterly entranced by this stunning man. His burning gaze dropped to her lips and she tilted back her head, wanting, no, needing this man to kiss her.

His head began to lower when a shout echoed behind them. Immediately, John pushed her behind him, changing to the protector in an instant. Peering around his arm, she saw a young man race toward a pretty, blonde woman who stood on the edge of the park. A sigh escaped Catherine when the man swept the lady up into his arms, capturing her in a passionate kiss.

"How sweet," Catherine whispered.

"How foolish," corrected John as he allowed her to step out from behind him. "They are completely unprotected and unaware. Anyone could sneak up behind them and pick their pockets or worse."

Her fingers trembled as she pressed them against her lips. "He's gone."

Lord Wykham frowned at her in confusion. "Who's gone?"

"John," Catherine replied with a sigh.

His frown deepened into a scowl. "I'm afraid you're not making sense again, Catherine."

"No, I'm probably not making sense to you, Lord Wykham, but I assure you John would understand."

An exasperated sigh ripped through him.

"Now, don't get all in a huff," she said, patting his arm. "I'm just glad that you changed back into your stodgy old self before I did something truly foolish, like kiss you." She ignored his indignant protest. "Why don't we go back inside, so you can return me, safe and sound, to my father?"

"Finally," he exclaimed. "A *reasonable* request."

Sighing over the loss of the enticing John, Catherine watched as the lady bestowed one last lingering kiss upon her lover's lips before hurrying away.

As they reached the entrance to the theater, Catherine stole one last peek back toward the end of the garden . . . and what she saw froze her to the core. "John!" she gasped in alarm. "Look!"

Responding to the tone in her voice, he turned immediately. Two men had set upon the young man, who had been gazing after his now-departed lady. As they watched, one of the men grabbed the young lover's arms while the other brute bashed him over the head. "Stay here," John ordered before racing toward the helpless man.

The larger of the two assailants turned to face John, while the other man slung the young lover over his shoulder and headed toward the alley. Catherine watched, frozen in place, as John slowed, adopting a boxer's stance and warily circled the brute.

Not only did the thug stand a full head taller than John, but he was twice his width as well. The odds were certainly not in John's favor. As the thug swung a meaty paw at John who ducked gracefully out of the way, Catherine decided to even the score a bit and raced forward to help.

As she neared, she saw John connect with the assailant's face, sending his head snapping backward. The feral look on John's face intensified as he stepped closer, edging the brute backward despite the differences in their sizes.

But the moment John caught sight of her, his expression shifted into one of horror. "Catherine! Get back!" he cried.

The shift in John's attention was all the brute needed to send a fist crashing into John's midsection, then he delivered a knock-out blow under his chin, sending John sprawling onto the grass. "*John!*" Catherine screamed, racing forward and dropping on her knees beside him, uncaring that the assailant raced off after his companion.

Catherine cradled John's head in her lap, brushing the hair off his forehead. "Speak to me, John," she whispered.

His lashes fluttered upward, confusion clouding his blue eyes. "Catherine?" he murmured, his brows drawing together in consternation. "What are you . . ." He broke off as the fog began to clear from his gaze. Abruptly, he sat up and looked around before clasping her shoulders. "Are you all right? Did he hurt you?"

"No, no," she hurried to assure him, pressing her hands upon his chest. "I'm fine. After he struck you out, he ran off."

The hands holding her shoulders tightened. "He wouldn't have knocked me out if you'd listened to what I said and stayed back . . . then I might have been able to help that poor gent they dragged off."

Guilt mingled with her anger. "Fine," she snapped, shaking free of his hold. "Go ahead and blame me for your being knocked out in a fight. Next time, I won't lift a finger to try and help you, even though the man you're defending yourself against is twice your size."

"I understand that you were simply trying to help, Catherine, but what I want *you* to understand is that you would have helped me the most by doing as I'd asked," he returned calmly, before fingering his jaw. "Damn, but that fellow had a mighty punch."

As swiftly as it had come, her anger left. Leaning forward on her knees, she gently fingered the line of his jaw, searching the swollen skin for cuts. "I suppose we should be thankful he didn't have a weapon."

When John captured her hand in his, pressing her fingers against the curve of his jaw, Catherine raised her startled gaze to his. With a lock of hair across his forehead and the darkness in his eyes, John had once more become the wild, all-too enticing man who made her romantic heart melt. Slowly, he lowered their clasped hands, dragging her fingers along his jawline before releasing them. "Thank you for your concern, Catherine," he murmured, his voice low and husky.

Flustered, Catherine rose to her feet and brushed off her skirts. "My goodness, there is no need to thank me, my lord. I would have been concerned about anyone."

"So wonderful to feel special," he muttered beneath his breath as he levered himself to his feet.

"Pardon me?" she asked, uncertain if she'd heard him correctly. Did he *want* her to think he was special? Lord, he was confusing her. One moment he was the stuffy Lord Wykham, then the next he became the stunning John. How was a girl supposed to know how to handle him if he kept on changing in the blink of an eye?

"It was nothing." He straightened his jacket and smoothed back his hair before turning to face her. "Shall we now return to the theater? I fear our extended absence will have been noticed by now."

And like that, Lord Wykham had returned. Propping her hands on her hips, Catherine faced him boldly. "Return to the theater? Have you taken leave of your senses?" she demanded. "What of that poor fellow those two men abducted?"

"What of him?" Lord Wykham countered. "Do you propose that the two of us trail those men . . . one of whom has perfected the roundhouse punch . . . through dark, dangerous alleyways with little to no hope of finding them?" He shook his head. "More than likely, what we'd find would be more trouble, and risk our own safety in the process."

"But we must help that poor man!"

"I'm not disagreeing with you," John said. "I'm only disagreeing with your method of helping him. Lord, Catherine, you must stop being so bloody impulsive."

"Perhaps I am impulsive, but we need to help him!"

"Doing something utterly foolish won't help him." John took hold of her elbow and began to steer her back toward the theater. "Once I return you to your father, I shall contact the authorities. If I can't get any satisfaction there, I shall hire a Bow Street Runner and set him on the matter."

"Oh," Catherine said after a moment.

"Oh?" he asked incredulously, pulling them to a halt. "That's it? No apology, no comment on my idea being a sound one?"

Though he had a point, she wasn't about to admit it to him. Patting him on the arm, she resumed walking, effectively dragging John along behind her. "No need to be smug, my lord," she remarked blithely.

"You called me John a few moments ago," he grumbled, thoroughly disgruntled with her.

She smiled up at him. "That's because you *were* John a few moments ago."

A long-suffering sigh escaped him. "Lord, not this again."

Catherine's laughter accompanied them back into the theater.

9

Bleary-eyed and irritable, Richard tried to focus his attention on the accounting book before him, but the bloody numbers kept on wavering. "Blast and damn," he growled as he slammed the book shut.

Usually he found such contentment, such completion in his work, but all morning he'd been utterly distracted . . . and it didn't take a bloody genius to figure out why.

No, he could lay his current headache directly upon the shoulders of one Lady Elizabeth Everley.

It had been bad enough trying to keep her from his thoughts when he'd been at odds with her, but now it was downright impossible to block her from his mind. Instead of thinking of her laughter, he thought of how soft her lips were, how they molded so perfectly to his, how they tasted so incredibly sweet, making him hunger for more.

And more he'd had. Indeed, his hand itched with the urge to touch her again, to feel the generous curve of her breast beneath his fingers, to shape her softness against his palm. In his thoughts, he undid her gown, easing it downward, off her shoulders, giving him complete, uninhibited access to her breasts. He'd pressed kisses along the supple line of her neck just as he had last night, but this time when he reached the rise of her breast, he'd fulfill his desire to take her rosy nipple into his mouth, drawing deeply on her until he'd . . .

"Beggin' your pardon, my lord."

The voice snapped Richard from his wayward thoughts. Thanking God he was seated and able to hide the results of his daydreams, Richard cleared his throat and inquired, "Is there a problem, Mr. Perth?"

"Not a problem, my lord, just a question," he clarified. "Some water got splashed on my orders, making them difficult to read, so I wasn't certain if the order for The Bull and Boar Pub was for five hundred pretzels or for six hundred."

Flipping open the order ledger, Richard ran a quick finger down the most recent column. "Six hundred."

Mr. Perth nodded once. "Very good, sir. We'll get right on it." He paused at the door. "Mr. Burnbaum is here to see you, too."

"Please show him in," Richard asked, wondering what news his neighbor would bring today.

Stepping into the office, Aaron removed his hat, revealing his thick, dark curls. "Lord Vernon, thank you for seeing me."

"How many times have I told you to call me Richard?" he said as he rose from his chair. Rounding the desk, Richard offered Aaron his hand.

After a moment's hesitation, Aaron accepted the handshake. "I know you wish me to call you by your Christian name, but it doesn't seem right."

"Why not?" Richard asked. "We are fellow tradesmen."

Aaron shook his head. "Even so, that doesn't change

the fact that I am a Jewish merchant, son of a Jewish merchant, while you are a titled gentleman, son of a marquess."

Crossing his arms, Richard gave Aaron a level stare. "I consider that immaterial, Aaron. After all, without your help, my business would have floundered. I will never forget how you and the other local merchants helped me negotiate deals with the captains, found workers to help renovate the factory, and taught me how to keep my accounts." He raised his brows. "When weighed against that, the differences in our station mean less than nothing to me."

Aaron smiled at him. "Perhaps I am merely surprised to find wisdom in a member of the aristocracy."

Tossing back his head, Richard laughed aloud. "Now *that* makes sense. For I will admit to having possessed very little of it for far too long." As his laughter faded away, Richard noticed that Aaron's smile didn't quite reach his eyes. "So tell me why you came to see me today, Aaron."

"It's because of my Isaac," Aaron began. "You saw him yesterday, didn't you?"

Richard nodded. "Yes, I did. Isaac said that your wife wanted some of my fine pretzels for the noon meal."

"Did he say anything else?"

Thinking back on the brief meeting, Richard tried to remember their conversation. "Not much. I did mention that he seemed in a hurry, and he told me he was meeting his lady."

"The gentile."

He started in surprise. "The *gentile?* That's what you call your son's inamorata?"

Aaron waved his hand dismissively. "I ask him why he can't settle down with a nice, Jewish girl, like Mr. Klein's daughter, but my Isaac says that this girl is like no other, that she makes him feel brave and honorable." He made a sound of utter disgust. "Tell me why my Isaac needs a woman to feel those things. Those are things he should feel simply because he *is* brave and honorable."

"Ah, but surely you remember, Aaron, how it feels to have a young lady look at you in admiration," Richard said.

"No, I am not so old that I forget these things," Aaron agreed as he turned his hat over in his hands. "But when I ask Isaac to bring this girl to our home so we may meet her, he refuses me. He tells me that it is impossible for me to meet this girl." He slapped his hat against his thigh. "Why, I ask you, Richard? Why can this girl not meet us? Is it because we are simple Jewish merchants and she feels we are beneath her?"

"If she is allowing your son to court her, I doubt she would feel that way about you," Richard assured the man. "There could be plenty of other reasons why she couldn't accompany Isaac to your house."

"And what would those be?" Aaron countered quickly. "That she is married or engaged to another gentile? Or that she hasn't told her own parents that she is seeing a Jewish merchant's son? All of the possible reasons I come up with unsettle me." Suddenly, Aaron dropped into a chair, looking utterly defeated. "Worst of all, my son has now disappeared, and I fear he has run off with this girl, whose name I don't even know."

"Disappeared?" Richard sat down next to Aaron. "Are you certain?"

Propping his elbows onto his knees, Aaron leaned forward, holding his head in his hands. "Positive. After he gave his mother your package, he left without telling us where he was going . . . which usually means he is heading off to meet this girl. Marta and I will often hear him returning late into the night, but last night we fell asleep before we heard him return. This morning we found his room empty." He lifted his head to look at Richard. "He never came home last night, and I worry that he's gone and done something foolish."

The bleakness in Aaron's gaze touched Richard. "Like raced off and married at Gretna Green?"

Aaron nodded dismally.

"Come now, Aaron," Richard said softly, putting a hand upon his new friend's shoulder. "Surely this won't be the worst thing in the world. Your Isaac is a sensible young man and you must trust him to make the right decisions. When he does return, you must accept his new bride, welcome her into your home, or you will lose your son."

A heavy sigh ripped from Aaron. "You are right, Richard. I know you are, but I don't know if I have it in me to welcome a stranger into my heart."

"Who said anything about your heart?" Richard asked with a slight laugh. "All I said was make her feel welcome in your home. Anything else will come with time."

"I can do that," Aaron murmured softly. He straightened in his chair. "I can do that," he repeated a bit louder this time.

Richard patted Aaron on the back. "I know you can."

Both men rose, and when Aaron offered his hand, Richard readily accepted. "Thank you, Richard, for letting me burden you with my troubles."

"Burden me?" Richard scoffed. "Hardly. I myself am familiar with familial woes."

"I would be honored to share your burdens as well."

"I appreciate the offer, Aaron, but I would never wish to bore you with my dull tales," Richard said lightly.

"Very well." Putting on his hat, Aaron headed toward the door. With his hand on the knob, he turned to face Richard once more. "Perhaps you would like to dine with my wife and me one evening?"

"I would be honored," Richard accepted without hesitation.

"Excellent. We shall be pleased to have you as our guest."

"Why don't you invite me when your son returns with his new bride? Think on it, Aaron. Two gentiles at your table at once! Will you still be welcome at temple after that?"

Grinning, Aaron shook his head. "Why do I have a feeling that I will come to regret using that word?"

"Because you will," Richard countered. "I'll see to it." With laughter coloring his voice, Richard knew Aaron wouldn't take offense at his reply.

"You are good for me, Richard. You make me question the old beliefs, and realize that I am far too young to be so set in my ways."

A side of Richard's mouth tilted upward. "I do have a habit of disturbing people . . . only very few of them actually thank me for it."

It felt good to give her croquet ball a strong, hard whack.

"My goodness, Elizabeth. What's got you in a snit?" Catherine asked as she stepped toward her green striped ball.

"I'm not in a snit," Elizabeth protested, glancing

around Lady Atherton's lawn to make certain no one at the afternoon party could overhear them.

"Oh, no? Then why did you hit your ball so hard it flew into the bushes?"

Elizabeth stiffened. "I simply misjudged my shot."

Glancing up from her ball, Catherine smiled in mocking amusement. "Mm-hmmm."

She glowered at her sister.

Tapping her ball lightly, Catherine sent it gliding through the first wicket. "It's your turn again," she said as she stepped back. "Try not to knock your ball out of the lawn this time."

What she'd really like to do, Elizabeth thought to herself, was knock herself in the head to rid herself of these plaguing memories from last night. Immediately, she was assailed by the image of herself in Richard's theater box, kissing him frantically, arching up into him. All evening she'd been tormented by that image . . . and by the emotions it invoked within her.

Why, oh, why couldn't she be repulsed by her act of intimacy with Richard? Why couldn't she think of the way he kissed her and shudder with disgust? Instead of remembering his rejection, she only remembered the passion. Elizabeth groaned softly as she lined her mallet up with the ball. No, she wasn't lucky enough to think of herself as one of many. Instead, whenever she thought of those moments in his arms, she forgot everything that came after the passion and she craved another taste. She found herself longing for more of his caresses, more of his mind-shattering kisses.

Dear God! Something needed to be done about this, she thought, panicking at her uncontrollable thoughts.

She didn't want to give Richard up as a friend, but neither could she become his next conquest. If she gave into her desires, she would be risking . . .

"Are you *ever* going to hit the ball, Elizabeth?"

Startled from her thoughts, Elizabeth instinctively drew back her mallet and hit the ball with all her might, sending it bouncing over the bushes, across nearly the entire expanse of lawn, and into an ornamental pond. Splendid. Just splendid.

Catherine's gales of laughter did little to improve her mood. Glaring at her sister, Elizabeth stalked over to the pond to fish out her ball.

"Ohhh, there's John . . . I mean, Lord Wykham," exclaimed Catherine. "Do you mind if we end this game, Elizabeth? I must speak with Lord Wykham about an urgent matter."

"Mind that I am saved from fishing my ball out of this water?" Elizabeth asked dryly. "Not at all."

"Thank you," Catherine called brightly before setting down her mallet and hurrying off toward Lord Wykham.

Noting the excited expression on her sister's face, Elizabeth wondered if her sister were falling in love with Lord Wykham. *Wouldn't that be delightful?* Elizabeth thought, *if one of them ended up happy.*

Surely their father would relent in his decision that Elizabeth must marry first when he saw how in love Catherine was with the marquess. Then, after Catherine was happily wed, Elizabeth could move back to their country home and live out the remainder of her life in peace without the pressure of trying to conform to society's standards. For it had become fairly obvious that she was destined to fail miserably . . . regardless of how hard she tried.

Deeply troubled, Elizabeth set down her mallet and went to enjoy some lemonade.

"So, what did the magistrate say?"

Holding in a smile, John glanced down at Catherine, who practically danced beside him with anticipation. "Good day to you, too, my lady," he said calmly.

"Yes, yes," she replied impatiently, waving her hands. "Let's dispense with all that polite nonsense for once, so we can move on to more important matters."

He lifted a brow. "I happen to consider behaving in a polite fashion quite important."

"John!" she hissed in exasperation.

He chuckled; he couldn't help himself.

Narrowing her eyes, she fixed a steady gaze upon him. "You're enjoying tormenting me, aren't you?"

"Immensely."

"I'll wager you wouldn't find it so enjoyable if I told everyone that we left the theater together, the two of us all alone. . . ."

"Do you want to hear about my meeting with the magistrate or not, my pretty little blackmailer?"

Her smile held immense satisfaction. "I most certainly do."

The clever minx thought she'd outsmarted him . . . and she had, John acknowledged ruefully. She'd known perfectly well that he would have done anything to protect her—even from herself. Afraid their discussion might be overheard by the guests mingling on the lawn, he suggested, "Why don't we try our hands at the garden maze, my lady? I've often heard Lady Atherton speak highly of it." At Catherine's nod, John tucked her hand onto his arm and directed them toward the large maze.

Surprisingly enough, Catherine had the good sense to keep silent until they were enveloped in the privacy of the shaped hedges. "Now, tell me of your meeting, John."

John. Hearing his name on her lips caused his gut to tighten . . . just as it had last night, when he'd almost made the utterly foolish mistake of kissing her. Thank God they'd been interrupted. For, as enticing as she might be, a lifetime of her antics would drive him mad. And by accompanying her on her adventures, he played a role, willing or not, in compromising her.

His determination to avoid any more of Catherine's evening escapades was precisely the reason behind his appearance here at the Atherton's lawn party. John already knew Catherine well enough to realize that she would launch herself at him the moment she saw him again to hear about the magistrate he'd spoken to. He allowed himself a smug smile at the accuracy of his prediction.

By seeing her during the day, he could avoid any more reputation-threatening incidents. Congratulating himself on a well-executed plan, John led them deeper into the maze. After all, it was perfectly acceptable for a couple to enjoy a stroll through a maze, so there wasn't any risk to Catherine's reputation.

"Are you ever going to tell me about your meeting with the magistrate, or am I going to be forced to call upon him myself?"

"You would, wouldn't you?" he asked, knowing the answer even as he finished the question. "Don't even bother answering, Catherine, as we both know the answer."

She pinched his arm in protest.

"As I feared, when I spoke to the magistrate, they promised me they'd look into the matter, but informed me that they held little hope of ever finding the perpetrators. Because of their lack of enthusiasm, I engaged the services of a gentleman named Mr. Lewis, who will try to locate the young man we saw abducted. I gave Mr. Lewis as accurate a description as I could, though we were too far away to see them closely enough for a detailed description. I then went to the magistrate and offered them the same information, though they were less hopeful of finding the gentleman. They seemed to feel that perhaps the man had outstanding markers with the wrong sort of people."

"That could very well be true," Catherine conceded. "But what about the lady? Are you trying to find her as well?"

"No," he said, confused at her question. "Why would I? She was unharmed."

"She won't be if she believes her true love has abandoned her!"

Catherine's dramatics made him smile. "I assure you, madam, many a lady has had her heart broken and lived to tell the tale."

"Quite the sensitive gentleman, aren't you, my lord?" Catherine asked frostily. "Very well, then, I see I shall have to take matters into my own hands."

Still wincing over her sarcastic remark, John warily focused in on her declaration. "What the devil do you mean by that?"

"Precisely what I said." When she tugged her hand off

his arm, John ignored the urge to snatch it back again. "I shall begin to make inquiries as to the lady's identity."

"Inquiries to whom? The patronesses of Almack's?"

"Why not?" Catherine retorted, obviously catching the sarcasm in his question. "After all, the mavens of society know everyone who is anyone, so I'm certain they would be a help in identifying the young lady."

John shook his head over Catherine's faulty logic. "How can you be so certain that she is a member of polite society?"

"Her dress was of the finest quality, my lord, which leads me to believe she is indeed a lady," replied Catherine, tilting her chin up as she gave him a haughty look.

John poked holes in her argument. "Just because she has excellent fashion sense doesn't make her a lady. Many merchants can afford to clothe their daughters and wives in the finest apparel."

"But not every lady wears a gold crest upon the left shoulder of her gown." Her eyes snapped with annoyance. "If I cannot find anyone within society who can identify the lady, then I shall begin to approach the finest modistes and see if one of them can claim the woman as a patroness."

"Do you have any idea how many dressmakers there are on Bond Street alone?" he asked. "It would take you weeks, no, *months* to question all of them . . . with no guarantee that you would ever find an answer."

"If it takes that long, then so be it," Catherine pronounced as they rounded yet another corner in the maze. "But I cannot forget that some poor woman is out there, thinking that her lover has abandoned her."

Good God, the woman was a hopeless romantic! John almost pointed out to Catherine that the lady they saw might have been no more than a well-paid prostitute. Then again, even if he did offer that as an option, John knew that Catherine would reject it out of hand.

There couldn't possibly be two people more opposite than he and Catherine. With her rose-colored view of the world, she'd seen two people madly in love while he saw two people enjoying a passionate kiss. She'd seen something that only true love could create, while he'd seen something that could be purchased for a few pounds.

"I'm afraid I cannot allow you to investigate into the matter of the lady's identity."

"Allow me?" Catherine burst into laughter. "Who are you, Lord Wykham, to presume you can dictate my actions?"

"I'm the one who saw how swiftly those men disarmed that young fellow, I'm the one who felt the power behind that thug's fist, and I'm the one who will go to your father if you dare ask one question about the lady's identity."

"And tell him what?" she asked, widening her eyes with such blatantly false innocence it almost made him smile. "I'll easily be able to convince him that I have no idea what you're talking about, that I never saw anyone abducted outside the theater." She brushed her hand slowly down his lapel. "Then I'll finish by saying to my darling Papa that I know it was very wrong of me to kiss you and let you touch me so intimately outside the theater, alone in the park, but you overwhelmed me with your raw passion."

With every word she said, John felt his mouth dropping open further and further. Good God! And she'd do it, too, he knew. Snapping his mouth shut, he glared at her. "I never kissed you," he hissed in pure annoyance.

"I know that and you know that, but Papa doesn't know that."

Her complacent smile snapped his self-control. "Then if I'm to be damned as a sinner, I might as well have a taste of sin," John rasped.

He had the satisfaction of seeing her eyes widen with shock when he clasped her shoulders and tugged her against him. Capturing her lips, he boldly explored her mouth . . . and lost himself in her. The taste was sweeter than any he'd known as she accepted his kiss. Needing more, he slid his hands from her shoulders to her back, pressing her nearer, until he could feel every inch of her against him.

When Catherine suddenly moved, wrapping her arms around his neck, bringing them closer still, John sent his tongue gliding inward to entwine with hers. A soft moan reverberated through Catherine as she tipped her head back, deepening the kiss.

His entire body began to shake with desire as the urge to claim her for his own rose up within him, a hot, needy emotion. As his hand curved around her waist, Catherine suddenly slid her hands onto his chest and pushed him away, breaking off their kiss.

"What are we thinking?" she gasped, pressing the back of her hand against her lips.

But that was the whole point. They hadn't been thinking at all, John realized, as his body and inflamed senses began to cool. He felt the blood drain from his face at the thought that he'd allowed his emotions to completely rule him. He had completely lost control.

Utterly shaken by that thought, John stumbled backward, ignoring the low thrum of desire within him. He shook his head, trying to clear it, unable to answer Catherine.

"Sometimes I think you're a dreadful stick-in-the-mud," Catherine said finally. "And you think me an irresponsible, romantic twit."

John opened his mouth to protest, but snapped it shut the next instant. How could he protest when she was right? Still, he had to say something. Stuffing his hands in his pockets, he cleared his throat. "I'm sorry I kissed you like that," he said stiffly. "I allowed myself to get caught up in my frustration and lost control for a moment."

"Oh, for Heaven's sake," Catherine sputtered. "You make it sound as if you were the only one who was at fault. In case it escaped your notice, Lord Wykham, I was kissing you right back."

No; it hadn't escaped his notice, John thought, remembering the feel of her mouth moving upon his, her arms threaded around his neck, her fingers toying with his hair. Bloody hell! There he went off again, lost in his thoughts. With this woman, he had absolutely none of his prized control.

"I propose that we simply forget this ever happened," Catherine declared firmly.

Forget it? Not bloody likely. Still, to Catherine, he offered a succinct nod. "Very well, my lady."

"Excellent," she returned in clipped tones. Running her hands over her hair, Catherine drew in a deep breath before spinning on her heel and marching down the maze path. Left with no choice but to follow, John thrust his fingers through his hair to straighten it as best he could.

As the end of the maze came into sight, John reached forward to touch Catherine's arm. She stopped abruptly at the gentleness of his touch and fell still. "You will remember what I said about getting involved in discovering that woman's identity, won't you?"

Turning her head, she gazed coldly at him over her shoulder. "If I say no, will you kiss me again?"

He clenched his teeth, ruthlessly pushing aside the desire that burst to life at the mere suggestion. "I thought you wanted to forget that ever happened."

A chagrined expression crossed her face. "My mistake," she said after a moment. "Good day, Lord Wykham."

Shaking free of his hold, she stepped from the maze and into the sunlight.

Damn. If only he could rid her from his thoughts as easily.

10

"What is *wrong* with you, Elizabeth?"

Elizabeth started guiltily at her sister's demand. "N-n-othing," she stammered.

Apparently her lie sounded as utterly pathetic as she'd suspected, for Catherine simply narrowed her eyes and stared at her. "All afternoon you've been on edge, looking as if you fear a big, bad monster is going to jump out and grab you."

No, not a big bad monster, Elizabeth thought, holding in a hysterical laugh, *just a handsome, tempting Richard.* "I have not," she protested weakly, before deciding to ask a question that had haunted her all afternoon, after she'd seen Cat disappear into the maze with Richard's brother. "Though I did wonder if Lord Wykham mentioned anything about last night," she said, trying to sound completely casual.

The distinct blush staining Catherine's face alarmed Elizabeth. Oh, dear God, had Richard actually told his brother about the torrid kiss last night? After a telling hesitation, Catherine replied in a high-pitched tone. "No, not really, I mean, not at all."

Her silver-tongued sister stuttering? Now Elizabeth *knew* something had been said. "What did he say about last night?"

Catherine's eyes widened with shock. "Last night? What do you know about last night?"

"Everything," Elizabeth replied, confused by the question. "I was *there* after all."

"You were?" Catherine sighed in relief. "Thank God! Now you can help me find her."

Elizabeth was completely lost. "Find who?"

"Why, that poor, tragic lady, of course."

"Whatever are you talking about?" Elizabeth asked, utterly bewildered.

Catherine blinked twice. "I'm speaking of the woman whose lover was abducted last night."

Now it was Elizabeth's turn to stare in shock. "What woman?"

"That's what I wish to discover," Catherine said, exasperation coloring her voice. "And you can help me uncover her identity by making discreet inquiries about her."

"I haven't the faintest idea what you're talking about," Elizabeth stated.

"Then why did you tell me you were there?"

"Because I thought you were speaking of what happened . . ." Elizabeth broke off her explanation. It was perfectly obvious that Catherine hadn't heard a word of what had happened between her and Richard . . . and she would be an utter fool to tell her fanciful sister. Lord, Catherine would start planning a wedding!

A slight frown marred Catherine's features. "What else happened last night?"

"Nothing of importance," Elizabeth replied, lifting a

shoulder nonchalantly. "I merely stumbled into the Wykham family box and watched the second half of the play with Rich . . . er, Lord Vernon."

With a nod, Catherine accepted the explanation. "So, will you help me?"

"Find some unknown woman with blonde hair?" Elizabeth gazed out onto the dance floor and saw at least two dozen blonde heads dance by them. "I see quite a few right here."

"But none of them are the particular lady I seek."

Elizabeth glanced down at her sister. "Then how can I possibly be of help to you? Can you give me more of a description?"

"You're right," Catherine conceded, tapping her slipper against the floor. "And I suspect that their meeting was a secret one, so it's highly unlikely to be common knowledge." She chewed on her lower lip. "Finding this lady seems a daunting task, to be certain, but I can't allow her to believe her lover has left her when, in reality, he was forcefully taken."

Catherine's words gave Elizabeth pause. "How forcefully?"

"There were two men—one held the young man while the other knocked him out," Catherine explained. "When we saw what was happening, Lord Wykham bravely charged forth and tried to stop them, but he was knocked down as well."

A frisson of unease raced through Elizabeth. "These men sound dangerous."

"Which is precisely why they must be stopped and that poor fellow found as soon as possible. Lord Wykham has set a Bow Street Runner on finding the man, but he did nothing to locate the lady." Wearing an expression of displeasure, Catherine shook her head. "He hadn't even considered how that poor woman would feel if she believed herself abandoned. And when I informed him that I would find her on my own, well, he . . ." Catherine paused for a moment, her cheeks reddening once again. ". . . let's just say he was less than pleased."

Concern filled her as Elizabeth placed a hand upon her sister's arm. "Perhaps you should heed his lordship's advice and refrain from inquiring after this woman. If you don't know who abducted that man, then you don't know who you will upset if you begin to ask questions." She felt a moment of panic. "What if they come after you?"

A sigh of utter disgust ripped from Catherine. "Good Heavens, Elizabeth. You sound just like John," she muttered before walking away.

John? The casual use of Lord Wykham's first name surprised Elizabeth. She hadn't been aware that the romance between her sister and the marquess had progressed so rapidly. Still, the matter was of little import when weighed against the dangerous task Catherine was determined to undertake.

Though her attempt to dissuade Catherine had failed miserably, Elizabeth knew she had to try again. She was considering different arguments to use on her younger sister when Catherine's words came back to her. *You sound just like John.* That was it! If she enlisted Lord Wykham's aid in dissuading her sister from pursuing this matter on her own, perhaps the two of them could succeed together where they had each failed on their own.

Knowing time was critical, Elizabeth immediately began to search through the crush for the marquess. Having no luck, she headed toward Lady Jersey and Lady Cowper, who sat watching the festivities from their chairs near the fireplace. The closer she came to the two matrons the more nervous she grew, but her need to find Lord Wykham outweighed her fear of approaching the two dragons.

Stiffly, Elizabeth came to a halt in front of the ladies. "I wondered if you'd seen Lord Wykham," she asked politely.

Lady Jersey pressed a hand to her chest and shot a look at her companion, before murmuring, "Well, good evening to you, too, Lady Elizabeth."

Flustered, Elizabeth tried again. "Many pardons if you found my greeting lacking, my lady. I did not intend to offend you."

"One very seldom *intends* to offend, madam," sniffed Lady Cowper.

This was getting her nowhere. With her lack of social graces, she'd been a fool for even attempting to approach these ladies. Lifting her chin, Elizabeth nodded stiffly. "I shall bid you a good evening, then," she said, pausing for a moment before adding, "and hopefully you won't take offense to that as well."

Turning on her heel, she took one step and bumped directly into a gentleman's back. Lord, this evening couldn't get any worse.

The gentleman turned around . . . and she discovered she'd been wrong. It *could* get much worse.

Richard's gaze swept over her with burning intensity for a second. But the next instant, he gave her such a cold look that Elizabeth was surprised she didn't begin shivering. Then, to her horror, without a single word uttered, he simply turned back around, cutting her directly.

Even the cruel snickers bursting around her couldn't cover her pained gasp. Utterly mortified, Elizabeth struggled to remain composed as she headed toward the ladies' parlor, where she could hide from the vicious whispers and avid stares.

"Oh, my, you are the wicked one, Lord Vernon," murmured Lady Jersey as she sidled up beside Richard. "Just yesterday you were sharing a box with Lady Elizabeth, appearing quite cozy in fact, and now you give her the direct cut." She raised both her eyebrows, not bothering to hide her eagerness to hear the gossip. "Whatever happened between you two, my lord?"

Lady Cowper appeared to his right. "Indeed, Lord Vernon. Do tell."

Dear God, what had he done? When he'd turned around and seen Elizabeth, a wave of desire had swept over him, making him want to sweep her up in his arms and kiss her the way he'd thought about all day.

Unable to look at her one more minute and resist his desire, Richard had simply turned around so he wouldn't be tempted by the sight of her. He hadn't even considered how it would appear to others. Bloody hell, he'd given Elizabeth a direct cut. Still, perhaps it was for the best. After all, she certainly would avoid him in the future.

The matching expressions of salacious avidity worn by Lady Jersey and Lady Cowper turned Richard's stomach. "I'm sorry to disappoint you, my ladies," he began smoothly, hiding his distaste, "but I've never been one to gossip about a lady."

Lady Cowper tapped Richard on the arm with her fan.

"Oh, come now, Lord Vernon. Don't turn high-brow on us now."

Richard stared coldly down at her for a moment. "Refusing to tarnish a lady's good name is hardly cause for insults, my lady."

"How dare you reprimand me!" exclaimed Lady Cowper, pulling back her shoulders. "After all, I'm not the one who publicly insulted Lady Elizabeth, now, am I?"

Guilt raked through him, but Richard refused to buckle beneath it. "What does one incident have to do with the other?" he asked coolly.

Lady Jersey waved impatiently at her companion. "Lady Cowper's actions are neither here nor there, my lord," she said briskly. "I am merely inquiring as to the reason behind your sudden . . . dismissal of Lady Elizabeth. Have you had a falling-out? If so, I'd find that most interesting, because she just approached us and asked if we'd seen Lord Wykham."

"My brother?"

Nodding once, Lady Jersey flicked open her fan. "One and the same. As you know, I'm not one to gossip," she said, lying through her aristocratic teeth, "but I have heard tales of your brother seeking a match with Lady Elizabeth as well. Though that was before she was seen with you at the theater." She fanned herself quickly. "It is quite confusing us all, so if you can clear up this matter as to who is courting whom, I would be more than happy to spread the truth. After all, I feel it my moral obligation to set the gossip right."

If Richard had been less consumed with thoughts of why Elizabeth sought out John, he would have laughed at Lady Jersey's pronouncement. Moral obligation, indeed.

"I appreciate your interest, my lady, but I shall relieve you of this burden now."

Lady Jersey's expression reflected her disappointment. "I assure you, Lord Vernon, it is no trouble to . . ."

"While I appreciate the generosity of your offer to clarify the gossip, my lady, I cannot allow you to become embroiled in this affair," he replied easily, leaving her no room for a gracious protest. "Thank you for your concerns." With a bow to both ladies, Richard excused himself and strode across the room, headed for the study to find his brother. What on earth had Elizabeth wanted with John? He intended to find out.

He wasn't hiding.

Perhaps if he kept telling himself that, he might come to believe it. Disgusted with his own thoughts and more so with the possibility that he was hiding from Catherine, John splashed more brandy into his snifter and tried to focus his attention on the conversation flowing in Atherton's study.

". . . say I shall win my wager about Lord Hancroft," protested Lord Atherton. "After all, everyone knows he was left a penniless estate, so marrying a wealthy merchant's daughter is his only way out of his current bind, as no self-respecting nobleman would allow his daughter to marry Hancroft now."

"I think Atherton has the right of it," John agreed before taking a sip of his drink. "Hancroft's less than savory reputation would put off any heiress, leaving him the choice of marrying beneath him or being tossed into debtor's gaol."

"I don't know which is worse," remarked Lord Weatherby with a laugh.

John shook his head. "Don't be such an elitist, Weatherby."

Scowling, Weatherby glared at him. "I am no such thing! I just feel it best not to mix the classes."

"That is an antiquated view, sir," John pointed out. "More and more estates are being run to the ground, bled dry of any income, leaving the heirs little choice but to marry for money. And, at this point, the merchants are making money hand over fist, enough to purchase a titled gentleman for their daughters." Lifting his glass, John toasted Lord Weatherby. "And voila—the classes are mixed forever."

"Doesn't that bother you, Wykham?" asked Lord Atherton in a disbelieving tone.

"Not at all."

Laughing, Weatherby slapped a hand onto John's shoulder. "For all your fine claims, sir, I don't see you showing interest in a merchants' daughter."

"Nor do you see my financial situation floundering, Weatherby," John reminded him.

"True enough. Though you don't seem opposed to the idea of marrying for money." Lord Weatherby's expression grew sly. "I've heard that Shipham has settled a large portion on each of his daughters."

Atherton nudged John with his elbow. "I always knew you were a clever one, Wykham. Never can have too much money, as I always say."

"Too bad your younger brother isn't as smart." Weatherby drew in on his cigar. "He all but had the eldest daughter eating from his hand, then he goes and publicly cuts her."

John almost dropped his snifter. *"What?"*

"It shocked me as well," Weatherby agreed. "Imagine being that close to securing the hand of an heiress, only to destroy all of your hard work with one careless action. And from what I've heard, your brother is something of a spendthrift, and could use the funds to replenish his holdings." He shook his head. "Wouldn't have believed it if I hadn't seen it myself not ten minutes ago." Before John could respond, Weatherby gestured toward the door. "Here's your foolish brother now." Raising his glass, Weatherby called a greeting to Richard as he stepped into the study. "Evening, Vernon, we were just discussing you."

"In only the best context, I presume," Richard drawled.

Before Weatherby could reply, John set down his snifter and moved toward his brother. "Pardon me, gentlemen, but I need a private word with my brother."

As John moved toward Richard, he heard Lord Atherton call out to him. "Talk some sense into the boy. He shouldn't be so quick to toss away a fortune."

But John wasn't concerned about the bloody fortune. No, his concern was for the insult to Elizabeth, a fine, upstanding young lady who deserved better than to have her name tossed about in a gentlemen's study. "I need to speak with you in private," John said without preamble.

Richard's expression revealed nothing of his thoughts. "Perfect. I wanted to speak with you as well."

"Me?" John asked in confusion. Usually Richard went out of his way to avoid him whenever he'd done something foolish.

"Not here," Richard said abruptly before heading out of the study.

John followed Richard into the next room. As soon as

they were both in the library, Richard shut the door behind him.

"Why was Elizabeth looking for you?"

Richard's question caught John completely off guard. "Pardon me?"

"Why was she looking for you?" Richard repeated, revealing his anger. "Apparently Elizabeth approached Lady Jersey and Lady Cowper and asked if they'd seen you. Now why would she do that?"

"I haven't the foggiest," John returned testily. "But if the story I just heard from Weatherby is true, you have some nerve, pretending to have concern for the lady."

"What story?"

Richard's expression grew wary. "Weatherby told me that you just gave Lady Elizabeth a direct cut . . . in front of the entire assemblage."

A dull flush crept onto Richard's cheeks. "Indeed, I did."

Bracing himself against a chair, John realized he'd been hoping the story had just been false. "Dear God, Richard. Why?"

"That is none of your concern," Richard stated firmly.

Accustomed to his brother's prevarications, John blinked twice at the cool, collected man standing before him. "I beg to differ, Richard, as I consider Lady Elizabeth to be a friend."

"And do you interfere in all your *friends'* squabbles?"

"No," John admitted readily, "but then again, I've never before claimed a lady as a friend."

Sighing in frustration, Richard thrust both of his hands through his hair. "Just leave this one alone, John. Trust me when I say that it is a personal matter, one between Elizabeth and me . . . and my actions were in her best interest."

"How could publicly insulting her, besmirching her reputation, be in her best interest?"

"I didn't intend to harm her reputation," Richard admitted quietly. "It was for the sake of her reputation that I turned my back on her." His jaw tightened. "I'm not the man she wants; she just doesn't realize it yet."

It wasn't the anger and frustration John heard in Richard's voice that stopped him from pressing for more details; it was the hurt. For the first time in his life, John heard raw pain echoing in his brother's voice and, since Richard clearly understood the ramifications of his actions, John had no choice but to respect him.

Nodding once, he conceded the point. "Very well, Richard," he said slowly. "I shall trust you to handle the matter in the best way you see fit. Just try not to hurt her again."

"I shall," he agreed immediately. Lifting his eyes, he gave John a rueful look. "Though I don't think it will be a problem, as the lady will avoid me like the plague in the future."

John rubbed at his forehead. "Lord, I wish Catherine would follow suit."

"Really?" Richard shook his head in confusion. "I thought things were going well between the two of you."

"Not at all," John said with a laugh. "I vow the lady is determined to drive me mad. For instance, Catherine's now taken it into her head that she wants to become an investigator of sorts."

"How's that?"

Swiftly giving Richard the background of what had

happened yesterday, John settled his hip against the chair. ". . . so that's why she's determined to find the identity of the blonde lady."

Richard rolled his eyes. "All this romantic rot is enough to make you wonder at a woman's sanity."

"True enough." Straightening, John tapped his fingers against the chair. "I wonder if that was the reason Lady Elizabeth wanted to speak with me. Perhaps Catherine ignored my warning and has gone off on this foolishness."

"It's a possibility," conceded Richard. "Why don't you find Elizabeth and make certain she's all right, and I'll see if I can't locate Lady Catherine in this crush."

"Excellent plan," John declared as he moved forward to clap Richard on the back. "After I'm finished speaking with Lady Elizabeth, we should confer."

Nodding in agreement, Richard suggested, "Why don't we meet back here?"

"Perfect."

In unison, the two brothers stepped from the library and headed off to complete their mission.

11

Why was she so different?

Elizabeth sighed softly as she stared at her reflection. Why couldn't she be more like all of the other ladies, like Catherine, and sail successfully through social events? Instead, they were becoming increasingly more painful.

But in her heart, she knew why she felt so awful. Richard's cut. He'd made it perfectly clear that he had no wish to be around her anymore; what she didn't understand was why. When had things gone so dreadfully wrong between them? At Mr. Dunfee's shop, they'd connected in a manner she'd never experienced, but then he'd withdrawn. Still, when he'd kissed her so passionately at the theater, she'd hoped he had gotten over his strange withdrawal, then he'd pulled back yet again. Yet she'd never expected him to insult her publicly. It was obvious she would never understand him.

Weary, Elizabeth closed her eyes briefly, wishing this night were over. Perhaps she could sneak out and no one would notice, but even as she thought it, she knew she didn't have a chance of leaving undetected. Even now, the gossips were waiting for her to emerge from the ladies' salon.

Anger surged within her as she straightened in her chair. Was she really going to let those old biddies make her hide? Elizabeth glared at herself in the mirror. "You're made of tougher stuff than that," she muttered to her reflection.

No, she could only be defeated if she played their game.

And she wasn't about to allow a bit of gossip to dictate her actions. So Richard gave her the direct cut? So what? She was still standing, still breathing, still able to show everyone that it would take more than an insult to destroy her. Inhaling deeply, Elizabeth calmed herself as she lightly powdered the tear tracks staining her cheeks. It wouldn't do to have anyone notice how upset Richard had made her.

Instead, she was going to march out of this room and onto that dance floor with her head held high, pretending that his insult hadn't cut her to the quick.

Satisfied with the repairs to her person, Elizabeth stood slowly, looked at herself in the mirror, and repeated the mantra her mother had taught her. "You're as good as anyone and better than most."

Saying Mama's silly statement out loud brought a smile to her face. Elizabeth felt a peace settle over her as she imagined Mama standing right behind her, a hand on her shoulder, urging her forward. Drawing strength from that image, Elizabeth strode from the safety of the parlor.

The door had no sooner shut behind her when she heard the first snide comment. Elizabeth faltered, but then she imagined her mother next to her, holding her up, guiding her through the treacherous waters. Taking a steadying breath, Elizabeth continued down the hallway without further pause. With her head held high and her stride firm and sure, she felt confident that no one would ever suspect her nerves were raw inside.

As soon as she entered the ballroom, Lord Wykham appeared at her side. "Lady Elizabeth," he murmured politely, bowing over her hand in a gentlemanly fashion. "It is so good to see you this evening." As he straightened, he ran his gaze over her face, as if searching for signs of upset.

The fact that he apparently had heard of Richard's cut didn't surprise Elizabeth. She was well acquainted with how swiftly hurtful gossip could spread. Still, Lord Wykham's concern was a balm. "As you can see, your brother didn't manage to do me in just yet."

"As one who has long suffered Richard's insults, I assure you I bear my own scars from those encounters." He smiled gently at her. "Still, I hated to hear that such a kind lady as yourself must bear one as well."

Elizabeth warmed at his comment. It was little wonder that Catherine was so attracted to Lord Wykham . . . despite her protests to the contrary. Again, Elizabeth wondered what was wrong with her that she'd been more interested in the wild, outrageous Richard than the kind, gentlemanly John. It was, Elizabeth realized, a most dreadful character flaw.

"Please be assured, my lord, that while your brother's antic stung, it has done no permanent damage and will not leave a scar." Suddenly, Elizabeth remembered the reason she'd needed to speak with Lord Wykham in the first place. "Though I appreciate your concern, my lord, there is a more pressing matter to which we both must turn our attention." Glancing around to be certain no one could overhear them, Elizabeth leaned in closer. "Earlier this evening, my sister told me of your dreadful encounter with those ruffians last night. I do hope you are unharmed."

Lord Wykham nodded with a chagrined smile. "The fellow wouldn't have been able to land a blow if your sister had remained where I'd told her," he admitted, his voice tinged with embarrassment.

"Catherine never was very good at doing as she was told," Elizabeth said with a laugh. Her amusement quickly died as worry over her sister's latest act of defiance filled her. "I fear she is once again disregarding your advice, my lord."

John's fierce gaze rooted her to the spot. "She's going to make inquiries after that blonde woman."

It was a statement, not a question. "I believe she means to begin this very evening."

"Blast that foolish twi . . ." John broke off as if he had just realized he was speaking with Catherine's sister. "Forgive me, Lady Elizabeth. I meant no disrespect."

"None taken," Elizabeth assured him. "After all, if she's going to act like a *foolish twit,* then she deserves to be called one."

Elizabeth could tell from Lord Wykham's broad grin that he was in complete agreement. "Shall we go look for Catherine?"

Lord Wykham shook his head. "Richard is searching for her and, once he finds her, he will let me know where she is and what she's been doing. We're to meet back in the library at half past the hour."

Elizabeth had no desire to see Richard again . . . ever. "I highly doubt if Catherine will have made more than a few inquiries tonight, so why don't you call upon us tomorrow and we can speak to Catherine together? Perhaps she will listen to the two of us."

"Do you really think so?" he asked dryly.

His doubt made her smile. "No, I don't," she admitted, "but it is worth a try, don't you think?"

"We must try something." His eyes darkened with concern. "Your sister has a most romantic nature."

Elizabeth smiled over the statement. "How long did it take you to notice?"

"A moment," he countered with a laugh. "Still, I worry that her tendency to romanticize everything will get her into trouble. In all good conscience, I can't allow her to be wandering about town, getting involved in something that might prove harmful to her."

"I feel the same." With their plans made, Elizabeth fell silent, uncertain of what to say. She'd never excelled at making small talk. Remembering Lord Wykham had to return to the library by half past, she glanced at the clock. It was only ten past. Well, she certainly couldn't stand here mute for the next twenty minutes. Struggling to think of something to fill the awkward pause, Elizabeth grasped at a conversational gambit she'd heard Catherine use before. "Would you care to get some refreshments?"

"No, I believe we should use this time to try and undo some of the damage done to you this evening, my lady. However, if you're thirsty, I shall be glad to accompany you."

She shook her head.

"Very well then." Shifting in front of her, Lord Wykham proffered his arm toward her. "Might I have the honor of this dance?"

Elizabeth hesitated. "I assure you it is quite unnecessary to dance with me simply to squelch the gossip."

"On the contrary, my lady, I consider it not only necessary, but enjoyable as well. Since it was a Vernon who hurt you, it should be a Vernon to help set things right." He tilted his head to the side. "Are you truly going to allow me to stand here with my arm offered to you and not accepting it?"

Feeling the weight of stares upon them, Elizabeth took his arm and accompanied him onto the dance floor. "You are a true gentleman."

John exaggerated a grimace. "Please don't say things like that too loudly," he returned with a laugh. "Your sister is already convinced I'm a staid, old bore. I should hate to make things worse by having her overhear you."

"Very well, kind sir," Elizabeth countered brightly. "I shall only repeat tales of your wild antics."

His mouth twisted into a rueful smile. "If you're only going to speak of my wildness, I fear you'll never speak of me."

Laughing at Lord Wykham's jest, Elizabeth found it easy to ignore the rustle of whispers behind fans and the unwavering stares. With a fond smile at the marquess, Elizabeth couldn't help but think that if Catherine allowed this fine gentleman to slip away, then her sister was completely, utterly, no, *certifiably* crazy.

"You've got cheek to approach me after what you did to my sister!"

Staring down at the mutinous expression upon Lady Catherine's face, Richard shook his head. Lord, what was he thinking, to approach yet another Everley female? As both he and John could attest, both girls had their share of maddening qualities. "I didn't mean to get this close, actually," Richard admitted without compunction.

"Oh, really," drawled Lady Catherine. Glaring at him, she stabbed her finger into his chest. "Were you spying on me, then? For that overbearing brother of yours, no doubt." She scoffed with disgust as she crossed her arms. "Is there no depths to which you two won't sink?"

Rubbing at his chest, Richard couldn't help but laugh. "Ouch," he said mildly. "You've got quite a sharp fingertip there."

"Do you find this amusing?" Lady Catherine demanded. "I suppose you had a hearty laugh over the way you completely humiliated my sister, didn't you?"

Richard sobered immediately. "I didn't mean to humiliate her."

"Then why did you cut her?"

"Because it is best if she stay away from me," he ground out.

"I'm quite certain that won't be a problem in the future."

Richard's eyes blazed with frustration. "Excellent. Then it makes the cut worthwhile."

Suddenly, Catherine stilled, her gaze fixed upon his face. "Are you saying you cut her for her own good?"

"Yes."

"How could your insult possibly help her?" she asked, her voice dark with bewilderment.

"It keeps her away from me." Richard thrust a hand through his hair. "I can't explain everything to you, Lady Catherine. You'll just have to trust me when I say your sister is better off far away from me."

"Why?"

"You're just going to have to trust me on this, my lady."

She lifted her brows. "I find it trying to believe someone who just embarrassed my sister."

"I understand," he said, flinching from the lash of guilt. It was for the best, he reminded himself.

Her eyes narrowed. "Dear Heavens, you're in love with her, aren't you?"

Richard's head snapped up. "Of all the preposterous . . ."

"There's nothing preposterous about it at all," Catherine returned swiftly. "You say that she's better off without you, so you cut her in order to save her from you."

Her words were on the mark. Richard stiffened, but remained silent. Dear God, were his feelings so bloody transparent?

Slowly, Catherine nodded as if she were considering this new development. "If you'll excuse me, Lord Vernon, I need to see to my sister."

Bowing, he watched her walk away, praying she didn't disclose his feelings to Elizabeth. *Not that she'd believe Catherine anyway,* Richard thought bitterly. No, he'd seen to it that Elizabeth despised him.

Lord, he'd never realized how regret soured a man's thoughts. Though he wanted nothing more than to be left alone, Lady Atherton moved to his side.

"Good evening, Lord Vernon," she said to him, even though her gaze was still trained upon Lady Catherine's retreating back. "I couldn't help but notice what a . . . spirited discussion you were having with Lady Catherine."

Lord save him from all the busybodies of the ton! Plastering a smile onto his face, Richard nodded politely. "Lady Catherine has a wit that lends itself to spirited conversations," he said politely.

"So true." Lady Atherton tapped her fan against her gloved hand. "I don't mean to be intrusive, my lord, but one thing piqued my curiosity. Does Lady Catherine have an ailment that affects her voice?"

Frowning over the odd question, Richard shook his head. "No."

"Oh." Lady Atherton's brows drew downward. "Then why were you standing so close to one another during your conversation?" Adopting an air of remorse, she pressed her hand to her chest. "Please pardon my bluntness, Lord Vernon. I mean no offense; it's just I couldn't help but wonder at the reason."

Because I didn't want gossips like you overhearing our conversation, Richard thought even as he kept his polite expression firmly fixed on his face. To Lady Atherton, he merely lifted a shoulder negligently. "With the large crush, I found it difficult to hear her replies, so I simply moved closer."

"Hmmm, yes, that makes sense, but . . ."

"Excuse me, my lady," Richard said, interrupting her, for it was clear she was like a dog with a bone and had no intention of letting go. And if she thought for one moment that he would reveal the intimate comments he'd exchanged with Lady Catherine, then she'd been enjoying a few too many glasses of claret. "I'm afraid I must take my leave now, as I have an appointment."

"Now?" she exclaimed. "In the middle of my ball?"

"Yes. I'm sorry, but it was something I arranged before I received your invitation. Naturally I wouldn't want to miss your affair, a premier event of the Season," he interjected, lying without a qualm, "so I arranged for a very late meeting." With a quick bow, he was gone.

Lady Atherton was watching him leave when Lady Jersey moved to her side. "I must say, Ellie, with all the intrigue between Lord Wykham, Lord Vernon, Lady Elizabeth, and Lady Catherine, your party has become the finest of the Season."

"Thank you, Florence. I agree that the romances between the Wykham sons and the Shipham daughters has become first tier." She nodded knowingly. "And just when you think you know which brother is interested in which sister, they switch on you again."

Lady Jersey remained silent for a moment, savoring the delightful observation. "Isn't that fascinatingly scandalous? Last night, Lord Wykham was seen with Lady Catherine in the Shipham box and Lord Vernon was with Lady Elizabeth in the Wykham box, but this evening, Lord Wykham danced with Lady Elizabeth while Lord Vernon gave her the direct cut and then spent time with Lady Catherine engaged in a most . . . passionate exchange," she finished, completely out of breath by the end. "It is all so confusing . . . and more than a bit scandalous."

"Delightfully so," agreed Lady Atherton. "I can't wait to see what happens tomorrow night!"

His ears still rang from the alarmed predictions of close friends and casual acquaintances alike. Weary to the bone, Douglas shut the door to his room, leaning back against it. Try as he might, he couldn't sort through all the gossip to reach an understanding as to why society was so aghast with his daughters, the marquess, and his brother. As far as he was concerned, they hadn't done anything more scandalous than speak to each other.

Pushing away from the door, Douglas struggled to find

the harm in their discussions. To his way of thinking, the number of females and males were equal, so what did it matter who wound up with whom? Rubbing at his temple, Douglas looked toward the fireplace for his wife. Margaret had always been far more adept at understanding the follies of the ton. Certainly she would know if he should intervene or if he should merely allow fate to play its course.

"Margaret?" Looking around, he didn't see her ethereal form anywhere. "Are you here, my love?" But no vision appeared.

Panic clawed at him as Douglas called for his wife's ghostly presence once again. "Margaret? Please come to me," he pleaded, his voice breaking on the last word. Dear God, how could he survive if he couldn't see her every night? He *needed* her still. He drew strength from her spirit to face the next day, found soothing peace from the demands of his life while in her presence, and garnered the courage from her nightly visits to awake, alone and cold, every morning.

Shaken, he sank down into his usual chair. "Please, Margaret," he whispered, dropping his head onto his hands. "I need help sorting out this mess with our daughters."

His heart sunk even further when the room remained silent. Douglas buried his face into his hands. How would he be able to go on?

A knock on his door broke through his dark thoughts. Lifting his head, he bade the person to enter. Expecting one of his daughters, Douglas was surprised when his butler entered. "Pardon the intrusion, my lord, but you have a caller."

"At this late hour?" Douglas asked in surprise. Rising,

he retrieved the card from his butler's tray. Mary Vernon, Marchioness of Wykham.

"I tried to send her away, but she insisted upon . . ."

"It's quite all right," Douglas said immediately. "I shall see the lady."

Ignoring his butler's shock, Douglas strode toward the front parlor. The minute he stepped into the room, Lady Wykham spun to face him.

"Lord Shipham," she murmured, relief filling her voice. "I wasn't certain if you would see me at this hour. I'm dreadfully sorry to be calling upon you so late, but it is an urgent matter."

"Don't concern yourself with the hour." He gestured for her to take a seat. "Now what can I do for you, my lady?" he asked as he settled into the chair opposite Lady Wykham.

Wringing her hands together, Lady Wykham glanced away. "Did you hear about the events this evening?"

"Between our children?" At her nod, he replied, "Yes, I did."

"What are we going to do?" she asked urgently, leaning forward in her chair.

Douglas began to drum his fingers upon the arm of his chair. "I was thinking about this matter as well. I find myself uncertain if I should begin to intervene or if I should allow fate to guide them."

"This situation has gotten too precarious, my lord," she stated emphatically. "We must do something! This evening all anyone spoke about was our children. If we aren't careful, this entire affair will become a mockery. People speak of my sons as if they're rakes, and they are beginning to question the moral character of your daughters."

Oh, lord, the situation was more dire than he'd realized. Douglas turned the problem over in his head, fervently wishing he could speak with Margaret about the matter. She would know what to do about this mess.

But she wasn't here.

No, it was up to him to muddle his way through and protect his daughters. He glanced at Lady Wykham, who gazed at him with such a hopeful expression, he knew he couldn't bear to let her down either. Reaching deep inside, Douglas drew a deep, calming breath and focused on the issue. "I believe what we need to do is decide which daughter should marry which son and see that it happens," he said decisively. "If we become matchmakers of a sort, we can see that the proper two stay together instead of this back-and-forth nonsense."

Lady Wykham straightened in her chair. "I do believe that might work," she agreed in a hopeful tone. "It is obvious that our children aren't able to decide for themselves, so, as parents, it's our duty to choose for them, isn't it?"

"Indeed," Douglas agreed readily, feeling confident in his decision. "Shall we match your eldest with my eldest?"

Pausing for a moment, Lady Wykham finally nodded her head. "Perhaps that might be best."

"Very well, then. We shall begin to arrange for the marquess to spend time with my Elizabeth and Lord Vernon to be with my Catherine."

A worried frown tilted Lady Wykham's lips downward. "Are we interfering too much?"

"Not at all," Douglas replied. Though he felt uneasy about the decision, it was obvious that his daughters needed guidance. If he were to inspire confidence in everyone involved, he needed to first convince the marchioness that he didn't have a doubt in the world. "Now what we need is a plan." He considered their options for a moment. "Tomorrow I shall send a note around to the marquess, asking him to call upon me at a specific time. In addition, I shall invite Elizabeth to join me for a ride shortly after your son is due to arrive. When Elizabeth comes to find me, I shall claim I'm far too busy to accompany her, and will ask the marquess to go in my stead."

Lady Wykham looked at him as if he were brilliant, making him feel more useful that he'd felt in years. It was, Douglas acknowledged, a feeling he'd missed. "What a clever plan!" she exclaimed. "And how will you bring Richard and Catherine together?"

"The exact same way . . . only an hour later."

Lady Wykham's nervous expression eased. "I believe this will work marvelously," she pronounced, rising from the chair. "I knew I was right in coming to you, my lord."

"Thank you for your confidence," he replied, meaning every word. "I believe everything will work out for the best."

"Quite true." Lady Wykham smiled brightly. "In fact, I believe they will even thank us for our assistance."

Douglas nodded in agreement. "Sometimes even fate needs a helping hand."

12

"Can I help you with something, Mother?" John asked as his mother strolled past the open door to his study for the third time in as many minutes.

"Oh, no, no," she said offhandedly.

Closing his ledger, he rose and came out from behind his desk. "I thought you wished to speak with me."

His mother's eyes widened. "Why on earth would you think that?"

"Oh, I don't know," he murmured with a smile. "Perhaps it had something to do with the fact that you've been milling about in this hallway for quite some time now."

Though his mother's cheeks grew pink, she waved off his comment. "I was merely checking to see if the maids have been doing their jobs properly."

The blatant lie made him smile. "Indeed."

As he stepped past her, she asked, "Are you going somewhere?"

"As a matter of fact, I am," he returned. "Lord Shipham sent around a note, asking me to call upon him this morning."

"He did?"

The lilt in her voice set off warning chimes in his head. Had she somehow learned of his arrangement with Elizabeth to call upon the Shipham household in order to talk some sense into Catherine? Impossible. All his mother knew was that he'd received that wonderfully well-timed note from Lord Shipham. John didn't know why Catherine's father wished to see him, but he wasn't about to question his good fortune.

As far as John was concerned, he now had a reason to call upon the Shipham household that wouldn't make Catherine suspicious. After he spoke with Lord Shipham, he would simply finagle a way to visit with Catherine and Elizabeth, so he could point out the foolishness of Catherine's grand plan.

Confident his mother knew nothing of his ulterior motive to call upon Lord Shipham, John smiled down at her. "In his note, he indicated that it was an urgent matter." He shrugged lightly. "Perhaps he wishes my opinion on an investment matter that is time-sensitive."

"That would make sense." His mother frowned slightly as she smoothed down the edges of his cravat. "Is this what you're going to wear?"

A laugh escaped John. "Yes, of course."

Pressing her lips together for a moment, his mother studied his attire. "I think the gray silk would be more suitable for this . . ."

"Mother," John said, interrupting her prattling. "I love you dearly, but I really don't have time for a fashion consult at this time." He pressed a kiss onto her hand to soften his rebuff.

"A gentleman should always make time to look his

best," she returned smartly. "After all, you never know who you might see."

An image of Catherine flashed into his mind. Perhaps he did have the time to change. "The gray silk, eh?" With a tug, he removed his blue cravat. "Excuse me, Mother." Bellowing for his manservant, John took the stairs two at a time.

If he'd taken a moment to glance back at his mother, he would have caught her satisfied, cat-in-the-cream smile.

"What do you mean, you're going for a ride?"

Elizabeth just stared at her father. "I mean just what I said, Papa," she returned slowly. "It's the first sunny morning in a week, so I wished to go for a ride and enjoy the fine weather."

"I understand. In fact, I was going to suggest it myself, b-b-but a little later," he stammered.

Frowning over Papa's odd comment, Elizabeth asked, "Is there any particular reason I can't go now?"

"This is hardly a fashionable hour to go riding," he said in a rush, as if he was searching for reasons to keep them from riding.

"Since when have I ever been concerned with appearing fashionable?" Elizabeth countered with a laugh.

"Why all this concern, Papa?" Catherine asked.

"Concern?" he blustered, puffing out his chest. "Simply because I enjoy having my girls around me doesn't mean I'm concerned."

"Fine then, Papa." Smiling, Elizabeth pressed a kiss to her father's cheek. "We're off, but I promise we'll return in a short while . . . so you don't get too lonely."

Muttering about disrespect, their father disappeared

into his study. Together, Elizabeth and Catherine headed out into the sunlight, mounted their horses, and set off for the park.

"Why do you think Papa was acting so strangely?" Catherine asked as they walked their horses down the wide path.

Considering the question for a moment, Elizabeth finally shook her head. "I don't know. Perhaps he's just missing Mama more today."

"You're probably right," Catherine conceded. "But he's been so much better lately that his behavior today surprises me."

"Everyone's entitled to a bad day. Whenever I'm feeling less than social, I simply hide in my workshop," Elizabeth admitted.

A dimple appeared in Catherine's cheek as she grinned. "Is that why you're there so often?"

"My, my, aren't you amusing?"

Catherine nodded briskly. "I think so. In fact, I do believe that . . ." A loud gasp escaped her. *"There she is!"*

Elizabeth looked at the few people riding near them in the park. "There who is?"

"The blonde lady," exclaimed Catherine. Before Elizabeth could ask another question, Catherine slapped her horse into a canter.

"Catherine, wait!" But her sister didn't even slow her horse, leaving Elizabeth with no choice but to follow.

Unfortunately, Catherine reached the woman and her escort before Elizabeth could stop her. Pulling back on the reins, Elizabeth brought her horse alongside her sister's in time to hear Catherine's opening remark.

"Excuse my boldness, my lady," she said sweetly.

"Allow me to introduce myself. I'm Lady Catherine Everley, and I saw you near the theater this past Friday."

The young lady's eyes widened. "Pardon me?"

While the woman's reaction would have stopped Elizabeth cold, it apparently left Catherine undaunted, for she forged onward. "I saw you the other evening in the gardens next to the theater," she repeated. "You met a gentleman there."

"I'm afraid you have me mistaken for someone else," the lady said politely. "I was at home alone that evening."

At her remark, the gentleman beside her twisted in his saddle and faced them for the first time. "Lord Morrow!" gasped Elizabeth, unable to hold in her surprise.

"Lady Elizabeth," he drawled. "What an unexpected delight."

The way his gaze ran down her made Elizabeth fight the urge to check to see that her riding habit was properly fastened.

"You know each other?" asked the lady.

"Indeed, we do. Lord Vernon introduced us." He shifted his gaze onto Catherine. "However, I've yet to have the honor of meeting this beautiful lady."

Catherine looked expectantly toward Elizabeth, but she wasn't about to introduce her sister to the loathsome Lord Morrow. "No, I don't believe you have," she murmured vaguely.

Apparently Catherine had little liking for Elizabeth's decision, for she took the matter into her own hands. "My sister is such a jester at times," she said, offering Lord Morrow a charming smile. "I'm Lady Catherine Everley."

"A pleasure." He dipped his head in acknowledgement. "And might I present my sister, Lady Serena Cole."

Annoyance flickered in Lady Serena's gaze so briefly that Elizabeth convinced herself she'd imagined it. "It is indeed a pleasure, Lady Elizabeth, Lady Catherine," she said softly.

"Lady Serena," began Catherine, the determined note in her voice alerting Elizabeth to her sister's intent, "I am positive that you are the woman I . . ."

"I hate to interrupt you, Catherine, but we really must be off now." Without giving her sister a moment to protest, Elizabeth reached out and swatted Catherine's horse, sending the animal jolting forward. "We promised our father we'd hurry home," she said in what she prayed was a somewhat polite reply.

Elizabeth kicked her horse into a gallop to catch up with Catherine, who now had her mount under control. "What on earth did you do that for?"

Ignoring Catherine's question, Elizabeth continued toward the house, this time leaving her sister to play catch-up. Catherine was again at her side when they arrived back home. After handing the reins over to the waiting groom, they entered the house through the gardens.

"I believe I asked you a question," Catherine snapped, yanking off her riding gloves.

"You want to know why I . . . hastened our departure?" Elizabeth asked as she, too, removed her gloves. "Very well, then. Reason number one is that we promised Papa we would return soon." Lifting her hand, she began to tick off her points. "Reason number two is that Lord Morrow is a detestable man who is best to avoid. And reason number three is you were about to launch into yet another, dare I say, *attack* upon that poor woman." Elizabeth tossed her gloves on the sideboard. "Lady Serena is cursed enough just by having a brother like Lord Morrow. The last thing she needs is to have you accuse her of running off and meeting a lover in the dark of night like she was a common trollop."

Catherine's eyes snapped with anger. "I never implied she was a trollop," she retorted sharply. "I'm the one who thought the whole thing desperately romantic and am concerned for her welfare."

"How do you know it's *her* welfare you need to be concerned with?" Elizabeth propped her hands upon her hips. "After all, you told me yourself that she was too far away to get a good look at her, not to mention it was dark and near the river, so fog was rolling in at the time." Tilting her head, Elizabeth pretended to be lost in thought. "Oh, yes, and there is that one last pesky reason to doubt she was the woman you saw." She stared at her sister. "Lady Serena denied the whole incident!"

"Well, well . . ." Catherine stammered, then suddenly a triumphant expression settled onto her face. "I know why she denied meeting her lover at the theater," Catherine announced confidently. "Undoubtedly the poor girl has yet to tell her brother about her own true love, so she couldn't very well admit to it in front of him." A dramatic sigh feathered from Catherine. "They are star-crossed lovers, just like Romeo and Juliet."

"Oh, for Heaven's sake, Cat!" burst Elizabeth. "How far are you determined to take this nonsense? It is time to stop weaving these ridiculous romantic fantasies about everything. Not everything in life has a happy ending."

"Do you think I don't know that?" Catherine asked quietly.

Elizabeth's annoyance faded at her sister's quiet admission. "I'm sorry, Cat, it's just that I fear you want so badly for your happy ending that you refuse to see reason."

Before Catherine could reply, their father stepped into the foyer. "I thought I heard voices," he said, moving to welcome them home with a kiss. "I appreciate you taking such a quick ride." He glanced over his shoulder toward the open door of his study. "So, what are the two of you planning to do now?"

"Since we're in the middle of an argument, I believe we might continue with that." Elizabeth lifted a brow at her sister. "How does that sound to you, Catherine?"

Catherine scowled at her. "Like the perfect plan."

"What, pray tell, are the two of you arguing about now?" asked their father as he rolled his eyes.

"And can we watch?"

Elizabeth was surprised to see Lord Wykham leaning against the doorjamb of her father's study. "When did you arrive, my lord?"

"Just a short while ago." A corner of his mouth quirked upward. "Your father invited me for a visit."

"How delightful. As for me, I'd prefer to hear more about your interest in watching two women argue," Catherine said flirtatiously. "Why, Lord Wykham, I never would have suspected."

"Ladies are usually so . . . inventive in their insults that I find it utterly fascinating to hear them argue," John said as he leaned against the doorjamb.

"You sound as if you have quite a bit of experience in this area, my lord." Catherine slid her gloves slowly through her left hand. "Yet another surprise," she murmured.

A corner of his mouth tilted upward. "Splendid . . . for

you see, I've been told recently that I am far too staid and boring and that I needed to ease up a bit." His mouth slid into a full grin. "How am I doing?"

"Positively wonderful," Catherine replied with a breathless catch to her voice.

"Let's go, Catherine."

Father's abrupt pronouncement made Catherine blink. "Go where?"

"Er . . . to the garden," he said as he stepped forward, clasped her elbow, and steered her down the hallway. "I promised you I'd tour your garden, and I'd like to do so . . . at this very moment." Pausing, he glanced over his shoulder at Elizabeth and John. "Don't mean to be rude, Wykham, but I am just too eager to see my daughter's work. Hope you don't mind." He waved to them. "Elizabeth, why don't you keep his lordship entertained until I return?"

And with that, he resumed tugging Catherine down the hall.

Surprised at this odd turn of events, Elizabeth turned toward Lord Wykham. "My goodness," she murmured. "That was . . . unexpected."

Suddenly, Lord Wykham started to laugh. "No wonder my mother was so concerned about my attire."

Elizabeth shook her head. "I'm afraid I still don't understand what's happening here."

"Our parents have apparently decided to become matchmakers," he informed her.

She blinked. "And they matched us up?"

Shrugging, Lord Wykham straightened away from the doorjamb. "It makes sense to match the two eldest children. It wouldn't surprise me if they've arranged for Catherine and Richard to spend time together as well."

"Hmmm," Elizabeth murmured, uncomfortable with the idea of Catherine being matched with Richard. Pushing aside the thought, she smiled at John. "Would you care for some refreshments, Lord Wykham?"

"Only if you agree to call me John."

Feeling at ease, she nodded. "And I'm Elizabeth."

"Done."

She gestured down the corridor. "Why don't you follow me and I can fill you in on what happened during our ride this morning?"

"Why do I get the feeling that this won't be a happy tale?"

"Well, isn't this a pleasant surprise?" their father said jovially as he rose to greet Richard. "I wasn't expecting to see you this afternoon."

Retrieving a note from his pocket, Richard held it out. "You weren't? But I received this . . ."

"Yes, yes," he said dismissively. "Whatever the reason, I'm glad you've come by this fine day . . . and just in time to take a tour of my daughter's garden."

Why, the old dear was matchmaking! Having a hard time holding in her laughter, Catherine rose from the settee, abandoning the tea she'd been having with her father. "It would be an honor, my lord, to show you my garden." She gave her father a pointed look. "And to explain exactly why you received an invitation to call upon us."

Her father had the good grace to blush. "I don't know what you're talking about."

She simply smiled at him before leading Richard into the garden. "I must apologize for this, Richard. Apparently, my father is bound and determined to play matchmaker for me and Elizabeth."

Richard looked slightly embarrassed. "I suppose I should be flattered."

"As should John, for he's with Elizabeth at this very moment."

Immediately, Richard began to look around the yard. "He is?"

His reaction spoke volumes. Whether or not Richard wished to admit it, he was in love with Elizabeth. He'd even cut her in order to protect her in some incomprehensible way. Though Papa had gotten the whole matter mixed up, his idea was still a solid one. Lord knew, Elizabeth and Richard seemed to need all the help they could get.

"I do believe you owe Elizabeth an apology," she said firmly.

Richard took a step backward. "That's true, but I think it best if I stay away from her."

Crossing her arms, Catherine shook her head. "Are you trying to get out of apologizing?"

"No," he denied. "It's not that at all."

"Then you shouldn't wait another moment to beg her forgiveness." Catherine pointed to a small building off to the left of the house. "I believe Elizabeth and John are in her workshop at this very moment."

"Her workshop?" Richard turned toward the building. "Where she builds her machines?"

"Precisely," she said, pleased at the curiosity she heard in his voice. "Now why don't you head over there and apologize to my sister?"

"If you insist . . ." He didn't even bother to finish his sentence as he headed off toward the workshop.

Catherine smiled as she watched him hurry across the lawn. Matchmaking was a tricky business, and best not left in the hands of their father . . . despite his good intentions. He'd almost managed to make a muddle of everything.

13

After consulting her notes on da Vinci's experiments into alchemy, Elizabeth carefully measured out the assorted elements. Humming softly, she added them to a large, stone chalice. Everything was progressing perfectly, she decided, as she walked to the other side of her workshop to retrieve a pestle. John sat in the corner, reading a newspaper. He'd tried to leave earlier, but her father had insisted she show John her workshop. It had seemed easier to simply do as he asked rather than argue.

Like the gentleman he was, John hadn't offered a word of protest at her father's blatant attempts at matchmaking. John had simply claimed the newspaper and settled into the corner, leaving her to her experiments.

Feeling a bit guilty, she glanced at John. "I doubt if you'll need to stay much longer."

"It's quite all right," John assured her. "I'm actually enjoying a few moments of quiet."

She smiled at him before returning to her work. Elizabeth set down the pestle and carefully retrieved her bottle of nitric acid.

"Hello, Elizabeth."

At the sound of Richard's voice, she bobbled the bottle and almost dropped it. Breathing a sigh of relief, she gently set the explosive substance down before turning toward the door. "Richard," she said, pleased that her voice didn't waver. "What are you doing here?"

"I came to see you," he returned, before looking toward John. "Hallo, John. Fancy meeting you here."

John grinned broadly. "Got an invitation, did you?"

Nodding, Richard patted his pocket.

"Is Catherine with you then?" he asked, leaning forward to see if she stood behind him.

"No. She's still in the garden, though, if you'd like to keep her company," Richard suggested.

"I think I shall." Folding the paper, John stood and glanced at Elizabeth. "If that's all right with you, that is."

"Perfectly fine with me," she said, waving John off, even though she selfishly wanted to keep him next to her. With John gone, it was just her and Richard. Immediately, she shifted her attention back onto her experiment. "What do you want, Richard?"

"To apologize."

Her hands stilled at his unexpected reply. "Will you go away if I accept?"

"Probably not," he informed her wryly.

She tried to keep her hands from shaking as she retrieved the pestle. "Pity."

"That's my Elizabeth," he said with a laugh.

The remark stung. "I'm not *your* anything."

"Pity," he murmured softly, echoing her.

She dropped the pestle. Why did he persist in tormenting her? The last time she saw him, he'd given her the direct cut, and now he was making a comment like that. She couldn't take any more of his games. "Why is it a pity, Richard?" she demanded. "You made your . . . distaste for my company quite clear."

"I know, and I'm sorry if I hurt you with my actions."

Closing her eyes, she resisted the urge to forgive him. "Why are you here?"

"As I said, I received a note from your father, requesting me to call upon him. As he implied, the matter was of an urgent nature, I responded at once. However, upon my arrival, your father asked me to keep your sister company in her garden."

"I know that," she said in a level tone. "What I meant is, why are you still here in my workshop?"

"Because I can't leave until I know you forgive me for my shameful behavior last night at the ball." A hint of redness stained his cheeks. "It was unforgivable of me to cut you like that, but I fervently hope you will accept my most sincere apology."

The pain she'd felt at his hands echoed inside her, making her ask him the one question that had plagued her all evening. "Why did you do it?"

He remained silent for such a long time that Elizabeth thought he wouldn't answer. "Because I'm not the man for you."

His reply was so low she almost didn't hear it. She shook her head, completely confused. "I don't understand."

Frustration flashed in his gaze as he thrust both hands through his hair. "I can't explain my reasons to you, Elizabeth. Just please understand that I did what I thought best for you."

"Don't expect me to thank you for it," she said dryly.

A side of Richard's mouth tilted upward. "I won't."

He nodded toward her worktable. "I don't suppose you'd agree to show me what you're working on, would you?"

Elizabeth wanted to tell him no, to send him away, but the lure of having someone to share her experiment with was strong. Richard didn't trust her enough to tell her why he'd hurt her, and he'd bruised her heart dreadfully, but that didn't take away from the fact that he shared the same passion for experiments as she did.

Perhaps this was all that could ever be between them.

Elizabeth waved him closer. "Why don't you come see what I've been working on?"

Wearing a curious expression, Richard moved to her side, looking down at her copious notes.

"Da Vinci dabbled in alchemy for a while, and I found his writings on the subject most intriguing," she explained as she added ground-up coal and a touch of sulfuric acid to the stone bowl. "I'm trying to recreate his mixture to see if it does indeed turn ordinary metal into gold."

"Fascinating," Richard murmured, reaching to pick up the bottle she'd set down earlier.

"Careful with that, it's . . ."

But even as Elizabeth gave the warning, Richard tilted the bottle, sending a drop into the marble bowl. A loud explosion shattered the quiet of the workshop as billowy smoke arose from the container.

". . . nitric acid," Elizabeth finished, snatching the bottle from his hand and replacing it on the shelf.

A fine coat of dark powder covered Richard's face. He blinked at her, then his teeth flashed white within the dark cover as he grinned boldly. "Oops."

His silly comment sent her into gales of laughter. "Oh, Lord, Richard," she gasped when she finally had herself under control. "How can you have me spitting mad one moment and rolling with laughter the next?"

Swiping a finger along her cheek, he lifted it to show her that she must be covered in the same black film. "I guess it's just a gift."

A loud explosion ripped through the air.

"What the devil was that?" exclaimed John, leaping up from the bench in the rear garden of the Shipham house.

"Undoubtedly something my sister is working on," Catherine said without concern. She'd lived with Elizabeth long enough to know that strange noises and smells often came from the awful workshop of hers. "Why don't you sit down again, so I might finish telling you *my* version of my encounter with Lady Serena?"

"I'd rather if you didn't," John said ruefully.

Catherine snapped her head up. "What? Aren't you interested in helping that young man?"

"Please, Catherine, let's not get into this old argument again." Sitting down on the bench, he shifted toward her. "You know perfectly well that I am working toward finding that gentleman, so I refuse to even respond to that accusation."

As she opened her mouth to reply, John lifted his hands, stilling the words. Snapping her mouth shut, she waited for him to continue.

"Now as for Lady Serena, I don't know what you expect me to say. You claim that she is the woman we saw . . . yet the lady herself denies it. And when I consider that it was dark, foggy, and we were too far away to see the woman's features clearly, it seems fair to say that you are probably mistaken."

"But I'm not," Catherine insisted. She'd never been more certain of anything in her life. "It's more than the way she looks. Lady Serena tilts her head in the same manner, she uses her hands when she speaks just like the woman did that evening, and her profile is an exact match. I just *know* she's the woman we saw."

John stared down at her for a long moment, before nodding once. "Very well, Catherine. Since you're convinced Lady Serena is the woman, I shall speak with her." Even as Catherine began to thank him, John cut her off. *"But* . . . if she denies it again, I shall allow the matter to drop." He leveled a finger at her. "And you must promise me that you will do the same."

If he thought for one moment that she would agree to such a demand, he was sadly mistaken. "I shall do no such thing," she protested. "How can I be certain that you won't call upon her, ask a few questions, then leave without probing further into Lady Serena's answers?"

"You will simply have to trust me."

His pompous answer annoyed her. "Why am I the only one expected to trust in this matter? You wish to speak with Lady Serena alone and expect me to *trust* you. Then you want to speak to the runner alone, and once again, you expect me to sit back quietly and allow you to handle the entire matter." She thrust out her chin. "Why can't you trust me to discuss this issue with Lady Serena or even the runner?"

"It's not that I don't trust you . . ."

"Then prove it!"

Silently, John stared down at her. Finally, he sighed loudly. "If I allow you to come to the meeting I have scheduled tomorrow with Mr. Lewis, will you promise me you won't badger poor Lady Serena anymore?"

Though she took offense at the word "badger," she was far too satisfied with the rest of his concession to reprimand him. "I promise."

John slanted her a look. "Why do I know I'm going to regret this?"

"Oh, no. Stodgy old Lord Wykham has returned," Catherine lamented. "So much for spontaneity and carefree thinking."

"Might I point out that I am currently sitting alone with you—in your garden—after having been called to your home—by your father—with his poorly hidden guise of an important matter." His smile was laden with masculine satisfaction. "Yet here I sit, pleasant and amenable. Hardly the actions of a stodgy old man, Lady Catherine."

"I suppose you have a point," she conceded. Her heart began to race at the glimmer of attraction she saw in his gaze. As she watched, John's smile slid away, leaving taut lines and shadows of desire on his face.

All she had to do now was lean closer, press against him, and offer him her lips. Then she could again feel the magic she'd discovered in the maze. One touch, and John made her ache for a deeper understanding of passion, for a way to satisfy the burning needs inside her, for him to show her the ways of love.

But then what?

The thought halted Catherine's forward motion. After this afternoon, she had hope that he could, that he *would,* continue to change, to loosen, but was she willing to risk her heart on a possibility? Her fear held her back.

Unfamiliar with caution, Catherine heeded it nonetheless. Clearing her throat, she straightened, clasping her hands in her lap to keep from reaching for him. "Tell me, John, what do you wish for?"

He blinked and straightened as well. "What do I wish for?" he repeated with a shake of his head.

She knew she'd confused him with her sudden change in topic, but Catherine wanted to know more about this man who was beginning to occupy far too many of her thoughts. "Yes. When you're all alone or just before you fall off to sleep, what do wish for?"

Leaning forward, John propped his elbows on his knees. "Promise you won't laugh?"

His question touched her deeply. "I promise."

"I wish I were climbing the mountains of Scotland with no destination other than wherever my feet chose to go . . . or sometimes I think of journeying to the colonies and learning more about the Indians there." As he spoke, his voice softened, taking on a dreamlike quality that wove itself straight into her heart. "Or I could go to Crete and tour the ruins there or to Egypt and sail down the great Nile." Sitting back, John laughed self-consciously. "I suppose all that sounds rather foolish to you."

"No," she whispered, her voice breaking on the word. Swallowing, she tried again to speak. "It sounds wonderful." She had to clasp her hands even more tightly to keep from reaching out to him. "But all of those dreams are attainable," she pointed out. "Why don't you fulfill at least one of them?"

She felt like crying as she saw the dreams drain from his eyes and the proper expression of Lord Wykham remove all the animation from his face. "Because of all my responsibilities," he said, his voice once more crisp and clear. "I can't very well hie off to foreign lands and leave my estates to molder, now can I?"

Not an ounce of the dreamer colored his tone. "Surely you could hire an efficient man-of-business to manage your estates for a short while."

"And what of my mother? Who would care for her while I was gone?"

"She's a mature woman, John," Catherine pointed out dryly. "I do believe she's capable of caring for herself."

"Then you don't know my mother," he muttered under his breath. "She's a delightful woman, but rather . . . fickle. She was always getting into one mess after another until I took over the household. She's just one of those women who needs someone to care for her."

"You do have a brother, remember?"

"Richard, care for Mother?" John shook his head. "He has too many demands upon his time and couldn't care for Mother and my business affairs as well."

Catherine tapped her foot impatiently. "You are bound and determined to place insurmountable issues between you and your dreams, aren't you?"

"*I* haven't placed them there!" he protested.

"Yes, John, you have. You know as well as I do that your mother, your brother, and your precious estates would be perfectly fine without you for a few months."

Thrusting up from the chair, John stared down at her. "Have you heard nothing that I've said?"

Catherine rose as well, meeting him on equal ground. "I've heard everything you said . . . and everything you left unspoken. Do you know what I think the problem is, John?" Without waiting for him to respond, she answered her own question. "I think you've been so burdened with responsibility for so long that you don't know how to be any other way."

"Rubbish."

"Is it?" she countered. "You wouldn't waltz on a deserted balcony with me because you've taken it upon yourself to protect my reputation; you won't allow me to speak to Lady Serena because you've taken it upon yourself to protect me; and you won't let yourself believe that your life wouldn't be destroyed if you take a short respite from it." She placed a hand on his arm. "Don't you see any of this, John?"

Jerking his arm away, he shook free of her grasp. "Well, pardon me if you find someone who takes responsibility seriously to be deadly dull."

"No, I just find it sad," Catherine whispered, her heart aching for the wonderful man she sensed trapped inside him. "All of your dreams are of escape, John. If you let go of some of the unnecessary burdens, if you set your inner spirit free, you might find all you are searching for without setting foot from London."

"Forgive me for pointing out, Catherine, that your father handles all of your financial and physical needs, leaving you free to indulge in all of your flights of fancy," he said stiffly. "You know nothing of a gentleman's burdens."

A single tear slipped down her cheek. "I feel sorry for you, John."

His shoulders snapped back. "Save your pity for someone who needs it, my lady," he advised coolly. Bowing his head in farewell, he strode off without another word, leaving Catherine alone in the garden.

14

Douglas whistled a happy tune as he shut the door to his bedchamber. Tugging on his cravat, he tossed it onto the bed with a chipper flick of his wrist.

"Margaret!" he exclaimed when he saw his wife's ghostly, translucent form near the fireplace. "I'm so glad you're here," he began, excited to share his marvelous day with her. "I've so much to tell you about our daughters. Last night, Lady Wykham called upon me. She was most upset about the situation between our children." Douglas paused in his tale to reflect upon that meeting. "A most delightful lady, she is, and quite intelligent as well." Suddenly he remembered he was speaking with his *wife* about another woman. Flustered, he cleared his throat and continued with his story. "Anyhow, I was at a loss as to the best way to handle the problem, but then . . . all of a sudden . . . inspiration struck." He gripped the back of a chair. "I know I usually discuss matters concerning our daughters with you, my love, but you weren't here. I'm sorry, but I had to make the decision on my own . . . especially since Lady Wykham was depending upon me, as well as our daughters."

"I'm positive you handled the situation perfectly," Margaret said reassuringly.

"As a matter of fact, I did," Douglas confirmed, pride puffing up his chest once more. "Today I've played matchmaker and done a fine job, if I do say so myself. Our Elizabeth spent quite a bit of time in her workshop with Lord Wykham, and our Catherine took a long stroll with Lord Vernon." He beamed at his wife. "And a splendid time was had by all."

Margaret floated closer. "Wonderful, Douglas."

"It was, wasn't it?" he murmured, distracted as it struck him that his wife was beginning to *move* more like a ghost now as well. "Did you just *float?*"

Her laughter sounded like chimes in a soft wind. "That is what we ghosts do, my love."

"No, it's not," he protested vehemently. "You've suddenly begun to look like a ghost, so pale I can barely see the color of your eyes."

The smile she gave him was filled with love. "I know, Douglas, and I'm so happy for you."

"Happy for me?" he repeated as a horrible suspicion began to form in his head. "You're leaving me, aren't you?"

"I won't go anywhere until you're ready to let me," she assured him.

That stopped the panic clutching at him. "You promise?"

"Yes."

"Then why weren't you here last night?" Douglas demanded, fear making his voice harsher than he'd intended.

"Because you didn't need me."

"I bloody well did!" he exclaimed. "Didn't I just tell you that I was confused about what to do for our daughters?"

"And didn't you also tell me you'd found the perfect solution all on your own?" she countered softly.

Feeling weary, he sunk into the chair. "Yes. Yes, I did."

As she floated closer to him, cool air whispered across him. He wondered if that was her form of a caress. "You have to let me go sometime, Douglas," Margaret said softly.

Tears filled his eyes as he gazed upon her beloved face. "Why?" he rasped. "I love you with all that I am, Margaret. I *can't* let you go."

"Yes, you can, Douglas," she murmured achingly. "You've already begun."

He spread his hands helplessly. "But I still miss you so dreadfully."

"I know you do, my love, but it is time for you to move on toward your future." Margaret drifted away from him. "Hold me in your heart, think of me with fondness, speak of me with joy, but don't keep my spirit tied to you, for it keeps you locked into the past as well."

"But I don't mind," he protested.

"Ah, but I do." Clasping her hands together, she pressed them against her heart. "You are such a wonderful man, Douglas. You have a great capacity for love . . . and you need to find someone new with whom to share your gift."

"Someone new?" Horror filled him at the mere thought. "I shall never love again."

"Yes, my darling husband," Margaret whispered. "You will. It is your destiny, you see, for you have many years to live yet . . . and you are far too good a man to live them alone."

Rejecting even the thought of it, he put up both of his hands as to ward the idea off. "I don't even want to think about that, Margaret, much less discuss it."

"I know, my sweet, but someday, after I'm the warm memory I was meant to be, you'll learn to live again."

"But not now," he insisted fiercely. Closing his eyes, he leaned his head back against the chair, knowing in his heart that Margaret was right, even though he desperately wished he could deny it. "I'm not ready to say good-bye to you yet, Margaret," he rasped, lifting his lids to gaze at his wife's fading form. "Not yet."

He felt rather than saw her smile. "Soon."

The ghostly whisper touched him with bittersweet softness. "Yes," he agreed after a moment. "Soon."

"Please come in, Lady Catherine," John said formally as he opened the door to his study. Before Catherine could make one of her flippant remarks about the polite title, he gestured toward the short, well-groomed gentleman who rose from his chair. "Mr. Lewis, might I have the pleasure of introducing Lady Catherine Everley."

"My lady," Lewis said, bobbing into a bow.

In her usual fashion, Catherine greeted him warmly as she stepped into the room. "Good day, Mr. Lewis. I'm glad to have a chance to meet you, sir."

Obviously uncomfortable around ladies, Lewis swallowed and jerked his head into a nod.

Taking control of the situation, John laid a hand upon the back of a nearby chair. "Lady Catherine, you may have this seat."

She murmured her thanks as she gracefully accepted the offer. John had to bite back a smile over Catherine's ladylike compliance. Reclaiming his own chair, John turned his attention to Lewis. "Have you any new information for me . . ." As Catherine cleared her throat, he glanced over at her, then corrected himself. ". . . any new information for *us,* Mr. Lewis?"

"After receiving your note last night, I did some digging into the lady's background."

"Excuse me," Catherine said, raising her finger. "Sorry to interrupt, but I seem to have missed a portion of the discussion. What note did you receive, Mr. Lewis? And about what lady?"

Shifting toward her, Mr. Lewis explained, "Lord Wykham sent me a note last night stating that there was a possibility that the woman you seek might be Lady Serena Cole."

The warmth and admiration in Catherine's eyes as she looked toward him made John feel like twice the man he was. Lord, it amazed him that with one look she could turn him into a love-starved swain.

"As I was saying," Lewis began again, "I checked into Lady Serena's background and found little of interest. Having lost both her parents when she was five, she's been raised primarily by her brother."

"Anthony Cole," Catherine supplied, surprising John with her answer until he remembered she'd met Morrow in the park.

"Precisely, Viscount Morrow," Lewis confirmed. "Now here's where it gets interesting, for Lord Morrow has a besmirched past and, if he doesn't reverse his fortunes soon, a very bleak future."

"Many gentlemen have a spotted past," John pointed out.

"True enough, my lord," conceded Lewis. "But very few have ever been accused of blackmail."

Immediately intrigued, John leaned forward. "Blackmail?"

Lewis nodded firmly. "More than once, according to my informants. Apparently, the gent would cuckold a wealthy personage, then blackmail the female by threatening to tell her husband or protector of the affair." A look of disgust crossed Lewis' face. "Nasty business."

"As distasteful as that might be, Mr. Lewis, I don't see how that has any connection with our case," Catherine said politely.

"I think it might," Mr. Lewis disagreed. "The last time Lord Morrow tried to blackmail a . . . kept woman, she got nasty right back and hired a few fellows to . . . dissuade Morrow from his course of action."

Catherine's eyes widened. "You mean she hired someone to hurt him?"

"Indeed, she did, my lady, but you must remember that she was fighting for her life . . . or at least her livelihood." Shrugging, Mr. Lewis dismissed Catherine's shock. "In my mind, fair is fair."

"I suppose," Catherine murmured, but John could tell she found the woman's behavior shocking. Then again, Catherine had never been faced with such a dire situation, never had to fight to keep from losing everything, so she had no idea as to the lengths someone would go.

"I take it Morrow lost his taste for blackmail after that incident," John remarked dryly.

"Apparently so," confirmed Mr. Lewis. "However, it did nothing to curb his expensive lifestyle. At this moment, the gent is mere days away from being tossed into debtors' gaol."

Rubbing his chin with his forefinger and thumb, John

made the logical conclusion. "So, if he was truly desperate for money, perhaps he would return to his old ways to acquire funds . . . only add a new twist. He might use his sister as a lure."

Mr. Lewis nodded in agreement. "It's a possibility, and since we have no other leads, I think we should follow this one up."

"Catherine," John said, forgetting to use her title. "Do you truly believe that Lady Serena was the woman we saw?"

"Without question," Catherine agreed firmly.

"Then let's assume that Lady Serena was indeed the blonde lady at the theater that evening." His thoughts whirling, John thrust to his feet and began to pace as he worked out a possible scenario of events. "What if she'd garnered the interest of a nobleman's son, a fellow whose father would be displeased if he knew his son was interested in a penniless lady. But let's say that the boy's love was stronger than his fear of his father, so he met Lady Serena in secret." He warmed to the tale he was spinning. "If Morrow discovered their liaison, it would provide him with the perfect opportunity to kidnap the son and ransom him back to his father, wouldn't it?"

"What of that, Mr. Lewis?" Catherine asked, looking expectantly at the runner. "Doesn't that make perfect sense?"

Mr. Lewis shifted awkwardly in his seat. "Er, it does sound logical . . . but you're making quite a few assumptions."

"Ungrounded assumptions," John stated. Leaning against the mantle, he gave Lewis an apologetic smile. "Forgive me, Mr. Lewis, for getting caught up in my own imagination."

"But you didn't," Catherine protested, thrusting to her feet. "Nothing you said was outside the realm of possibility."

"No, just *probability*," John countered. "And Mr. Lewis can hardly accuse Morrow of committing such a serious crime as kidnapping without more proof than my fanciful imaginings."

"I know that, my lord, but that doesn't mean that he can't look into the situation and see if perhaps Lord Morrow was behind the entire matter."

"That's quite true, my lady," interjected Mr. Lewis, who rose as well. "I shall look into Lord Morrow's whereabouts on the night in question, then I shall put my ear to the street to see if anyone's squawking about a kidnapping job; it's doubtful that an earl would do the actual nabbing."

Catherine smiled at the runner. "Very clever of you, Mr. Lewis."

Flushing a brilliant red, Mr. Lewis scraped a booted foot against the carpet. "Thank you, my lady." He bowed to John. "I shall be in touch as soon as I have any additional information."

"Thank you, Mr. Lewis." Slapping a hand upon the runner's back, John walked him to the door. "Good day, sir."

"Good day to you, my lord." Mr. Lewis looked at Catherine and swallowed again. "To you as well, my lady."

As John shut the door behind Mr. Lewis, he turned to find Catherine beaming at him. "Delightful fellow, your Mr. Lewis," she observed. "And I do believe he shall find that poor man . . . especially since you told him about Lady Serena." Her expression softened as she pressed a hand against her heart. "I can't tell you how much it means to me that you not only heard what I had to say, but really *listened* to me as well."

"Of course, I did," he said, feeling uncomfortable with the weight of her gratitude. "I know I promised you I would meet with Lady Serena, but I couldn't devise a way of doing that without making her feel hunted." He lifted a shoulder. "So, instead I asked Mr. Lewis to look into the matter."

"Most commendable, John." Walking toward him, Catherine placed a hand upon his lapel. "But what impressed me most was the way you created that brilliant scenario. I couldn't have done better myself."

"Catherine, I . . ." he began, uncertain of what he could say to make her understand how much she tempted him, so he fell silent once more.

"Thank you for including me in this meeting, for making me feel like an equal." A soft smile curved her lips upward as she lifted her hand to his face. "There are times, John, when I think you could be so easy to love."

His heart contracted at her softly spoken words and, for that moment, all his concerns and fears were swept away beneath the surge of desire. "Catherine," he rasped, lifting his hands to cup her face, his fingers burrowing into the wealth of her silky hair.

Claiming her mouth, he boldly took all she offered and returned it with a matching hunger of his own. Need pulsed through him, hardening him into a mass of aching desire. Lord, he could so easily lose himself in this woman.

Catherine's moan vibrated against his mouth as she slid her hand from his face onto the back of his head, clutching at his hair as if she were using him to steady herself. But he didn't want her steady. No, he wanted her reeling with passion, weak with desire, swaying with need.

Curving his hand downward, he trailed his fingertips down her neck, along her collarbone, onto the lace edge of her high-cut bodice, and finally over the peaked rise of her breast. Satisfaction roared through him as he claimed her breast with his hand, molding the soft flesh to his palm, feeling her pebbled nipple pressing against his fingers.

Breaking off the kiss, John bent his head further into the curve of her neck, touching his lips to the slender arch. "Catherine," he murmured softly, hearing the aching need in his voice.

"Yes, John." Her whisper feathered along his ear, sending a shiver along his spin. "Oh, yes."

Dear God, he wanted to unfasten her bodice, bare her to his hungry eyes and hands, sweep her onto the floor, and . . . and . . . what? Take her like a whore on the floor of his study?

That thought sobered him from the heady spin of desire. Lord, had he really sunk so far that he would even consider, for one moment, fulfilling his passion upon an innocent like Catherine? Jerking back his head, he gazed down at her, seeing her passion-swollen lips. Dropping his eyes further downward, he looked at his hand, still holding onto her breast, like she was no better than a demimonde.

"Oh, God, Catherine," he rasped, pulling away from her as if he'd been burned. "I'm so sorry."

She offered him a soft smile. "I was as swept away as you, John."

The innocence blazing out of her eyes made him feel even more the heel. It was up to him to treat her with respect. She was an innocent, well-bred lady who had been swept along with his passion. True, she hadn't protested his touch, but that didn't make it any more acceptable for him to take advantage of her inexperience.

John raked his fingers through his hair. Lord, another minute and he would have pulled her to the floor of his study and . . .

Shutting his eyes against the erotic images burned into his mind, John forced himself to take calming breaths and ignore the pounding hunger inside him.

"John?" Catherine said softly, placing her hands onto his chest.

Sweet Heaven, he felt her touch clear through to his bones. His eyes flew open as he stepped backward, breaking her hold upon him. "I'm sorry," he said again. "I took advantage of you, and it won't happen again."

Catherine's brows drew together. "But I enjoyed your kiss," she said hesitantly.

"Bloody Hell, Catherine! Don't say things like that to me," John snapped harshly. Didn't she realize that he was a hairsbreadth away from claiming all she offered in her innocence? No, she didn't, he realized, which was precisely the problem. If he took what she offered, he'd be making a different offer to her the very next day . . . and tying himself to her for the rest of his life.

With his thoughts in a tangle with his emotions, John needed time to sort through the mess. Time without Catherine around to muddle everything up again. While he wanted her more than he wanted anything else in his life, did he want to spend the rest of his life a jumble of emotions?

John pressed two fingers to his temple, trying to still the pounding inside his head, before he inhaled deeply and looked at Catherine. "I will show you out now, Catherine. If I hear from Mr. Lewis, I shall contact you immediately."

"That's it?" she demanded, her mouth opening in surprise. "We share a kiss, and all you can say to me is 'I'll show you out'?"

John took another calming breath. "I know you wish to speak about what is happening between us, Catherine, but I just can't right now. I need to sort through things in my head before we can talk."

Her head snapped back as if she'd been struck. "I didn't realize that it was so complicated you needed to think it over so carefully, John."

"You didn't realize . . ." He broke off. "Do you remember how we argued last night? Then today you come here, acting sweet as cream, and we end up in each other's arms again." He shook his head. "How can you *not* find all of this complicated?"

"Because I don't fight my emotions, John; I just feel them."

The glimmer in her eyes looked suspiciously like tears. Dear God, if she started crying now, he was done for. "I'm willing to feel my emotions as well . . . but I have to understand them first. All I'm asking for is a little time to sort through everything."

"And put it in a neat, orderly fashion, where you can control everything you feel and when you feel it." Catherine's lips began to tremble. "Sorry, John, but life doesn't work like that. You can't help how you feel any more than you can stop the sun from setting." A tear slipped down her face. "Because, believe me, if I could stop myself from falling in love with you, I would do it."

His breath got lodged in his throat at her quiet admission.

Lifting her chin, she looked at him with disdain. "So when you're finished *sorting* through your emotions, John, you may call upon me. And perhaps, just perhaps, I might still wish to see you."

And with that parting line stinging in his ears, he watched her walk out of his study . . . and wondered if she was walking out of his life as well.

15

A knock on the door of her workshop broke Elizabeth's concentration. Unwittingly, she wiped her oil-covered hands upon her gown as she bid the servant to enter.

"Blast!" Elizabeth exclaimed the moment she caught herself smearing oil all over her skirts. She smiled ruefully at their butler. "I'm forever ruining my clothes this way. Terribly careless of me, isn't it?"

She could tell from his expression that their butler didn't know how to reply. Laughing, Elizabeth waved her hand. "Just ignore me, Tibbs. Now, what can I do for you?"

Holding out a tray, he announced, "You have a caller, Lady Elizabeth."

Not wishing to stain the card with oil as well, she nodded toward Tibbs. "Who is it?"

"A Lady Serena Cole," he announced.

Just dandy. "Is my sister home yet?" Elizabeth asked, praying Catherine had come home from her meeting with Lord Wykham.

"No, my lady." Tibbs lowered the tray. "The young lady asked me to mention it was a most urgent matter."

Elizabeth knew she couldn't avoid seeing Lady Serena. "Very well, Tibbs. Please inform her I shall be along momentarily." Glancing down at her hands, she explained her delay. "First I'm going to try and wash off some of this grease."

"A most daunting chore, my lady," Tibbs remarked with a nod.

All of the servants had witnessed Elizabeth's past attempts to remove the stains from her hands. She'd tried everything from lemon juice to tea leaves, yet nothing seemed to easily remove the oil from her skin. "Very true, Tibbs, but I can hardly entertain her like this."

Tibbs' mouth twitched. "Indeed not, my lady."

"I only wish I had time to change my attire," Elizabeth muttered as she glanced down at the large oil prints now discoloring her pale blue gown. *Ah, well,* she thought. Lady Serena can't call unexpectedly and expect her to be suitably dressed, Elizabeth decided with a nod. "Please arrange for tea and refreshments to be brought into the parlor, Tibbs." After all, she didn't have to be completely unsophisticated.

"Very well, my lady," he said before bowing and heading out the door.

In her washbasin, Elizabeth scrubbed at her skin, trying to remove as much of the oil as possible, until she finally managed to get the discoloration down to a dull gray. Shrugging, Elizabeth headed into the house for a dreaded visit with Lady Serena. Again, Elizabeth tried to put her finger on what she'd disliked about the young woman, but the answer evaded her.

As she stepped into the parlor, Elizabeth prayed she could handle this meeting with composure. "Lady Serena," she said in greeting, gliding forward to take a seat opposite the pretty blonde.

In a stunning pale rose walking dress, Lady Serena was the very essence of feminine grace and beauty, making Elizabeth even more self-conscious about her oil-smeared gown and stained hands.

"I'm so thankful you could see me," Lady Serena said in her breathy voice. "I . . . I . . ." A cry broke from her as she buried her face into her hands.

Good Heavens! What was she supposed to do now? Elizabeth wondered, completely at a loss as to the best way to handle a weepy stranger. "Can I get something for you? Tea? A handkerchief?" she asked, grasping at anything.

"No, no," murmured Lady Serena as she straightened, dabbing at the corner of her eyes with her glove-covered fingertip. "I'm so embarrassed." She fanned herself with her hand. "What you must think of me . . ."

"To be perfectly truthful, I don't know *what* to think," Elizabeth admitted.

A tearful laugh burst from Lady Serena. "I thank you for your honesty, Lady Elizabeth."

The surprise in Lady Serena's voice made Elizabeth wonder if she'd made yet another faux pas.

"I'm sorry for my outburst, but it's just that I've been under such pressure lately," Lady Serena explained, twisting her hands together. "Since you're acquainted with my brother . . ."

Elizabeth held up her hands . . . then snatched them back down again when she remembered the stains. "I couldn't claim having an acquaintance with your brother, my lady. We were merely introduced."

"Oh." Lady Serena blinked twice. "From the way my brother spoke to you, I thought you knew each other."

"Yes, well . . ." Elizabeth stammered, uncertain of

how to reply to that comment. Instead, she tried a weak smile. "You were mistaken."

Elizabeth knew from Lady Serena's flinch that she'd been too blunt yet again.

"It seems I was," Lady Serena finally murmured. "Oh, dear, this makes it even more awkward. For you see, I thought, if you were acquainted with my brother, then perhaps you could understand the reason for my fabrication that day in the park." She pressed a finger against her lips. "You see, my brother loves me, but sometimes he . . . frightens me," she finished with a whisper.

While Elizabeth had found Lord Morrow offensive, she hadn't thought him violent. "Frightens you in what manner?" Leaning forward, Elizabeth laid her hand upon Lady Serena's forearm. "I promise I won't betray your confidence."

She offered Elizabeth a wavering smile. "No, I don't believe you will." Closing her eyes briefly as if to draw strength to continue, Lady Serena finally lifted her lashes and met Elizabeth's gaze. "I *was* the lady your sister saw the other night," she confessed softly. "Please don't think ill of me. My brother forbade me to see my lover, so I was forced to sneak out in secret. When your sister recognized me in front of my brother, well, I had no choice but to deny her claim."

"I understand," Elizabeth said reassuringly.

A relieved sigh escaped Lady Serena. "Thank Heaven. I knew I was right in coming here. I just couldn't have lived with another lie." Determination hardened her delicate features. "It's time to end all this deception. When next I meet my lover, I shall . . ."

"Oh, no!" Elizabeth exclaimed as she remembered the

reason *why* Catherine had been so determined to find this woman. How was she supposed to look this woman in her innocent, blue eyes and tell her that the man she loved had been kidnapped?

Lady Serena gripped Elizabeth's hand. "What is it?"

"It's . . . you see . . ." No matter how she tried to begin her explanation, the words seemed to freeze upon her tongue. Taking a deep breath, Elizabeth tried again to find the words. "After you left your gentleman friend that evening . . ." Elizabeth broke off at the sound of their butler greeting Catherine. "Oh, thank God," she murmured. "Excuse me for one moment. My sister has come home and, as she was the one involved, I believe she would be far better at explaining everything." Squeezing Lady Serena's hand reassuringly, Elizabeth rose and hurried toward the door to beckon Catherine inside.

"What is it?" Catherine asked as she strolled into the parlor. "I've just . . . Lady Serena!" Dropping her gloves onto a sideboard, Catherine hurried forward with outstretched hands. "What a surprise."

As Lady Serena burst into tears again, Elizabeth sent thanks winging upward that Catherine was here this time to deal with the weeping. Without hesitation, Catherine wrapped her arms around Lady Serena, offering her comfort in a way Elizabeth never would have thought to do. Feeling out of place, Elizabeth nonetheless took her seat opposite Catherine and Lady Serena.

Pulling out of Catherine's hold, Lady Serena dabbed daintily at her eyes. "Oh, there I go again," she murmured brokenly. "I vow I'm a veritable watering pot today."

"You have every right to be," Catherine said soothingly. "Hearing that someone you care for has been abducted is an awful thing to experience."

All the color drained from Lady Serena's face. *"What?"* she rasped, her voice darkened with confused panic.

Catherine's gaze flew toward Elizabeth. "Didn't you tell her?"

Wishing the floor would open and swallow her whole, Elizabeth shook her head. "I hadn't the chance yet."

Catherine scowled fiercely at Elizabeth before returning her attention to Lady Serena. "After you left your . . . friend that night at the theater, two men set upon him, dragging him off down an alleyway. My companion, Lord Wykham, tried to stop them, but one of the brutes attacked him, so we were unable to help your young man."

Tears rolled from horror-stricken eyes. "My Isaac? They took my Isaac?"

"Yes," Catherine murmured compassionately. "I know what a shock this must be for you, but rest assured, we're already doing all we can to find him. In fact, we have a Bow Street Runner investigating the case right now."

Lady Serena snapped her head toward Catherine. "You do?" she asked in a strained voice.

Something about the sharpness of Lady Serena's tone struck Elizabeth as odd. It almost sounded as if all of her other responses had been tempered, while this one was unabashedly honest. "Why are you so surprised?" Elizabeth asked, unable to hold in the question.

"Well . . . because you are . . . were total strangers," stammered Lady Serena as her eyes began to fill once more. "I'm simply stunned that you would go to such lengths for someone you don't even know."

Sending Elizabeth a quelling look, Catherine patted

Lady Serena's arm. "We're only doing what anyone would do," she said with a shake of her head. "Are you up to answering a few questions?"

Lady Serena drew in a shaky breath. "If it will help my Isaac, then yes."

Nodding, Catherine asked the obvious question. "What is Isaac's full name?"

"Isaac Burnbaum," Lady Serena supplied. "Mr. Issac Burnbaum."

"Where is he from?"

"Here in London."

Picking up Catherine's lead, Elizabeth asked a question of her own. "Is he the son of a nobleman? Someone we would have met at a social affair?"

A delicate pink hue tinted Lady Serena's cheeks. "No, you wouldn't have met him," she admitted quietly. "He's a . . . a merchant's son." She pressed her hands against her stomach. "I know that sounds quite scandalous, but please try to understand how it was for me. I met Isaac when I accompanied my brother to the wharf area, and I fell in love at first sight." Her eyes glazed over as she lost herself in memories. "He was so gentle, so sweet, so charming that I couldn't resist him at all. When he delivered the items my brother had ordered, I had another opportunity to speak with him, and enjoyed myself so much that I agreed to meet him again in secret."

As Catherine sighed romantically, Elizabeth shook her head, knowing her sister was now lost within the story and would be of little help uncovering any other facts. "Where does Issac live?" Elizabeth asked, thinking they might learn more by speaking with Isaac's parents.

"I . . . I don't know," Lady Serena stammered. "I never met his family."

"If you didn't even know where he lived, how would you arrange to meet?"

Lady Serena twisted her handkerchief. "I would wait for a note from him, telling me where and when to meet."

"And what if you couldn't make it at that time? How did you let him know?"

"I would ask my maid—who is completely loyal to me—to meet Isaac. I'd give Lucy my appointments and have her make arrangements with Isaac for our next meeting." Lady Serena's smile grew dreamy. "Then I would wait breathlessly until the day arrived when I could see my Isaac."

Elizabeth tried to garner more information from Lady Serena. "With all the times that you met and spoke with each other, surely you must know more about his life than simply his name."

Lady Serena nodded eagerly. "I knew he was honorable, loyal, and a true gentleman."

Biting back a frustrated exclamation, Elizabeth tried again. "But what of his life? Did he tell you were he worked? What he did for a living? You said his father was a merchant. Did Isaac work for his father? Or did Isaac ever mention where his father's shop was?"

This time Lady Serena shook her head. I know his father sells linens and that his shop is near the wharf. I don't remember exactly where though. I never concern myself with mundane details."

Elizabeth barely managed to keep her mouth from dropping open in surprise. She hardly considered knowing where a person lived a *mundane* detail. "You never spoke about your personal lives?" she said, pleased her voice didn't betray her disbelief.

"No," Lady Serena replied without batting a lash. "We only spoke of love."

That brought another sigh from Catherine, while it was all Elizabeth could do to keep from rolling her eyes. Good Heavens! Lady Serena claimed to love Isaac, but how could she love him, *really* love him, if she knew nothing about him? Having witnessed the close, unshakable bond between her parents, Elizabeth knew that true love was more than stolen kisses and claims of passion. True love meant being best friends, having someone who understands you almost better than you do yourself, knowing that your mate will stand beside you, support you, when you need it the most.

When you love someone, you feel connected to that person in a way you've never known before. Even when you're angry with the person you love, you work together to overcome your differences. Much as she had with Richard.

Elizabeth's breath caught in her throat. Dear God, it couldn't be. She *couldn't* be in love with Richard. She just couldn't.

"Are you all right, Elizabeth?" Catherine asked, concern in her voice.

"Y-y-yes," she stammered, thrusting away her disturbing thoughts and refocusing her attention onto Lady Serena.

"I love my Issac with all my heart," Lady Serena sobbed as she pressed the back of her hand against her forehead. It was a gesture that would have earned her accolades if she ever took the stage.

Elizabeth didn't know what Lady Serena had with her Isaac, but she doubted very much that it was even close to being true love. Still, her opinion was hardly the sort of thing a crying woman needed to hear. Elizabeth smoothed her skirts and stood. "Thank you so much for coming to us, my lady."

Taking the gesture for what it was, Lady Serena rose as well. "I should be the one thanking you, for your forbearance."

Catherine stood as well. "No, please, Serena, don't consider it forbearance." She placed her hand over her heart. "My Heavens, that was the most romantic story I've ever heard. To be able to help reunite true loves is reward enough. Neither Elizabeth nor I want your gratitude," she assured her. "I'll keep your card and will send around a note as soon as I hear anything."

Lady Serena hesitated. "While I'm willing to do anything to help my Isaac, it would be better for me if you could refrain from speaking to my brother about this entire matter."

"Of course," Catherine replied without hesitation. "I shall pass along Isaac's name to our runner, Mr. Lewis, and see if he can't find Isaac's parents. After all, how many merchants named Burnbaum can there be in all of London?"

Elizabeth had no idea, and from Lady Serena's helpless shrug, it appeared she didn't either.

Undaunted, Catherine answered the question herself. "Not many, I'll wager." Placing a hand upon Lady Serena's arm, she guided her toward the door. "I think it might be best if you go home and rest now. This news has been quite a shock to your system."

"Yes . . . yes," she murmured vaguely, before impulsively leaning forward to press a kiss upon Catherine's cheek. "Thank you so much for your help."

Elizabeth stood perfectly still as Lady Serena repeated the familiar gesture with her. "We haven't done anything yet," she remarked, feeling uncomfortable.

"Not only have you hired a runner to find my Isaac, but you also listened to my problems, the problems of a total stranger."

When phrased that way, Elizabeth could see why Lady Serena would feel grateful, but that didn't make her any more comfortable with the situation. "I just hope that we are able to find Isaac for you."

Bidding farewell to Lady Serena, Elizabeth remained in the parlor while Catherine saw her out. As soon as her sister returned, Elizabeth sank down into a chair. "Thank you for your timely arrival, Cat. I didn't know how to handle Lady Serena's crying . . . and I hadn't even told her the worst of it yet."

Catherine smiled sadly. "Unfortunately, poor Serena will have a lot more tears to shed if our suspicions prove correct."

"What suspicions?"

"As you know, I was meeting with John and Mr. Lewis." At Elizabeth's nod, Catherine continued, "Mr. Lewis mentioned that Lady Serena's brother is in a dire financial situation."

"As is more than half of society," Elizabeth pointed out. "I fail to see what connection this has with Isaac's disappearance."

"That's because you won't let me finish!" exclaimed Catherine with a shake of her head. "I was about to tell you that, in the past, Lord Morrow has resorted to black-mail in order to refill his coffers."

Elizabeth was stunned. "Are you positive about this?"

"Absolutely. Mr. Lewis uncovered this information and, as you know, the reputation of the Bow Street Runners is unsurpassed."

"And if Lord Morrow will sink low enough to commit one criminal act, it isn't hard to imagine him shifting from blackmail into kidnapping," Elizabeth said slowly.

"That is precisely what John and I thought as well, so Mr. Lewis is going to look into the very strong possibility of Lord Morrow being the one behind the kidnapping."

"That makes sense," Elizabeth agreed. "Richard knows him."

"Mr. Lewis?"

Smiling over Catherine's response, Elizabeth shook her head. "No, Lord Morrow. In fact, Richard is the one who introduced us."

Catherine sat down opposite Elizabeth. "I wonder if he has any information he can give us about Lord Morrow."

"I don't know," Elizabeth replied. "I do know that Richard dislikes Lord Morrow now, but I believe they spent time together in the past."

Excitement sparkled in Catherine's eyes as she leaned forward. "Really? I wonder what happened to make Richard dislike Lord Morrow."

"I suppose I could ask him," Elizabeth offered, trying to hide the flare of eagerness she felt at the mere thought of seeing Richard again.

"Splendid!" exclaimed Catherine. "When will you see him again?"

"I'm not certain," she replied honestly. "However, I could send him a note, asking him to call."

Tapping her fingers against the arm of her chair, Catherine considered the suggestion. "I think that might be best. After all, time is of the essence."

"Very true," Elizabeth agreed, trying to hide the surge of excitement she felt at the prospect of seeing Richard. "If you'll excuse me, I shall go write my note now."

Catherine waved vaguely. "You go do that and I'll go to Lady Allton's salon. Perhaps I will be able to discover what the matrons think of Lord Morrow."

"I think that is a sound idea, Cat. After all, if anyone is bound to know the sordid tales about a person, it is one of the old biddies who attend Lady Allton's salon."

"Those *old biddies* are the premier matrons of our society."

Elizabeth tilted her head to the side. "Do you suppose that's why I dislike attending social affairs so much?"

Catherine laughed as she rose to her feet. "You are utterly incorrigible, Elizabeth."

"And without even trying," she retorted with a grin.

After Catherine left, Elizabeth sat down to write a note to Richard. With her quill in hand, she paused to consider the best way to start her letter. A large drop of ink spilled onto her paper as she held her hand poised to write. Mumbling under her breath, she set down the quill, tossed out the paper, and tried to begin again. Lord, it would be far easier to just speak to Richard in person.

That's it! If she simply called upon Richard, it would be far quicker, eliminating the need to write the note, then have it sent around, await a reply, and wait until Richard arrived. And Catherine *had* said that time was against them. Still, if she took a few moments to freshen up, it wouldn't make any difference.

Of course, she was not going to see him simply because she enjoyed spending time with him. Oh, no. Most definitely not. She had a reason, *an important reason,* to visit him.

Ignoring the taunting laughter she heard in her own head, Elizabeth rushed off to prepare for her visit with Richard.

16

Inside the hackney, Elizabeth pulled her shawl around her shoulders. Self-consciously, she tugged at her low-cut bodice as she realized it was scandalously early in the day to be displaying this amount of cleavage. What on earth had possessed her to change into one of the gowns Catherine had purchased for her? Elizabeth shook her head, then stopped abruptly as she felt the elaborately pinned curls bob precariously.

Dear Heavens, what had come over her? Here she sat in a hired carriage, wearing an evening gown, with her hair swept upward into a fashionable style and her body perfumed and powdered . . . while heading to a gentleman's house uninvited. A nervous laugh escaped Elizabeth. Even she knew enough to realize that if anyone discovered this little adventure, her reputation would be destroyed.

While Elizabeth cared not one whit about ruining her reputation, she did care that her actions might reflect poorly upon her sister and hurt her father. Still, she'd arranged for the hackney rather than take her family's carriage, in an attempt to keep her visit to Richard a private matter.

As the carriage rocked to a stop, Elizabeth glanced out the window, looking up at the stately home before her. The hackney bounced on its springs as the driver alighted from his seat to open the door for her. Elizabeth was just about to step from the carriage when she heard the clatter of wheels against the cobblestones coming from the rear of Richard's home.

She watched as Richard, driving a smart phaeton pulled by a set of well-matched grays, headed left onto the lane. "Blast," she muttered under her breath. If only she hadn't taken the time to make herself fashionable, she wouldn't have missed him. Now she could either wait for him to return home or she could go back to her house.

Or you could follow him, a little voice said inside her head.

Stunned at the outrageous thought, Elizabeth slumped back against the seat. Follow him, indeed, she scoffed to herself. To where? Richard was undoubtedly headed to one of his clubs. Still, by the time he made arrangements for his phaeton, she might be able to hail him, invite him into her carriage, and ask him a few questions about Lord Morrow.

Having taken time to talk herself into the plan, Elizabeth leaned out to see where Richard's carriage had gone. She breathed a sigh of relief when she saw it not fifty feet away. Pointing to the cream-colored phaeton, Elizabeth said to her driver, "Do you see that phaeton there?"

"Yes, my lady," the man answered politely.

"I'd like you to follow it."

Apparently the carriage driver had heard many unusual, scandalous things, for he didn't even blink. He simply nodded and shut the door. An instant later, they began to move forward. *Well, thank heaven,* she thought as she leaned back against the cushions, still feeling overly bold for chasing after Richard.

What she was doing was insane, utterly mad . . . but at least she wouldn't have gone to all this trouble to look glamorous for nothing.

The lanes to the dock were overrun with carriages and people, making it slow going for Richard, but he didn't mind. It gave him more of a chance to replay in his head the conversation with Elizabeth.

She'd looked so bloody beautiful, standing there telling him why she didn't wish to be attracted to him. Her words had sliced through him, creating cuts that even her healing praise couldn't close. He'd longed to shout at her that the man she feared was not the man he was today. He wanted to tell her of his new purpose in life, of his pride in his business, but he'd held his tongue. Yes, he'd remained silent for one simple reason.

Fear.

Richard's teeth clenched at the acknowledgement. Though he hated to admit he was afraid, he couldn't deny the emotion. Yes, fear of her complete rejection had led him to refrain from telling her his secrets. While Elizabeth didn't want to court him, she still wanted to be his friend. And oddly enough, he'd come to enjoy her company as well. He loved the way she would get that fire in her eyes and snap out a dry retort almost as much as he loved how she laughed so brilliantly when he told a joke . . . or how she enjoyed machines and odd gadgets.

Indeed, he enjoyed so many things about her. She wasn't like any other woman of his acquaintance and, even if he knew her for a hundred years, he was quite certain she would continue to surprise him. But would the underlying desire he felt for her remain over time, like a banked fire; would it eventually die out; or would it one day burst from its containment, burning both of them with passionate intensity?

Richard gripped the reins as he struggled to make sense of his feelings for Elizabeth. But that was the problem, he realized suddenly, his fingers slackening upon the leather.

He couldn't make sense of his feelings toward her. He'd *never* be able to make sense of them . . . because he was wildly, madly, insanely, deliriously in love with Elizabeth.

His heart pounded in his chest as he struggled to breathe. Dear God! Was love supposed to be this . . . this . . .

Richard began to laugh when he realized that he was so crazed for the girl that she'd even stolen his ability to think! He felt the curious stares of passersby as he sat in his phaeton, laughing aloud, but he couldn't contain this maelstrom of happiness, wariness, and sheer panic rolling around inside of him. When had it happened? When had he fallen in love with her?

Perhaps it had begun the very moment that she'd gazed at him with those cool blue eyes of hers, demanding he stop eavesdropping, unwittingly challenging him to break through her wariness. And break through he had. But he'd been so busy trying to overcome her shyness that he hadn't even realized she'd been weaving her way into his heart, thoroughly entangling him, until now he was in complete knots over her.

And she thought him a rake, a wastrel, an utter drain upon society.

That thought sobered him quickly enough. *So, what am I going to do about it?* he wondered as he guided his carriage into the alleyway beside his factory. Pulling back on the reins, Richard brought his phaeton to a halt and sat for a moment, staring at the brick wall in front of him.

"Absolutely nothing," he muttered to himself, knowing that it was the truth. He would bury his love for Elizabeth, hiding it from her in order to protect their friendship. While he might be consumed with love for her, he would never risk telling her, never risk losing her altogether.

To bloody Hell and back. Why did his life always have to be so damned complicated? Just when he'd thought himself back on track, just when he'd pulled himself together and gained a true sense of self worth, he had to go and ruin everything by falling in love with a lady who thought him the despicable man he *used* to be.

Would you rather she know that you're a pretzel maker instead? a voice inside of him sneered. It was bad enough that he was in trade, but making a fortune with something as ridiculous as pretzels? Lord, anyone would look down their noses at that!

Richard leapt down from his phaeton and tossed his reins to the lad he'd hired to water and care for his horses while he was working. Annoyed with himself, he slammed open the door . . . and stopped just inside the threshold. To his right, a man mixed a huge vat of dough until it formed a large, sticky ball. Then he passed the dough on to the group of men on his right, who would cut off small chunks, roll it out, twist it, and drop it into the pots of boiling water and baking soda. After a minute or so, another group of men, standing directly behind the dough rollers, would scoop the pretzels out of the water, drain them off, and place them onto trays covered in coarse chunks of salt.

At the rear of the building stood a huge coal oven with twelve narrow holes, the perfect size for one of the trays. The pretzels would bake until they were a golden-brown, before being pulled out and set onto cooling racks. The cooling racks would then be carried to the floors above and stacked, giving the pretzels their drying time. In a few days, he would have another shipment of crunchy pretzels ready for packaging and shipping.

This was his world now; a successful world he'd created from another man's ruins. This buzz of activity, the hum of contented workers, the satisfaction of achievement was something he had built . . . and in the process, had turned himself from a dissolute spendthrift into a prosperous businessman.

He'd be damned before he'd allow himself to feel another ounce of shame.

Richard smiled to himself at his newfound resolve. Hell, he was tired of hiding who he'd become like it was a dark, dirty secret that would embarrass him and his family. To hell with it.

He would tell Elizabeth of his business, and if she chose not to continue their friendship . . . well, then she wasn't the woman he thought her to be. Richard vowed he would indeed tell her, regardless of the consequences. Then, he would announce it to the world.

He would, of course, be ostracized by the ton, but what did he care? They thought him a despot now, but not beyond the pale, so they could speak to him and invite him to their events. How ironic that he'd finally made something of himself, finally found his purpose in life, and it would be the very thing that would make people look down at him and gasp in horror.

Richard actually grinned at that thought. He'd been fodder for gossips for as long as he could remember. Well, with this last announcement, he would be spoken about in hushed whispers for years.

A skirmish outside the door broke through Richard's thoughts. "You can't go in there, miss!"

Recognizing the voice of the lad who cared for his horses, Richard turned around and opened the door. "Is there a problem . . ." He forgot what he'd been about to say when he saw Elizabeth standing in front of him.

Only it wasn't an Elizabeth he'd seen before.

Gone was the high-necked stained gowns or the fichu to protect her modesty. Instead, she wore a low-cut dress, showing miles and miles of creamy, smooth flesh that made his fingers itch to touch it. Her hair had been pulled up and piled into an artful arrangement of curls and ribbons, leaving a few tendrils dipping down to play with the skin at her shoulders.

She was a goddess. She was perfection. She was . . . at his factory.

Richard's resolve to end the deception wavered at the realization that he would soon lose all hope of touching this vision. The warmth in her blue eyes would drain, leaving her gaze cool and flat. She would change from this smiling, enticing woman into a disdaining lady, offering him nothing but her scorn.

Though that thought made him want to rush her away from his factory before she discovered the truth, Richard forced himself to stand firm. He would do anything for Elizabeth . . . anything except be someone he was not.

"Elizabeth," he said finally. "I would say that it is a

surprise to see you here, but I fear you would find that pedestrian phrase far too obvious."

Blushing prettily, Elizabeth smiled in relief. "I would welcome it, Richard, for I thought perhaps I might anger you with my presence." She glanced at the lad listening in upon their conversation. "I followed you," she admitted.

"I gathered as much," he said, hoping his voice didn't sound as hollow as he felt. "After all, this isn't exactly Bond Street."

"No, it's not." Curiosity brightened her eyes as she looked around at the tall brick and wooden building. "What is this place?"

The question he'd been dreading. "It's my factory."

"*Your* factory?" exclaimed Elizabeth, shaking her head. "I don't understand."

Bracing himself, he stepped aside and bade her to enter. As he'd done mere moments before, Elizabeth stopped just inside the threshold and stared at the bustling activity. He watched her back, waiting for it to stiffen as she realized he was in trade, but all he saw was her head turning this way and that as she peered into every corner of the large, open room.

Finally, he couldn't stand it any longer. "This is my business," he stated firmly, just in case she hadn't understood that part. "These men work for me."

"What are they doing?"

The lack of censure in her question stunned him. Unable to resist, he spun her around to face him so he could look into her eyes. But all he read in the blue depths was an overwhelming sense of curiosity and even a spark of . . . was that excitement? Richard shook his head, finding it hard to believe what his own eyes were telling him.

"They're making pretzels," he rasped, his voice sounding raw. God, just saying it sounded like a jest.

Elizabeth's expression shifted into one of pure excitement. "You're a pretzel maker? I've heard of pretzels, but never had the opportunity to taste one. Are they good?" Glancing over her shoulder, she gestured toward her right. "And what are those men putting that dough into? Oh, and those machines over there, what do they do? Oh, yes, and how many . . ."

He kissed her.

He couldn't help himself.

Love for her, for his unique, one-of-a-kind Elizabeth overwhelmed him, and he had to express it in the only way he knew how. Wrapping an arm around her neck and one around her waist, he bent her over, staking his claim to the sweetness of her soft mouth in front of all and sundry. The whistles and cheers of encouragement simply added to his thundering sense of victory. He'd braved rejection, faced his greatest fear, and had finally won the prize.

Powerless against the surge of love, Richard poured himself into their kiss, reveling in the way her fingers clutched at his shoulders and how her lips eagerly parted to accept his possession. Feeling his control slipping, he slowly eased out of the kiss, pausing to nibble at her lips, nip at her chin, before he straightened and released her.

Gazing at her, Richard could read every nuance of her expression as she went from pure desire, to embarrassment at the cheers and well-wishes from his workers, and finally to bemusement before she looked back at him with a smile.

"Oh, my," she murmured, pressing the tips of her fingers to her lips.

Richard figured his grin looked perfectly ludicrous, but he didn't give a fig. "Oh, my, indeed."

Turning on her heel, she faced his workers, who began to clap and shout out congratulations. Uncertain of Elizabeth's reaction, Richard stepped to her side and had started to raise his hands to silence his men when the sound of Elizabeth's laughter reached his ears. Astonished, he looked at her, then goggled as she dipped into a curtsey.

Still laughing, she rose and slanted a glance up at him. Dear God, he wanted to kiss the laughter from her lips and swallow the happy sound inside of him until it filled him up and took away that awful emptiness he'd felt for far too long. Why had he worried that she would be mortified by his all-too-public kiss? Hadn't she already proven, by her easy acceptance of his business, that she was truly an original?

His original.

Satisfaction broadened his foolish grin as he raised his hands to silence the cheers. "Gentlemen, may I introduce the finest lady it has been my pleasure to meet, Lady Elizabeth Everley?"

Each and every one of his workers, from the most well-educated to the coarsest, gave Elizabeth their best version of a bow. Obviously touched, she pressed her hands to her chest. "Thank you, gentlemen, for your gracious welcome."

Pride burst through Richard as she gave his workers a reply worthy of the finest drawing room. Cupping her elbow, he shifted her to face his foreman. "Elizabeth, may I present Mr. Perth? He's the man who makes everything run so smoothly. Without him, I would be lost."

Without hesitation, Elizabeth grasped Mr. Perth's outstretched hand and shook it. "It is indeed a pleasure, sir," she said warmly. "I find this entire process utterly fascinating. Would you mind giving me the grand tour?"

"Don't know how grand it would be, miss, but I'd be pleased to show you the operation." Gesturing toward where the mixers stood, Mr. Perth led Elizabeth over to them. "Now, there's really nothing much to mix together, just some flour and water, but it's getting the right amounts of each that's the trick. Then you need to push it and pull it until it forms into a ball."

"Just flour and water?" Elizabeth frowned slightly. "Wouldn't that make them taste rather bland?"

Mr. Perth beamed at her as if she were a prized pupil. "Now that's a right fine question, miss," he agreed readily. "And it would indeed be not much to eat if it weren't for how we prepare them. If you'll come over here with me, I'll show you the next step."

Watching Elizabeth gave Richard new insight . . . and renewed hope. She greeted everyone easily, conversed with the men without reserve or hesitation, and moved with unconscious grace, an ease that seemed to be missing whenever she was amongst the ton.

Yet, here, in his new world, she was comfortable.

What else had he expected from a woman who wandered through junk parts stores and blew up her workshop?

Mr. Perth led her behind the narrow tables where the men were rolling and twisting the dough. Sawing off a chunk of dough, Mr. Perth handed it to Elizabeth, who accepted it with a murmur of thanks that brought approving nods from his men. "Take the dough and roll it between your hands and the board like so." Mr. Perth held his hands flat and, using his palms, rolled the dough beneath them, moving his hands steadily outward to lengthen the piece of dough. Copying him, she continued until Mr. Perth stopped her. "That's good, and now it's time for the shaping. First, you curve the dough up like this." He made a U-shape out of the dough.

Though she followed his direction, Elizabeth began to pepper him with questions. "How did you learn to make pretzels? Or did you create them?"

"I'm afraid Mr. Perth was born hundreds of years too late to have created them," Richard supplied, stepping closer until he stood on the opposite side of the table from Elizabeth. "Pretzels were created by the Benedictine monks over twelve hundred years ago. In fact, there's a reason why they're twisted like that."

When Elizabeth's eyes lit up with that fierce fire of curiosity, it was all he could do to keep from leaning over the table and kissing her again. "What's the reason?"

"The U-shape symbolizes arms open to receive God." As Richard spoke, Mr. Perth demonstrated with his piece of dough. "Then you twist it once for arms crossed in prayer." Taking the two ends of the U, Mr. Perth folded the right end over the left. "You twist again to symbolize the tightness of marriage and family," Richard continued as Mr. Perth again laid the right end over the left, creating a complete twist in the dough. "And finally, you fold the ends down onto the bottom of the U, to symbolize embracing God into your heart, home, and life." When Mr. Perth pressed the ends of his dough into the bottom of his piece, it created the pretzel shape she'd seen on the finished ones. "And in its final shape, those three openings symbolize the Christian Trinity."

Finishing up her pretzel as well, Elizabeth reached up

to tuck a strand of her hair behind her ear, brushing her hand against her cheek and leaving a streak of flour. Richard took in the picture she made, standing in the midst of his factory in a beautiful silk gown, with her hair done as if she were attending the finest ball . . . with a streak of flour smeared across her face and wearing a huge grin. He'd thought she was beautiful when he'd first seen her in her finery; she'd looked so perfect, almost too perfect, as if she might shatter if he touched her. But now she was real, stunningly real, and she stole his breath away.

"Here's the secret to pretzels, miss," Mr. Perth said as he walked over to the vats of boiling water. "We add baking soda to the water to give it some taste."

Elizabeth drew her brows together. "I know baking soda has some very unusual properties when combined with other elements, but I didn't think it tasted very good."

Chuckling, Mr. Perth dropped his pretzel into the water, letting it bob for a minute or so until he retrieved it with a scooper. "That's true enough, miss, but somehow it just comes out right. Then we place it on these salt-covered trays and bake it in those coal ovens." Guiding Elizabeth toward the back of the room, he retrieved one of the pretzels that had just come out of the oven. "Try one," he offered.

Elizabeth glanced back at Richard and he nodded encouragingly. As she bit into the pretzel, Richard watched her eyes close for an instant as she hummed her approval, the sound sending a shiver along his spine. Would Elizabeth wear that expression of sublime pleasure when he made love to her? Richard almost groaned at the erotic image.

"This is delicious." Elizabeth gestured toward the drying trays stacked along the wall to be brought upstairs. "Why are they laid out on those trays? Is that where they cool?"

"Cool and dry," Mr. Perth said. Heading around to the side of the ovens, he retrieved a pretzel that looked dark brown instead of light gold, like the one she held in her hand. "Here's the finished product."

Accepting the second pretzel, Elizabeth turned it over in her hand. "It's hard."

"Precisely," Richard said, strolling to join them again. "But it's still delicious . . . yet it lasts up to three months, which makes it a wonderful treat for pubs and clubs to serve."

"Because it doesn't spoil," Elizabeth finished correctly. Tentatively, she bit into the hard pretzel, snapping off a piece in her mouth. "This *is* just as wonderful."

Mr. Perth rocked back on his heels. "And that's the tour, miss. Grand or no, that's the lot of it."

"Thank you, Mr. Perth," she said before looking around the room to include everyone in her thanks. "I truly appreciate your time."

"Why don't you come upstairs to my office, Elizabeth?" Richard suggested as he slipped his hand into hers and led her out of the main room of the factory toward the staircase. "I doubt if my men will be able to do a lick of work if you're here. You, my dear," he murmured, pausing at the base of the stairs to tap a finger to the tip of her nose, "are just too much of a distraction for them."

She tilted her head to the side, a saucy move he'd never seen her make before. "And what of you, Lord Vernon? Do I prove to be a distraction for you?"

17

For a moment, Richard could only stand there, blinking in surprise at Elizabeth's very un-Elizabeth-like flirtation. "Most certainly," he returned, sliding his finger along the curve of her jaw, "but luckily for me, I don't have to work this afternoon."

"Really?" she purred, her voice soft and seductive. "Then what about . . ." Breaking off, she began to laugh and shake her head. "I can't do it," she finally gasped.

She'd lost him. "Do what?"

"Flirt." Elizabeth sighed dramatically. "I'd promised myself the whole way over to your house that I would be utterly sophisticated and devastatingly charming . . . just like I were any other proper lady of the ton." She held her arms out to the side. "Which explains my attire."

Hearing the doubt in her voice, Richard cupped her cheek in his hand. "But you're not like any other lady I've ever met . . . and I've met more than my share . . . but no other woman has ever captivated me the way you do."

"Are you telling me the truth, Richard?" she whispered. "Last night we promised to be friends, and I told you that's all I wanted from you . . . and I meant it." Confusion darkened her gaze. "But then I found myself dressing like this, wanting to impress you, wishing you would see me like one of the women you'd courted in your past, and then, when you kissed me, I . . ." She broke off and rubbed her cheek against his hand. "I'm so afraid, Richard," she admitted brokenly. "I'm afraid of how I feel for you, I'm afraid that you'll break my heart, but most of all, I'm afraid that I'll never feel this way about anyone else and if I don't tell you, don't push aside my fear and take a chance, I'll never know what it feels like to love."

"*Elizabeth*," he groaned hoarsely, before lowering his head to claim her lips once more. The kiss was bold, carnal, and unbelievably powerful, leaving Richard shaking with the need to make love to this glorious woman in his arms. He'd banished her wariness, melted the wall around her heart, and discovered beneath the cool facade lay a vibrant woman who awakened him to the true meaning of hunger, of need, of desire.

Breaking away from her mouth, he trailed hungry kisses along her neck, gently scraping his teeth along her flesh in an erotic torment. A booming order from Mr. Perth broke through the passion storming through him, reminding him that they were in an open foyer where anyone could come along and see them. Lifting his head, he gazed down at Elizabeth, his breath catching at the sight of her eyes half closed with desire, her mouth parted in welcome, and her cheeks flushed with unsated needs. With a groan, he leaned down, swept her up into his arms, and carried her up the stairs.

Elizabeth clung to Richard, not knowing where they where headed . . . and not caring. She'd stopped fighting the desires within her, finally understanding why her father had urged her to find someone to love. If the intensity of the emotions filling her even now, on the very threshold of love, were this powerful, she could only imagine the depth and commitment a person would feel after time had strengthened that love. Staring up at Richard, allowing herself to feel everything she'd suppressed, she knew she wanted to grow old with him, share her life with him, be one with this man who was so much more than she'd ever suspected.

Even when she'd worried so much over losing his friendship, she'd refused to acknowledge why he was so important to her. But when she'd come here, to this factory Richard had built, she'd realized that the depth and maturity she'd sensed in him had indeed been there all along, hidden beneath a facade of ennui and jaded airs.

And then he had kissed her. Right in front of everyone. She knew she should have been mortified, but the way Richard kissed her, pouring himself into their embrace as if he admired her, as if she were precious to him, as if he loved her . . . erased the twinge of embarrassment she'd felt. Indeed, when he'd finally lifted his head and she'd heard the good-natured cheers, she'd felt victorious, as if she'd just won something very, very important. So, instead of shifting awkwardly about, she'd pretended it was all a grand adventure, turning to curtsey to the men, and bringing that sparkling light of admiration into Richard's eyes. She hadn't felt nervous around Mr. Perth or the other men because, unlike the ton, no one was judging her, no one would find her lacking, so it freed her to behave like herself.

Down there, in that factory, something had changed between them. It was as if she'd passed a test she hadn't even known she was taking. But something in his gaze had reached inside of her, touching her very core, and made her acknowledge what had been hiding in her heart.

She loved him. Completely. Irrevocably.

The planes on Richard's face were taut with desire as he carried her up the stairs. Lifting her hand, she smoothed her fingertips down his cheek, the simple touch making him pause and bend down to press a swift kiss upon her lips.

The realization that she could so deeply affect this man shook Elizabeth to her very core. "You love me, don't you?" she whispered in wonder.

His lips curved upward as he gazed down at her. "Madly."

Joy, pure and sweet, burst through her. Setting her down, he opened the door in front of them and ushered her into a well-appointed room. A huge desk presided over the room, facing two high-back chairs and the long divan that rested against a side wall.

"This is your office," she murmured, taking in the organized stacks of paper upon the desk and the rows of ledgers standing in the book shelf on the rear wall.

"Yes." The single word possessed a wealth of pride. But before she even had a chance to praise him, Richard gathered her into his arms once again. "Seeing you here, in my office, standing among the things I hold most dear . . ." Choking on his words, Richard shook his head, unable to complete his thoughts.

But Elizabeth knew what he meant, and was even more touched that he felt it so deeply it robbed him of the words to express his feelings. What had changed him, made him want more than social flings and wanton pleasures? She didn't know, but she now hoped for a lifetime to find out. "I love you, Richard," she murmured achingly.

"My darling Elizabeth," he rasped before capturing her lips again.

Opening herself up to him, she gave back the love he offered, accepting his tender caresses along her spine and returning some of her own. When his hands slid into her hair, ruining the elaborate style, Elizabeth welcomed the freedom.

As he toyed with her mouth, Richard unfastened her gown, exposing the corset beneath. Needing to touch him as well, she slid her hands from around his neck to tug his cravat off, tossing it heedlessly upon the floor.

Breaking off their kiss, he gazed down at her as he slowly shifted her gown forward, allowing it to pool at her waist, exposing the curves of her breasts beneath her chemise. Richard reached behind her, pulled on the strings of her corset, loosening the garment. A heady sense of abandon filled her as the tight garment was loosened, then discarded, allowing her breasts to fill out the thin chemise.

Richard's breath caught in his throat. His hand shook as he lifted it to her chest, his fingers lightly stroking along the curve of her breast, brushing the softness of her chemise against her aroused nipple. A moan feathered from her as he cupped her flesh, skimming his thumb over her turgid nipple. The small movement sent a flash of heat straight to her loins.

"*Richard!*" Elizabeth arched her head back, curving her hands beneath his jacket.

"So beautiful," he murmured as he bent his head to capture her nipple between his lips, moistening the tip through her chemise.

She'd never even begun to imagine the pleasure a man could give a woman by suckling at her breasts. Clutching at his shoulders, she arched into his touch, silently begging him to continue educating her in the sensual ways of love.

As he lifted his head, Elizabeth murmured a protest, bringing a smile to his lips. He recaptured her mouth in an explosive kiss, before drawing back again, this time to lift her gown over her head, then tossing it onto the floor, a forgotten puddle of silk. Without pause, he raised her chemise up and tugged it off as well.

Realizing she was standing before him in nothing but slippers and stockings, Elizabeth gasped in alarm, crossing her arms protectively in front of her.

"No, no," he protested softly, clasping her hands within his to draw her arms back up to his shoulders. "Don't hide from me, Elizabeth," he appealed in soft entreaty. "Not from me."

He was right, she thought, calming her jittery nerves by meeting his love-filled gaze. She'd hidden from him . . . and from her feelings for far too long. It was time to change that.

Lifting her chin, Elizabeth dropped her hands to her sides, proudly meeting Richard's admiring gaze.

"Oh, love," he whispered, his voice hoarse. "I never knew such perfection existed in this world." Before she could utter a reply, he swept her up into his arms, carried her to the divan, and laid her down as if she were as fragile as delicate spun glass.

The way he touched her, making her feel utterly cherished, brought tears of joy to her eyes as he removed her slippers and stockings. Then he grew still, only his gaze roving over her as she lay there upon the divan like a wanton . . . and reveled in the sensation. The touch of his gaze made her ache for the erotic slide of his hands over her skin. Arching upward, Elizabeth silently pleaded for him to make the images in her head a reality.

Standing, Richard began to tug off his jacket, allowing it to fall unheeded to the floor, with his waistcoat and shirt following swiftly behind. As each layer was removed, revealing more of his masculine flesh, Elizabeth felt her heart beat faster. The curved muscles of his broad chest made her fingers itch to trace the taut lines, to tease his nipples, to feel if the hair trailing in a V pattern down to his stomach was as silky as it looked.

Propping his hip against the edge of the divan, Richard levered off one boot, then the next, before unfastening his breeches and sliding them off as well. With a swift movement, he removed his stockings, before turning toward her.

Eagerly, she reached for him as he laid down next to her. A soft moan ripped from him at the erotic glide of flesh against flesh. She'd never imagined that it would feel so good to have him pressed against her. Lifting her hand, she satisfied her curiosity, discovering the softness and springiness of his chest hair, molding along the enticing curves of his chest.

Not to be outdone, Richard mirrored her path, trailing the tips of his fingers along her breast, onto the slope of her stomach, and along her outer thigh. With a groan, Richard shifted until he rested on top of her and took her mouth with barely contained restraint. Moving his chest side to side, he teased her nipples, making Elizabeth lose herself in the delicious sensations battering her.

After thoroughly delving into her mouth, Richard broke off their kiss, tilting his head to the side to capture her earlobe between his teeth. A murmur of delight whispered from her as she arched into him, her fingers burrowing into his thick, dark hair to hold him close.

Slowly, he made his way down her body, pausing to lick her collarbone, tracing the hollow between her breasts, before moving on to capture her nipple with his lips. A cry broke from her as desire pulsed through her with every tug of his mouth. Restlessly, she entangled her legs with his, shifting her hip toward the turgid length pressing against her.

Having grown up in the country, she knew well enough what the hardness was and, from her studies, even understood the technical aspects of making love. But what the books had failed to tell her was how she would glory in the sensations pounding through her, making her crave him like she would food or air. Nor had the book mentioned how the mere touch of his tumescence against her would make her core tingle with anticipation.

Richard's hand moved from the outside of her thigh to trail along the inner flesh. Without direction, she let her leg fall to the side, opening to his touch, waiting breathlessly for his fingers to reach her aching womanhood.

"Richard!" she cried, unable to hold in her cry when he boldly pressed his hand against her. Curving his fingers inward, he rubbed against her moistness. Her eyes closed as beautiful, rainbow-colored sensations cascaded through her, pushing her higher and higher toward an unknown pinnacle. Suddenly the rainbow burst into a cascade of color, sparkling and glorious, as she fell over the edge.

Shivers racked her body as she wallowed in the wonder of it all. "Richard," she murmured, surprised at the huskiness of her voice.

"My beautiful, wonderful Elizabeth."

His words feathered over her breasts as Richard shifted further on top of her, moving until he lay between her legs and his manhood nudged at her core. Lifting her gaze onto his face, she saw the feverish light in his eyes, and it ignited the fire inside her that he'd so delectably doused moments before.

"Will you take me into you?" he rasped, his muscles quivering with the effort he was making to hold back.

"Oh, yes, my love," she said, tilting her hips upward to accept him fully into her.

Slowly, he eased forward, entering her body, becoming one with her. Her anticipation faded slightly as he joined them, his manhood stretching her beyond the point of comfort. Unconsciously, she tried to shift away, but Richard captured her hips beneath his hands.

"It's all right, Elizabeth," he said soothingly, though his voice was dark and deep with unsated passion. "It will only hurt for a short moment. I promise." And with that, he thrust forward. When he lay, buried to the hilt inside her, Richard stilled again, looking down at her with concern. "Are you all right, Elizabeth?"

"Yes," she replied. "I *think* I am."

A strangled laugh rumbled through Richard. "Ah, the overwhelming praise."

The vibrations from Richard's laugh created an interesting friction where they were joined. She'd *felt* what he'd felt. That erotic realization made her think of how he'd made her feel with the touch of his hand. Experimentally, she shifted her hips, recreating the little jolt of friction that sent a glimmer of that delicious rainbow sensation through her.

"Richard?"

"Yes, love?"

She arched her pelvis upward, the movement brightening the feeling inside of her. "Can you get on with it?"

Again, his laugh went from him straight into her, binding them in a way she'd never imagined possible.

Anticipating another intriguing flash of color inside her, Elizabeth found herself splashed into the heart of her desire when Richard stroked outward, then back in again. The explosion she'd experienced beneath his hands seemed like nothing when compared to the sensations bombarding her now. An intense burning, deep inside her, began to radiate outward, making her quiver with desperate longing as she clung to Richard.

The whole world narrowed down until all that remained was them, locked together in a delicious dance of love. His beloved features began to blur as the sensations rocked through her at a furious pace, driving her higher and higher, before thrusting her over the edge with a grand explosion.

A cry of fulfillment ripped from Elizabeth, frantically clutching at him as she embraced the wildness raging within her. Moments later, he stiffened beneath her hands as he drove forward with one last powerful surge and emptied himself inside her. Shaking with the intensity of his release, Richard slowly lowered himself onto her, shifting to the side to keep his full weight off her while remaining inside of her.

Lassitude overtook her as she curled against Richard. Lazily, she trailed her fingers through the hair on his chest. She almost purred when he began to gently run his hand along her back. She'd never realized just how much emotion could be demonstrated with a single touch. From passion to love, all it took was an easy touch to communicate.

Capturing her hand, Richard lifted it to his mouth and pressed a kiss onto her palm. "I love you, Elizabeth."

The satiation deepening his voice made her smile. "I love you, too, Richard."

He hugged her closer, pressing her against his warmth. "Marry me," he said simply.

She gave him the answer in her heart. "Yes."

18

Shifting her upward, Richard captured her lips.

Elizabeth felt his excitement in the kiss he pressed upon her lips. "We shall have a wonderful life together."

"I believe we will," she agreed happily, settling back onto his chest.

Richard hugged her tightly. "I'm certain my mother would be thrilled to help you plan the wedding."

Just the thought of planning a wedding daunted Elizabeth, so she was relieved to hear that Lady Wykham might be willing to help. "I will welcome her assistance," Elizabeth said truthfully. "I'm not even sure how one goes about arranging for one."

"Don't worry, love," Richard murmured reassuringly. "My mother is the consummate hostess and can easily plan any affair . . . even one that begins with a wedding."

His remarks struck her as odd. "What do you mean by an affair that begins with a wedding? The wedding *is* the affair."

"I know," he said, lifting her hand to kiss it again. "I meant the reception we'll have afterward." His chest shook beneath her cheek as he laughed softly. "If the gossip we generated this past week is any indication, everyone will be vying for an invitation to our wedding."

Her blood chilled at the thought. "A reception?" she stammered, her nerves already jangling at the idea of hosting a large affair. It was difficult enough for her to attend a party; she couldn't imagine actually hosting one. "Couldn't we have a quiet, private ceremony, perhaps back at my family's country estate, with only our family in attendance?"

"Not bloody likely if my mother has anything to say about it," Richard returned easily.

She shifted away from him. "But she *doesn't* have a say in this matter," Elizabeth informed him quietly, lifting her head to gaze down at him. "This is our decision."

Richard tucked a strand of hair behind her ear. "She's my mother, Elizabeth, and I have no wish to hurt her by excluding her from helping to plan the wedding."

"Neither do I," she insisted, "but I don't want a huge reception afterward, nor do I wish to be married in town. The best times of my life were spent upon our country estate, attending Mass at the local parish, socializing with the local gentry who never looked down their noses at me or judged me and found me lacking." She needed him to understand how she felt. "And whenever I imagined getting married, it was always before my childhood pastor, not by some stranger in a cold, foreign church here in town."

She drew a relieved breath at the compassion blazing from his eyes. "Very well, my love. We shall marry at your chapel," he conceded without another word of protest. "Instead, I shall let my mother plan a large soiree here in town after we return to celebrate our nuptials."

Again, his statement confused her. "Return to town? Why would we wish to do that so soon?"

"I'm afraid you've lost me," he said with a laugh. "After our wedding, I can't spend more than a few days in the country before we must return to town."

"But I have no wish to return."

Richard frowned slightly at her emphatic statement. "But we must, Elizabeth."

"Why?" she asked insistently. "I've tried to fit into the ton, but I've failed miserably. Besides, once people find out about your business, we will be ostracized."

"Perhaps, but I'm afraid I have no choice. We must live in town so I can be close enough to run my business."

She met Richard's serious gaze. "And while you're off running your business, what shall I do? You know as well as I that we will be shunned and I won't be welcomed anywhere."

"But you've never enjoyed social functions," he pointed out.

"That's true, but if we remain in town, I won't even be able to shop on Bond Street without running into some-one who will mock me."

Richard froze beneath her. "So what you're saying is that, while you might love me, you don't love me enough to weather the ton's disapproval."

"No, that's not what I'm saying at all." Elizabeth searched for the words to explain her apprehensions to Richard. "I want to marry you, Richard, but I don't want to live in town. Perhaps we could live nearby, and you could visit your business every few days."

"It would never work. I need to be here every day," he said, tucking a strand of hair behind her ear. "I know you're worried about the ton's reaction and I don't think your fears are unfounded. Still, I do believe we can find a place for us, a place where we can be happy together." His gaze grew intense, as if he were willing her to believe him. "Please trust me, Elizabeth."

Slowly, she nodded. "I shall."

A corner of his mouth lifted, easing the grimness of his expression. "You won't regret your trust."

"I better not," she said teasingly.

Lifting his hand, he gently traced the shape of her face, before rising. He retrieved her gown from the floor. Shaking out the hopelessly wrinkled gown, he laid it upon the foot of the divan, then picked up his own shirt and waistcoat. "Would you like me to help you dress?"

"No, thank you. I'll be fine," she murmured. Swiftly shrugging into his shirt and waistcoat, he paused to fasten them, then bent to pick up his cravat.

When Richard turned away from her, Elizabeth rose from the settee and donned her dress. She twisted her arms awkwardly behind her to fasten as much of her gown as she possibly could, but she had to leave the last few fastenings undone, causing her gown to dip precariously low.

Elizabeth stopped in surprise when she caught a glimpse of herself in the mirror. Her hair had been ravaged by Richard's impassioned caresses, leaving it hanging loose to flow over her shoulders, the curled tips flirting with the sides of her breasts. Her lips were reddened from their heated kisses, and there was a mark at the base of her neck where Richard had pressed a particularly delicious kiss.

Dear Heaven, Elizabeth thought in alarm. Anyone looking at her would know precisely what she'd been about. Searching the divan for her missing hair pins, Elizabeth twisted her hair into a bun and secured it as best she could. However, with her hair swept up, it made that mark upon her neck stand out even more. Carefully, she pulled a strand of hair from the bun, strategically placing it to cover the mark.

"Elizabeth?" Richard said from behind her. "Do you need my assistance now?"

"As a matter of fact, I do," she replied, thinking he could finish securing her gown, as she turned to face him.

The sight of Richard, looking utterly dashing and impeccably well-groomed, made her breath catch, and an insidious thought whirled around in her head—this glorious man was her lover.

Lover.

Something about the word jarred Elizabeth's memory. Suddenly, she remembered the reason behind her call—gathering information about Lord Morrow. She'd opened her mouth to ask Richard about Lord Morrow when another thought dawned on her. Richard was now a merchant, running a successful business near the wharf. "Richard, do you know of a family named Burnbaum?"

He lifted his brows at her question. "Quite a few of them. Why?"

Presenting her back to him, Elizabeth sighed in disappointment. "I was afraid of that," she admitted over her shoulder as Richard refastened the top of her gown. "I was just hopeful that you might know an Isaac Burnbaum."

"As a matter of fact, I do."

Elizabeth whirled to face Richard. "You do?"

"Three of them," he clarified with a smile.

The burst of excitement died. "Oh."

"Why do you ask?"

Telling him about the visit by Lady Serena, Elizabeth

finished, ". . . so I'd hoped that you might know who his parents were."

"I might," Richard said thoughtfully. "My friend, Aaron Burnbaum, mentioned that his son had become involved with a woman who wasn't Jewish and had begun sneaking around to meet this woman. However, last time I spoke with Aaron, he thought Isaac had run off with this woman to Gretna Green."

"What if that's what they'd intended, but poor Isaac was kidnapped before they could leave?" Elizabeth asked immediately.

"That is a possibility," Richard conceded as he shrugged into his jacket. "After I see you home, I shall call upon the Burnbaums and speak with them to see if they've heard from Isaac."

Elizabeth didn't budge an inch. "See me home first?" She shook her head. "I'd like to meet the Burnbaums."

"I think you'll like them," Richard predicted as he finished fastening her dress. "After you, my lady," he said gallantly, sweeping his hand toward the door while bowing.

Praying the Burnbaums wouldn't notice that her gown was completely inappropriate for this early in the day . . . or that it was a mass of wrinkles, Elizabeth drew back her shoulders and headed out the door.

The Burnbaums lived in a charming Georgian home on the outskirts of town. Having never been in this section, Elizabeth looked around, overcome with curiosity. "This is a beautiful area," she remarked, appreciating the beauty of the imposing homes separated by large, manicured lawns. "Why have I never been here before?"

"Because these homes are owned by merchants and

other commoners who have made their wealth," Richard explained, jumping down from his phaeton to hand the reins to a waiting groomsman. Reaching up, he placed his hands upon her waist and swung her down from the carriage. "No self-respecting aristocrat would ever frequent this part of town." As he lowered her to the ground, he stood for a moment with his hands at her waist. "Luckily, I've never considered myself an aristocrat . . . much less self-respecting."

She laughed as he'd undoubtedly intended. Laying a hand on his chest, she smiled up at him, knowing full well that he'd purposely been putting her at ease by acting like her friend once more. The funny thing was—it was working. With every laugh, every smile, every jest, he eased her fears, making them seem inconsequential and foolish. "Thank you," she murmured softly.

Wordlessly, he cradled her hand in his and lifted it to his mouth for a kiss. Still clasping her hand, he led her up the stone walkway to the elaborate front door. A moment after he sounded the knocker, a butler opened the door and bade them enter.

Richard and Elizabeth were shown into a spacious parlor to wait to be announced. "This is a beautiful home," Elizabeth whispered to Richard as she scanned the rich furnishings, marble fireplace, and brocade draperies.

Before Richard could reply, they heard footsteps heading toward them and, a minute later, a gentleman with dark, curling hair and deep brown eyes entered the room with his hand outstretched. "Richard!" he exclaimed, a wealth of pleasure in the single word. "Welcome to my home."

Shaking his hand, Richard returned the warm greeting. "I promised I'd come by, didn't I, Aaron?"

"True, but I'd hoped for a little more notice," he replied, his voice light and teasing.

Still smiling, Richard held out his hand for Elizabeth, who accepted it and glided forward. "Might I present my fiancée, Lady Elizabeth Everley?"

Richard's bold announcement robbed her of her breath for a moment, but, not wanting to make a scene in Mr. Burnbaum's house, she squeezed Richard's hand, silently promising retribution. "It is a pleasure, Mr. Burnbaum," Elizabeth said politely, curtseying as best she could with only one hand.

Surprise widened Mr. Burnbaum's eyes. "Please, my lady," he exclaimed, moving to lift her upward, but stopping inches away from touching her. "There is no need to curtsey to me."

"Of course there is," she replied as she straightened. "I am a guest in your home and, in my mind, it is far more important to honor matters of polite courtesies than worrying about all those silly rules on class distinction." She tilted her head. "Don't you agree, Mr. Burnbaum?"

"Y-y-yes, my lady, I do, and from the scolding I got from Richard the last time I tried to refer to him by his proper title, he does as well." He gave Richard a wry glance. "You are well-matched, my friend."

Richard stroked his thumb along the back of her hand. "I couldn't agree more."

Nodding, Mr. Burnbaum gestured toward the sideboard. "May I offer you some refreshments? Tea perhaps?"

"No, thank you, Aaron. We've come to ask you . . ."

"Aaron!"

The female voice echoing down the hall cut off Richard's explanation. Stepping toward the doorway, Mr. Burnbaum reached the threshold just as a lovely woman appeared. With her dark curls caught up in an elegant coiffure and her brown, almond-shaped eyes, she was one of the most beautiful women Elizabeth had ever seen. The warmth of the smile she gave Mr. Burnbaum made her seem even more beautiful.

Instantly, Elizabeth's guard began to rise, as it always did around ladies of quality. Snatching her hand back from Richard so as to not appear overly forward, she waited for the woman to glance at her, take in her wrinkled gown and simple hairstyle, and dismiss her with a sniff. Without even being aware of her actions, Elizabeth squared her shoulders as the woman turned her gaze on her.

But the judging look never came, nor did the insulting dismissal.

Instead, the woman's smile broadened. "Aren't you going to introduce us, Aaron?"

After Mr. Burnbaum had introduced them, he laid a hand upon the woman's shoulder. "And this is my treasure, Mrs. Marta Burnbaum."

A pretty flush stained Mrs. Burnbaum's cheeks. "Stop with that, Aaron. You're embarrassing me in front of our guests." The smile she turned upon Elizabeth didn't hold a trace of censure. "You must forgive my husband. He speaks his mind far too easily."

"I find it an admirable quality," Elizabeth replied hesitantly.

"As do I." The sparkle in her eyes belied the long-suffering sigh she released. "Though he is forever making me blush in front of my friends."

Slanting a glance at Richard, Elizabeth murmured, "I know the feeling."

A feeling of kinship spread between them as Marta nodded in complete understanding. For the first time she could remember, Elizabeth felt completely at ease in a stranger's home.

"It appears we have more in common than we realized, Aaron," Richard said, laying his hand on the small of Elizabeth's back.

Aaron smiled lovingly down at Marta. "Then you have been blessed as well."

"Blessed . . . or cursed," Richard replied, a wicked light in his gaze. "There are times when I wonder."

Covering his mouth with his hand, Aaron politely smothered his laughter. Elizabeth gave Marta a pointed look. "See what I mean?"

A moment later, both she and Marta chuckled as well.

"Are you quite certain I cannot offer you something to drink?" Aaron said when they quieted down.

Shaking again, Richard launched into his explanation. "As I started to say, Aaron, I've come to speak to you about Isaac."

"My Isaac?" All the blood drained from Marta's face as she lunged forward, gripping onto Richard's arm. "Have you seen him? Do you know where he is?"

"Marta, Marta," Aaron murmured, taking hold of his wife's hands and prying them off of Richard's arm. "Let him speak."

"Then you haven't heard from him?" Richard asked grimly.

Aaron's eyes held a well of grief. "Not a word. I even sent one of my servants on to Gretna Green, to see if

Isaac and his lady had been there, but there was no trace of him." He slid his hands onto Marta's shoulders and pulled her back against him, as if offering her his strength. "My wife . . . she worries."

"I'll wager she's not the only one," Elizabeth said softly.

Again, Aaron shook his head.

Richard's hand curled into her waist, making her aware of his nervousness. Knowing what he had to now tell these kind people, Elizabeth leaned into him, silently offering her support.

Clearing his throat, Richard began his unenviable task. "Aaron, Mrs. Burnbaum, I believe I might know where your son is," he said in a measured tone, obviously trying not to alarm them more than necessary.

"You do?"

The hope in Marta's voice was painful to hear. "I have recently learned that a young man named Isaac Burnbaum was assaulted the very night your son never came home."

"*Assaulted?*" rasped Aaron. "Someone hurt my son?"

"I don't know if he was seriously harmed or not," Richard replied. "All I know is that he was rendered unconscious and dragged off."

Tears welled in Marta's eyes as she shook her head, denying every word Richard said. "No, no. It's not true!" Her voice trembled with a mixture of fury and fright. "It can't be true."

Turning his wife toward him, Aaron enfolded her in his arms, murmuring consoling words.

"Excuse me, sir."

Shifting uncomfortably, the butler held out a rumpled note. "Someone just delivered this to the kitchens and said it was most urgent. I took the liberty of opening it and . . . well . . ." He broke off his stammering and began to wave the note.

Releasing Elizabeth, Richard retrieved the missive, opened it, and quickly scanned the contents. When he lifted his head, his expression foretold disaster.

"It's a ransom note."

19

The setting sun cast shadows through his study, but John didn't even notice. Ever since Catherine had stormed out of his house that morning, he'd been consumed by a single thought—she was falling in love with him.

And how had he responded?

By nearly pulling her down on the floor of his study and taking her as if she were a harlot. Closing his eyes, Richard leaned his head back, trying to ignore the taunting voice inside of him. *So what?* it said, over and over, until finally he allowed himself to argue the point in his head.

So what? What would have happened if he had pulled her down and made love to her?

First, he would have offered to marry her and, with that one stroke, destroyed his comfortable, organized existence.

What a shame! Especially since it was making him so deliriously happy.

All right. Perhaps he wasn't happy, per se, but he was comfortable.

And is that what you want out of your life? To be comfortable?

John squirmed on his chair, but finally he admitted to

himself that he wanted more than just to be comfortable. He wanted excitement, adventure, intrigue.

Ah, you mean everything you've begun to experience ever since you've met Catherine.

"That's not . . ." But before he could even say the words out loud, he knew he couldn't deny the argument. It was true that ever since Catherine had become a part of his life, he'd stopped dreaming about leaving London . . . and had started dreaming about her. She'd touched a part of him he hadn't even known was inside him, the part that longed to be free, to dance under moonlit skies, to laugh out loud without care of what people might say.

And she'd offered each and every one of those things to him . . . but he hadn't taken them. No, he'd been so locked inside himself, so determined to avoid taking on any added responsibility, that, in his blind ignorance, he had turned away the one person who could help him shed the burden he'd felt for years. My God, he had been a fool.

"John?" His mother called through the door, before peeking her head into the room. "You *are* here. It's been so quiet that I wondered if you'd left the house."

"No," he said softly. "I'm still here."

A concerned frown marred his mother's face as she came into the room. "Is something bothering you, John?"

"Other than the fact that I seem to have destroyed the one chance I might have had for happiness, no."

His bitter response brought a gasp from his mother. "Is that all?" she replied lightly. Gracefully settling down upon a chair, she gazed at him steadily. "Why don't you tell me about it, and we'll see if we can't figure some way out of this together?"

Her offer brought him out of his morose mood. His

mother, offering to help *him?* After years of caring for the family, it seemed an odd turn of events. "I doubt if you . . ."

"There you go again," she exclaimed, throwing her hands up in the air. "Always taking things upon yourself without accepting help from anyone. It's been like this ever since your father passed on."

"I had little choice in the matter," John said dryly, remembering how lost his mother had been. "If I hadn't stepped in, we would have been financially ruined within a year's time."

"That's true," his mother conceded readily, "but that didn't mean you had to do it all alone. I would have helped you, just as you helped me."

The concept was so foreign to John that he just shook his head in confusion.

"If you'd let me help you, John, I could have kept the books or paid the household bills or any other number of things. But you simply took over everything, patted me on the head, and told me to resume the life I'd once enjoyed before your father died." She sighed heavily. "Much to my everlasting guilt, I accepted your pronouncement and allowed you to carry the burden for the entire family. I'm sorry for that, John."

His mother's apology stunned him. He'd had vague memories of her offering to help him, but he'd assumed they'd simply been polite offers, not a true desire to help. Even Catherine had accused him of taking on burdens that no one asked him to carry, but he'd dismissed her words as nonsense. His heart began to pound as he remembered all the times he'd simply gone ahead and taken charge of something without being asked. And what had his actions done to Richard? Had he taken away so many of Richard's responsibilities that it had turned him into a wastrel because he'd never had to handle any of the responsibilities?

John pressed a hand to his temple, trying to stop the colliding thoughts all determined to bombard him at once. "I've been such an arrogant bastard," he rasped, raising his gaze to his mother. "How have you put up with me all these years?"

"Come now, darling, don't add this onto your already lengthy list of burdens," chided his mother. "You're merely rather bossy at times." She softened her words with a loving smile. "You held us together when I was destroyed from your father's death and your brother felt utterly lost." Burrowing into her chair, she leaned her head against the wing. "You are so much like your father, John. He was always so serious, so determined to care for his own, so . . . predictable." A girlish laugh better suited to a maid twenty years younger escaped his mother as she lost herself in old memories. "We were so very different, your father and I, which is precisely why our marriage worked so well. Whenever he got too gruff or pompous, I would tease him or do something utterly outrageous that would first make him sputter with outrage, then he'd laugh and hold me." Her gaze sharpened once again and focused upon him. "You need someone who can do that for you, John."

"I found her," he admitted, "but I pushed her away."

His mother smiled gently. "Are we speaking of Elizabeth?"

John frowned at his mother. "No. I meant Catherine."

"Catherine! I thought you were interested in her sister."

"Never," John said firmly. "It was always Catherine." Just the mention of her name made him ache with longing.

His mother threw her hands up in the air. "If you love her, then what are you doing sitting here? Go find that girl and propose to her."

John grinned at his mother's directive. "Yes, ma'am." Wearing a grin and carrying a smile in his heart, he hurried from the study to convince Catherine they were meant to be together. Who needed to climb mountains or visit old ruins when he could have the adventure of a lifetime simply by keeping her at his side?

Too excited to wait for his horse to be brought around, John slipped out of the house through the kitchens, out into the dusk, heading for the stables. Opening the rear gate, he stepped into the past, as the scene by the theater played itself out before his eyes again. Only this time, it was Mr. Lewis who was being set upon by the same two thugs.

"You there!" he shouted, running forward. "Leave him be."

"Bloody 'ell!" the larger man bellowed as he dropped Lewis to the ground like a deadweight and turned to face John. "It's 'im again."

Crouching down, ready to spring, John faced the larger of the two men. "Let him go, and I'll let you walk away."

"You're becomin' a real boil on my backside, govn'r," grumbled the larger man. "An' I think it's time ta thank you proper like for it."

The man's eyes shifted over John's shoulder, alerting him to the fact that, this time, there was a third person with them, but it was too late. Even as he spun to face the new threat, he felt the blow to his head . . . then nothing.

* * *

"I still don't think it's Morrow," insisted Richard firmly, meeting the mutinous gazes from Elizabeth and her sister. "I even lent him some money recently, so he shouldn't be that desperate for funds." Their expressions didn't change. "I know both of you have made up your minds that it is him, and, granted, I'll give you that he has the motive, but he's always been a womanizer, a cheat, and a liar." He looked at them both. "Not a kidnapper."

"Going from blackmail to kidnapping is the natural progression," Elizabeth pronounced, earning a nod of agreement from her sister.

"I wasn't aware crime had a progression," he remarked dryly. When Elizabeth pursed her lips at him, it was all he could do to keep from lunging across the Everley's parlor, snatching her up in his arms, and kissing the pout off her lips.

The trip to the Burnbaum's had produced unexpected results. While he'd hated going there and telling his friend that his son had been abducted, he'd found Elizabeth's interaction with Aaron's wife very interesting indeed. She'd stiffened and had almost radiated coolness when Marta had walked into the room, but after a few minutes of conversation, Elizabeth had seemed to connect with the woman in a way he'd never seen her do before.

Now all he could do was pray Elizabeth would think of how easily she'd conversed with Marta and realize that she *could* build a life for herself here in town.

Thinking of Marta was a grim reminder of the tragedy that had befallen the Burnbaum's. What was wrong with him, that he was sitting here thinking of his problems with Elizabeth when his friends were worried that their son might be dead? "I'm sorry for my remark. This is hardly a laughing matter," he said somberly. Wearily, he leaned forward, resting his elbows upon his knees, and dropped his head down. "I can't help but wonder if Aaron is getting together all of his money for naught." He lifted his head and looked straight into Elizabeth's eyes. "What if Isaac is dead?"

Reaching out, she pressed two fingers against his lips. "Don't even say that," she said fiercely. "Don't even think it. We must believe he's all right and that he will be returned safely to his family."

Not caring that her sister was watching them, he kissed her fingertips before she pulled away from him. "You're right," he said, pushing aside his dark thoughts. "What we need to do is try and help find him."

"Exactly," Catherine agreed as Lord Shipham walked into the room. "Have you sent someone for Mr. Lewis and for John?"

"More than half an hour ago, so we should be hearing from them soon," he surmised, heading to the sideboard to pour himself a brandy. "Nasty business."

"The worst," Richard agreed as he thrust to his feet. "I can't sit here any longer, doing nothing but twiddling my thumbs and waiting for news." Drumming his fingers against the back of his chair, he considered where he might better use his time to help his friends. "What if I find Morrow and speak to him, try to lead him around to see if he might say something telling? He's not exactly the snappiest sail on the boat, especially when he's been in his cups, so he just might reveal some information."

"But I thought you didn't believe he was guilty of this crime," Elizabeth asked, an adorable frown furrowing her brow.

"I don't, but he's the only suspect we have so far. So I'll speak with him, then follow him, just in case I'm wrong. I'll send word if I discover anything of importance." Deciding that he'd much rather follow a dead end than sit here and be driven mad, Richard bid them farewell, his gaze lingering upon Elizabeth for a moment, before he strode toward the door.

"Richard!" He turned in time to catch Elizabeth in his arms. "Be careful," she whispered, before stretching onto her tiptoes and pressing a swift but unbelievably sweet kiss upon his lips.

Taking her public display of affection as a positive sign, Richard squeezed her tightly for an additional minute before finally letting her go. "I will," he murmured softly, pausing to touch her cheek, then heading out of the parlor.

Pricking herself for the umpteenth time, Catherine tossed aside her embroidery in disgust. Elizabeth had disappeared into her workshop to fiddle with some silly experiment until Mr. Lewis or John arrived and Papa had his head buried in the accounting ledgers, claiming it helped keep him distracted. No, she was the only one being driven mad by the infernal ticking of the clock. In desperation, she'd tried to embroider, but the only thing she was doing to the piece was bleeding all over it.

The sound of the front knocker permeated the silence of the parlor, and Catherine leapt up to see if John had finally arrived. She struggled to hide her disappointment when their butler let Lady Wykham into the house. "Lady Wykham," she said as cheerfully as she could manage. "How nice of you to call upon us."

She nodded in a distracted manner. "Thank you, my

dear, but I confess I came because of your note," she said, removing the missive from her reticule. "Normally, I wouldn't have opened it, but as it came from your house and was addressed to John . . . well, I was understandably confused."

Now she was the one who was confused, Catherine thought, as she led Lady Wykham into the parlor. "I believe Papa's note was fairly straightforward."

"It's not what the note says," she insisted. "What confused me was that I thought John was already here."

"John? Here?" Catherine shook her head. "The last time I saw him was at our meeting this morning."

Lady Wykham frowned. "But he left to come here hours ago."

"Are you certain he was coming to see me?" Catherine asked, before admitting, "We didn't exactly part on the best of terms this morning."

"Yes, yes," Lady Wykham murmured, flicking her hand as if dismissing the comment. "John told me all about that when we discussed . . ." Breaking off, she pressed a hand to her chest. "I know John was coming here, Catherine, and if he's not here, then where could he be?"

Frankly, Catherine couldn't understand Lady Wykham's distress, but she offered comfort regardless. "Perhaps he stopped by his club," she suggested helpfully.

"Impossible," Lady Wykham stated emphatically. "The matter that he wished to discuss with you was far too important to be put off for a game of dice." Flustered, she laid the back of her hand against her cheek. "Dear me, I'm saying far too much, but I just don't understand where John could be."

As the front knocker sounded again, Catherine smiled

reassuringly at John's mother. "That's probably him now." Stepping back out into the foyer, Catherine steadied her nerves, wondering what "important matter" John wished to discuss with her. *Please God, let him have realized he loves me,* she thought, sending the quick prayer winging upward.

But instead of John, a complete stranger stepped into the house. Holding his hat respectfully in his hands, he bobbed his gray-haired head at her as their butler introduced him.

"Mr. David Baker from Bow Street, milady."

"Do come in, Mr. Baker," Catherine offered as he handed his hat and coat to the butler. "I assume you've come in Mr. Lewis' stead."

"On his behalf, not in his stead," he clarified.

For the second time in as many minutes, she was confused again. "I'm afraid I don't understand, Mr. Baker."

"You had a meeting with Mr. Lewis this morning." As Mr. Baker stated it as fact, Catherine didn't feel the need to confirm his statement. "When you sent around the urgent note for Mr. Lewis, we immediately tried to contact him, but none of my men have seen Mr. Lewis since early this evening."

"Is that unusual?" she inquired hesitantly.

"Most unusual, especially for a fine investigator like Mr. Lewis." Catherine nodded in understanding, allowing Mr. Davis to continue uninterrupted. "So, we began to retrace Mr. Lewis' steps today—which is how I know about your meeting with him—and we uncovered some disturbing news." Mr. Davis' expression grew foreboding. "A street urchin witnessed an incident near Lord Wykham's stables and, as soon as he heard we were looking for information, he came forward. He saw Mr. Lewis knocked unconscious by three men."

Catherine's hands flew to her cheeks. "Poor Mr. Lewis. Is he all right?"

"We don't know, my lady," Mr. Davis explained. "These men made off with Mr. Lewis." He paused, before adding, "But that's not all. Apparently, while these three men were abducting Mr. Lewis, they were interrupted by Lord Wykham, who tried to help Mr. Lewis, but he was assaulted and abducted as well."

"John?" Catherine fought back the panic that threatened to consume her. "They took John?"

At Mr. Davis' nod, Catherine's knees began to wobble, her head grew light, and the room seemed to spin. She was going to faint, she thought hysterically, unable to stop the terror clawing through her. *She could faint, but that wasn't going to help John.*

Catherine didn't know where that voice of reason had come from, but she clung to it, drawing strength from the knowledge that John needed her now. He'd tried to protect her so many times in the past, but, as it turned out, he was the one who needed protecting.

Swallowing her panic, Catherine drew in a shaky breath and shored up her nerves. "Please come with me into the parlor, Mr. Davis, while I inform my family and Lord Wykham's mother of this horrible incident." She embraced the dark anger filling her. "Then we can discuss how to find Lord Wykham and Mr. Lewis and bring them *home.*"

20

Checking the reputable clubs had been an utter waste of time, Richard decided with a disgusted shake of his head. He should have known he'd find Morrow in a disreputable gaming hell.

"A gentleman who can't afford to lose should never join a game," Richard drawled lazily, noting the small pile of markers in front of Morrow.

"Just having a run of bad luck," Morrow replied cheerfully. If the smell emanating from Morrow was any indication, the man was definitely foxed. "Care to join the game?"

"I'll pass." Snatching Morrow's cards from his hand, Richard set them on the table, folding for him.

"What'd you do that for?" demanded Morrow.

Richard yanked Morrow from the chair, snagged his few remaining markers, and herded the man outside.

"Why'd you go and spoil all my fun, Vernon? There was a time when you would have been right beside me," Morrow asked.

The truth of that statement made Richard wince. "As I've said before, Morrow, times change." He watched his old companion carefully. "But not for you apparently. I heard you've been up to your old tricks."

Panic flickered in Morrow's eyes before he glanced away. "Have you come to preach to me again, Richard?" He clicked his tongue as he shook his head. "You've become quite the bore lately."

But, like a blood hound chasing the scent of the fox, Richard knew Morrow was hiding something. "Let's not talk about me, then, old friend," he murmured in a smooth tone, to invite confidences. "Let's discuss you, for you're far more interesting these days, aren't you?"

"That's a wager I'd bet a pound note on," he remarked with a drunken laugh. "And I'll soon have plenty of pounds to wager."

Perfect. Luckily for him, Morrow was so stinking drunk he couldn't even tell he was being manipulated. Leading Morrow into loosening his tongue even more, Richard slapped him on the shoulder. "Congratulations are in order then, my friend, are they not? It's not every day a man recoups his fortune."

"No, indeed not." Morrow's chest puffed out. "Only the most clever of us can manage that one." He frowned slightly, narrowing his gaze upon Richard. "How did you get yours back again?"

"Through hard work," Richard offered.

Morrow found that extremely amusing. "Christ, you sound like a bleeding tradesman," he remarked when he'd finished laughing. "If I added up all the bloody money I spent on gaming and my other entertainment, it would amount to a damn fortune." Crooking his finger, Morrow leaned closer and whispered, "I'm far smarter than you, 'cause I've discovered a way to have my cake and eat it, too."

Moving in for the kill, Richard asked, "How's that?"

"By using my head and encouraging . . . free trade." He smiled, pleased at his phrasing. "That's it indeed. I get something someone else wants and trade for something I want—their money."

With every word that passed through Morrow's mouth, Richard became more convinced that Elizabeth and Catherine had been right all along. "It sounds as if you've discovered a far better way to recover your fortune, Morrow." He slung a companionable arm across Morrow's shoulders. "Care to share your knowledge with an old friend?"

In an instant, Richard knew he'd gone too far. With a jerk, Morrow pulled away, turning to glare suspiciously at Richard. "So that's your game, is it, old chum?" he murmured darkly. "You've had nothing to do with me for years, then all of a sudden you're sniffing around me, trying to get a piece of my action." Shaking his head, Morrow began to stumble backward. "Well, I'm too clever to be fooled by your trickery."

Richard tried to regain some of the ground he'd lost with that one misstep. "It's not like that, Morrow," he insisted, adding a note of sincerity to his voice. "We never stopped being friends. Didn't I just give you some blunt?"

Again, Richard sensed he'd made another mistake. "You might have tossed a paltry sum at me, true, but you also told me to never speak to you again," Morrow snarled bitterly. "You thought you were too good for the likes of me . . . so don't be thinking that just because I'm going to get some of my own that you can come around looking for my help." He spat at Richard's feet. "We'll just see who's better than whom."

As Morrow stumbled off, Richard waited until he'd rounded the corner of the alley before he began to follow. With a bit of luck, the drunken fool would be motivated to check on his . . . investment, and would lead Richard straight to Isaac. Making certain he stayed far enough behind, Richard trailed Morrow through the dark streets into the very bowels of London.

Finally, Morrow paused in front of a dilapidated building, looking right, then left, before slinking inside. Blood pumping through his veins, Richard neared the building, heading around the outside to see if there was another way in. At the rear, Richard found what used to be a staircase leading to a second-floor landing, but it had long since broken, leaving only a portion of the structure behind.

With all the lower windows boarded up, Richard didn't think he'd find another way into the building when he happened to notice the house right next door. At the rear of that structure, there was a staircase as well, but this one appeared intact and led to an upper balcony . . . that was mere feet from the upper landing on Morrow's building.

Not waiting another moment, Richard hurried next door and carefully made his way up the stairs. He easily jumped to the upper landing of Morrow's building. Pressing against the outer wall, he peered into the dingy window. Through the dirt, he thought he saw someone sitting along the opposite wall. Excitement pulsed through him as he used his shirt sleeve to wipe the window clean.

The excitement chilled in his very bones when he saw just who was sitting against the far wall, trussed up like a hog on the way to slaughter. John. And off to his right lay a bound Isaac, while a third man, tied up as well, lay to John's left.

Swearing under his breath, Richard sank back down against the wall. How the hell had John gotten in there? Not that it mattered. No, all that he needed to know now was how was he going to rescue the three men without being detected. Turning, Richard looked through the window again, this time trying to see John's captors. While he didn't see them, he heard two other male voices besides Morrow's distinctively slurred one.

The odds against Richard being able to sneak undetected into the room, free all three of them, help them outside and down the stairs, then get them away from the building were horribly slim. So, as much as he wanted to charge in and save his brother, Richard forced himself to think logically. The only way to save his brother was to leave him here and go for help.

Resolve tightened his gut as Richard peered through the window again, pressing two fingers against the glass as if to touch John, to tell him that help was on the way. Then, he backed away, making his way down from the building . . . and leaving his brother behind.

It was one of the hardest things Richard had ever done, and he prayed it wasn't the biggest mistake he'd ever make.

Sitting forward, Elizabeth gazed at Mr. Baker. "What if Mr. Lewis was getting close to finding Isaac? Too close? Perhaps they took Mr. Lewis to keep him from leading Lord Wykham and the authorities to Isaac."

Mr. Baker rubbed his chin. "There is always that possibility, because we believe Mr. Lewis was the intended victim. Unfortunately for the marquess, he simply got in the way."

"Then why take him?" Catherine asked, obviously distraught, but still controlled. "Why not simply knock him out and leave him?"

"Perhaps John saw their faces more closely this time," suggested Lady Wykham. "From what you've told me, the last time you encountered these horrid miscreants it was dark and foggy. You yourself said that you hadn't gotten a good look at their faces."

"That has solid reasoning," Mr. Baker agreed.

"Everything you've suggested does make sense to me," her father said, before shaking his head. "But what I don't understand is why it took the kidnappers so long to send a ransom note."

"Who can say?" replied Mr. Baker, lifting his shoulders. "Perhaps they wanted to give the Burnbaums a taste of life without their son, making them so eager to get him back that they would pay any amount."

Papa's hand shook as he rubbed it down his face. "It wouldn't take me a few days to be willing to hand over my fortune to get back one of my daughters."

Elizabeth knew by the inflection in her father's voice that he was thinking of losing one of them . . . just as he'd lost Mama. "Luckily, you won't need to worry about that, Papa," she assured him. "Both Catherine and I are right here, safe and sound."

Blinking rapidly, her father nodded.

Everyone jumped at the sound of the front door banging against the wall. "Elizabeth!"

Richard's bellow shook the house. "In here," she called out, hurrying to reach him. "What is it? What's wrong?"

Skidding to a stop inside the parlor, Richard swept his

gaze over the people in the room, before coming to rest on her. "It's John," he panted, completely out of breath. "They've got John."

"I know," Elizabeth murmured, reaching out to comfort Richard.

But he shook her off. "You don't understand. *I know where he is.*"

Everyone in the room erupted at that pronouncement, until Mr. Baker shouted for quiet and explained to Richard that he was Mr. Lewis's colleague. "John is being held in a building near the river," he explained as quickly as possible. "Isaac Burnbaum and a third man I didn't recognize are there as well. All of them are tied and appear groggy or unconscious." Pausing only to take a breath, he continued. "While I couldn't see the captors, I did hear three distinct voices coming from an area off the second floor room where my brother is being held."

"Where is the exact location of the building?" After Richard told Mr. Baker, he headed from the room, pausing only to give directions. "I want all of you to wait here. I'm going to collect my men and we'll soon have the marquess home where he belongs, as well as Mr. Burnbaum and Mr. Lewis."

Without waiting for a reply, Mr. Baker rushed from the house.

"I don't know about the rest of you, but I'll be damned to Hell and back before I sit here and wait while my brother is held captive."

"I'm coming with you," Elizabeth said immediately, and an instant later Catherine, Papa, and Lady Wykham all chimed in as well.

Nodding brusquely, Richard began to issue orders.

"I've come up with a plan, so I want all of you to do exactly as I tell you. I don't think we'll need to use it, now that the runners are going to be there, but it's best to be prepared."

As Elizabeth, Catherine, and Lord Shipham raced off to retrieve the items Richard requested, his mother came up to him and cupped his face. "You sounded just like John now, barking out those commands."

"I'll get him back for you, Mother," Richard promised, pressing her hand against his cheek.

She gave him a teary-eyed smile. "I don't doubt it for a moment." Sniffling, she pulled away from him, straightened her back, and looked him in the eye. "Now, tell me what I can do so I don't feel like such a useless old woman."

They'd had a devil of a time convincing the hackney driver to let them off in such a dangerous section of town, but the flash of Richard's money had eased the man's worry. Sneaking down alleyways, they'd finally come to the building where John was being held. Weak light shone from the second-story window like a beacon calling them forth to rescue John, Isaac, and Mr. Lewis.

Still, they sat, quiet and watchful, awaiting the arrival of the runners. "Must we wait?" Catherine asked for the third time.

"It is the sensible thing to do."

Looking at Richard's taut back, Elizabeth realized that, while he might be behaving very responsibly, all he really wanted to do was burst into that building and rescue his brother. It was exactly how she would feel if it were Catherine in that horrid place. Odd, how she was sitting here in this dingy alley, terrified for the welfare of three people, cold and frightened, yet she felt completely in tune with Richard.

In this horrible situation, where their welfare was in jeopardy, life was stripped of everything but its essence. And at the core of her heart lay Richard.

Wishing she could tell him, Elizabeth settled for placing her hand upon his back. He started beneath her hand when a loud crash came from the second-floor room, followed by shouts of anger.

"I don't think we can wait any longer," Richard said, turning to look at them. "Does everyone remember what they're supposed to do?"

At their nods, Richard met Elizabeth's eyes for one heart-stopping moment before gesturing to her father and heading up the stairs. Gathering up her materials, Elizabeth hurried to the rear of the building and began mixing her special concoction, while Catherine and Lady Wykham went round to the front of the building to await the arrival of the runners.

Tilting her head back, she waited until Richard and her father were in position on the second-floor landing; then, at Richard's signal, she stepped back and tossed the acid into the bowl. The explosion shook the foundation of the house as Richard, with his pistol drawn, kicked out the window and disappeared inside the building, followed by her father.

Following Richard's instructions, Elizabeth slid back into the shadows behind the second building to await his next signal.

Elizabeth's explosion had worked like a charm, alarming John's captors, making it easy for Richard and Lord

Shipham to get into the room undetected. The two kidnappers turned themselves over to Richard and Lord Shipham without a fight. "Where's Morrow?" demanded Richard as he tied up the two men.

"Gone," said the shorter man, a veritable font of information.

As soon as the two captors were secured, Richard and Lord Shipham began to untie John and Mr. Lewis. He'd only begun to undo the ropes binding John when he heard something behind him. Rolling to the side, he barely managed to escape being knocked unconscious by none other than his old friend, Morrow. Elizabeth's father lay at Morrow's feet in an unconscious heap.

"I knew you couldn't resist sticking your nose into my business," sneered Morrow as he pointed a pistol at Richard. "You're a fool, Vernon."

Out of the corner of his eye, Richard saw John working his hands out of the ropes. But he knew John was still groggy, so he wasn't about to rely upon him for help. "I used to be a fool," Richard agreed without hesitation. "But not any more."

Morrow stepped over Lord Shipham, closing the distance between them. "From where I'm standing, I'd say that's a lie."

"Really?" Richard said in a considering tone. "Then I suppose I'll have to prove to you that I'm a changed man." Before he even finished uttering the last syllable, Richard launched himself at Morrow's legs as Morrow fired, sending the lead ball harmlessly into the wall. As Morrow fell to the ground, Richard scrambled on top of him and plowed his fist into Morrow's face, knocking him unconscious.

Richard drew back his fist to give in to one last punch against the man who had threatened his family.

"I think that's quite enough."

Richard's gut churned as he watched first his mother, then Catherine step into the room . . . followed by another woman, who held a gun to Catherine's head. "Lady Serena, I presume," Richard said, as all of the pieces clicked together.

"Aren't you the clever one?" she murmured, her beautifully shaped blue eyes dead. "But then you'd have to be, to spoil all of my plans."

He gestured toward Morrow. "I knew he didn't have the intelligence to pull off a kidnapping." He remembered the runner's report on Morrow. "Were you the mastermind behind his blackmail schemes?"

"Heard about those as well, did you?" Her smile chilled him to the bone. "My brother is a drunken sot who ran through all of our money within a year of our parents' death." Her jaw tightened. "For a while, I allowed him to manage our lives, until he completely bungled everything, leaving us penniless and homeless." Her dead eyes began to shimmer with madness. "Well, I've had enough of being poor, of relying on the generosity of others for a place to live."

"So you decided to capitalize on your one remaining asset," Richard concluded accurately. "Your beauty."

"And why not? Women have been making money off men's foolish lust for hundreds of years." She tossed her head proudly. "I'm just smarter than the rest and figured out a way to do it without selling my body."

Pointing his thumb at Isaac, he kept Serena looking toward him, hoping she wouldn't notice John shifting his legs to untie the final knots that held him. "So you enticed young Isaac here, making him believe you'd fallen in love with him, when all the while, all of you planned to kidnap him and ransom him back to his parents." He caught the mocking glimmer in her expression. "You never intended to return him home alive, did you?"

"He'd seen us, all of us. What do you think?" Serena remarked, leaving no doubt in Richard's mind. "My brother was supposed to have killed him and disposed of the body, but he managed to bungle that as well. He said he didn't have the stomach to do the job. I would have done it myself, but it was too dangerous for me to be seen down here until we had our money."

"So when Catherine recognized you in the park, you must have panicked, because you began to make mistakes."

"I don't make mistakes."

Holding up his hands, he warded off her anger. "Fine, fine. You don't make mistakes." He paused before pointing out, "Yet when you arranged for Mr. Lewis to be taken, someone saw the entire incident." He tapped his finger against his knee. "Ah, yes, and let's not forget that I did manage to find this hideaway."

"Only because of my idiot brother," Serena snapped, gesturing toward Morrow with the gun.

"But you're the one in charge; you were the one responsible for making certain things were done right."

When Serena swung the pistol from Catherine onto him, Richard rallied at his success. "I cannot be held accountable for the mistakes of others," Serena sneered.

"Ah, but you are," Richard taunted her.

"Enough!" Serena's shriek echoed throughout the room. "I can still make this work."

"How?" Richard demanded, pushing her to the brink. "By killing every last one of us, then collecting the money from Isaac's parents?"

"Precisely," Serena agreed with an evil smile.

"And what of the runners who are on their way here at this very moment?"

"I shall be long gone before they arrive." She began to pull back on the trigger. "But first, I need to clean up this mess."

Looking into Serena's face, Richard knew he was a dead man.

What was taking so long?

Elizabeth kept an unwavering gaze upon the now open window, expecting to see Richard give her their agreed-upon all-clear wave. But as the minutes began to tick by, she grew more and more worried that something had gone wrong.

As another minute ticked by with no sign of Richard, she *knew* something was wrong. But what should she do? All Richard had needed from her before was a distraction. Perhaps if she provided him with another one, he might be able to get himself out of whatever trouble had befallen them.

Then, if that didn't work, she would climb up and help them herself.

Opening her valise, she withdrew the catapult she'd been working on for so long. Guessing at the tragectory angle, she positioned it in place, before beginning to mix together another explosive. But this time, she would use baking soda instead of the more dangerous acid. It would be safer for everyone in the room, but would provide the same smoking effect.

Her tour of Richard's factory had inspired this new mixture, so it was only fitting that she use it to help him. She soaked a rag in the base mixture, then tied it around the largest rock she could find and placed it in the cradle of the catapult.

After one last check of the releasing mechanism, she poured vinegar over the cloth to start the chemical reaction before releasing the arm, sending the now fizzing, smoking cloth flying upward into the window.

Bull's-eye.

As Richard prepared to dive off to the side, another loud explosion reverberated through the night air. Smoke filled the air, and Richard made his move. Holding his breath, he headed toward the thickest part of the smoke, hiding inside the cloud as Serena regained her senses and began to swing her pistol around in search of him.

"Where are you, you bastard?" she screamed, turning toward where he stood in the now dispersing smoke. When she began to smile at him, Richard understood true evil for the first time in his life. "It's time for you to die," she murmured as she leveled the pistol directly at his heart.

Serena pulled the trigger, and Richard dropped to his knees, falling out of harm's way, just as John grabbed hold of her legs, sending her crashing to the floor. When Catherine and his mother retrieved the rope they'd used on John, Richard bound Serena tightly, before moving on to tie up the still unconscious Morrow. His mother untied

Mr. Lewis and Isaac, while Catherine cradled both John and her father's heads in her lap.

Tightening the last knot on Morrow's bindings, Richard stood as Elizabeth stumbled into the room, followed by Mr. Baker and a small army of Bow Street Runners. Frantically, she scanned the room until she saw him. In an instant, she was in his arms.

And all was right with the world.

21

"I never suspected a thing," Catherine admitted, her mouth tightening as she remembered how she'd been duped. "And I even let her cry on my shoulder."

John's laugh turned into a groan as he held his head where they'd hit him.

"My poor darling," Catherine murmured, leaning down to press a kiss onto the injured spot. They'd left that horrid building . . . after hearing an earful from Mr. Baker on how they could have all been killed—as if they hadn't already figured that out for themselves . . . and they'd all come back to her home.

Elizabeth and Richard were off somewhere together and Lady Wykham was tending to Papa, leaving Catherine alone with John on the terrace, sitting side by side on a cool marble bench.

"The whole time I was in that awful place, I wasn't certain if I was ever going to leave it alive," John said quietly. "And as I thought back on my life, I realized there are a lot of things I've come to regret, but do you know what the largest regret was?"

Catherine shook her head, not even willing to take a guess.

Lifting his hand, he trailed his fingers along her hairline, coming to curve around the back of her neck. "I regretted not accepting your offer."

"What offer?"

Releasing her, John rose and held out his hand. "May I have the honor of this dance?"

Understanding and love flooded her as she placed her hand within his, allowing him to tug her off the bench and into his arms. Humming softly, he waltzed her slowly around the terrace. "I have died and gone to Heaven, but no one has the courage to tell me," John murmured against her hair.

"Your head wouldn't be pounding if you were in Heaven," Catherine pointed out with a laugh.

Arching her back against his arm, John gazed down at her. "I've been such a fool, Catherine. I nearly let life pass by me with never once enjoying the simple pleasures, like waltzing with the woman I love beneath a star-kissed night."

"Woman you love?" she repeated, her mouth suddenly dry. "Just how hard did you get hit, John?"

He laughed again, wincing as he did it. "Don't worry. I came to my senses before the blow to my head." The smile slid off his face and he brought their dance to a halt. "I know exactly what I'm saying when I tell you I love you, Catherine Everley. When you came into my life, you terrified me. I was convinced that you would drive me mad with your impulsiveness, your zest for embracing all life has to offer, your sheer unpredictability." The look in his eyes spoke volumes. "But if this is madness, then I willingly commit myself, for to be without you would be like living in a world without light." Slowly, he bent his head and tenderly kissed her, his touch promising a wealth of happiness. "Please say you'll marry me and save me from my horrid fate," he finished with a smile.

Tilting her head to the side, she gazed up at him. "As proposals go, my lord, that one was decidedly humorous in nature, utterly unsuitable for a proper young lady . . ." Pausing, she slid her arms around his neck. ". . . and utterly perfect for me."

With a groan, John captured her smile with his kiss, just as surely as he'd captured her heart.

". . . and when you created that second explosion in . . ." Richard broke off, frowning slightly. "How *did* you do that?"

Clasping her hands behind her back, Elizabeth strolled next to a soot-streaked Richard through the quiet garden behind her house. "Since I wasn't certain where you would need me to set off the explosion, I brought along the catapult I'd designed. When you didn't signal for me, I knew something had gone wrong, so I thought you might need another diversion."

Richard grinned down at her, his teeth gleaming white beneath his darkened skin. "Have I told you you're positively brilliant?"

His words pleased and embarrassed her. "Have I told you you're positively a mess?"

Holding his arms wide, he reached for her. "Come give me a hug," he murmured as he enfolded her close, leaving streaks of soot all over her.

Laughing, she pushed against him, trying to break free. "Stop it, Richard."

He grew still. "I have no intentions of stopping," he said seriously. "Now, or ever."

Elizabeth stopped writhing in his arms. "Good."

He stared down at her with such intensity it seemed as if he were trying to see clear to her very soul. "Do you mean it?"

"Mean what?" Holding onto his hopelessly stained lapels, she met his eyes. "Do I mean that I love you? Most definitely. Do I mean that I believe I might find happiness living in town? As long as I'm with you, I do." The certainty she'd felt in that awful alley rested securely within her. "Do I mean I plan on holding you to your proposal?" Sliding up onto her tiptoes, she came within a hairsbreadth of his lips. "Just try to get away from me now."

"Elizabeth," he whispered before claiming her mouth with a passion, a hunger, a love she knew would never end. "I'll make you happy, I promise."

She smiled at him. "I'll make *myself* happy," she said confidently. "But having you in my life will make me even *happier.*"

"It's a bargain." Bending his head to kiss her again, Richard pulled back at the last minute. "Would you demonstrate your catapult to me? It seemed amazingly accurate and I . . ."

"Later," she murmured, drawing him toward her. "Much later."

Richard went along with her plans most willingly.

The evening was almost gone when Douglas finally entered his bedchamber, more at peace than he'd been in a long time. Margaret hovered near the fireplace, little more than a hazy shadow.

"It's time, Douglas," she said, her voice sounding very faraway.

"Yes," he finally agreed. "It's time." Pushing away from the door, he walked over to the chair where he'd sat many a night, talking with her, gazing at her, longing for her. "I love you still, Margaret, but tonight, as I watched our daughters endanger themselves for the men they've grown to love, I realized how unfair I'd been to them, to you, even to myself." He held onto the back of his chair, trying to find the right words to explain what was in his heart. "If John had been killed, I would have held Catherine as she'd mourned, then urged her to let him go, for she's still a young woman with a life left to live." Lifting his hand, he pressed it against his chest. "And tonight I realized that I have a life left to live as well. Not quite as much as Catherine, granted, but enough that to squander it would be a crime."

Margaret's ghost seemed to glow. "That's so true, my love," she whispered, an airy sound that caressed him.

"Nor is it what I would have wanted for you if I had been the one to die." He smiled at his wife. For the first time since her death, he didn't feel anger, only quiet acceptance. "You've been very patient with me, Margaret, staying with me all these years. If our positions had been reversed, I wager I'd have railed at you nonstop."

Slowly, she shook her head. "You *needed* me, Douglas."

"Indeed, I did," he admitted, knowing he would have sunk into a dark abyss forever without Margaret guiding him out of the darkness. "I will always love you, Margaret, and I'll always miss you, but I've finally learned how to live without you." He blew her a soft kiss, wishing briefly that he might kiss her in earnest to say farewell, but he let that wish go as well. "Good-bye for now, my love."

Touching her hands to her lips, Margaret gently blew him a kiss, her breath a soft, sweetly scented breeze that washed over him. Closing his eyes, Douglas inhaled deeply, and when he opened them again, she was gone.

The first morning's rays of sunlight pierced his room, ridding every corner of shadows. Sliding his chair away from the darkness by the fireplace, Douglas moved it directly in front of the window and sat down to watch the sun come up.

It was being touted as the Wedding of the Year.

Elizabeth nearly laughed out loud at the thought, but managed to hold in her amusement. It would hardly do to be caught laughing at the altar. Feeling his gaze upon her, Elizabeth looked across the expanse of marble . . . and directly into her husband's eyes.

Her husband.

Just saying the words sent a shiver of wonder and delight down her spine. Two weeks earlier, they'd been married in the chapel at Godmersham, with close friends and family in attendance. Even the Burnbaums had traveled all the way from London to attend. The image of Richard awaiting her on the altar, with John standing at his side as best man, would forever remain in her heart.

Now Richard stood at John's side as Catherine and John united. In front of a crush of people. Surprisingly, Elizabeth felt at ease. She'd finally found the acceptance she'd craved for so long. She and Richard lived next door to the Burnbaum's in that lovely section of town, and their new house came complete with a large shed out back that she'd immediately converted into her new workshop. She'd already begun working on one of Richard's designs to build a machine that would help him in his factory.

As predicted, the ton had ostracized them upon learning of Richard's trade. Yet, it didn't matter one bit to either of them. They'd built a new life for themselves, filled with friends, love, and family. Elizabeth smiled across the altar at her husband. No, she'd never regret losing her social status; she was far too busy being happy.

As the organ music swelled, Elizabeth watched her sister glide down the aisle upon their father's arm. Leading Catherine to the altar, he handed her into John's care and stepped back. And in her heart, Elizabeth knew that somehow, someway, Mama was here today . . . just as she'd been at her wedding two weeks ago.

Seeing the adoration in John's face as he gazed down upon Catherine's loving expression, Elizabeth knew they, too, would find the happiness she and Richard had found. Her sister would make a perfect marchioness.

And as for her, well, she'd make a perfect pretzel maker's wife.